HEAR, O ISRAEL

A Novel

Sam Jon Wallace

1123

HEAR, O ISRAEL

ISBN 978-0-578-09635-3

Hear, O Israel, ye approach this day unto
battle against your enemies.
Deut. 20:3

I accuse you all!
Naturally.
Because I am always, always the victim.

Ephriam Sidon
"Fighting and Killing Without End"

For S.

One

L eaning against the ruin of an old Crusader castle, her back pressed against the warm sandstone blocks, Noa Kagan first noticed the tan SUV when it was far down the beach. Vehicles were not allowed on the beach in Herzliya unless they were military or security. She wondered what it was doing here. Her horse, standing in the sand with its reins hanging loose over its head, ignored the SUV and, after her first glance, Noa tried to do the same.

She'd been watching the sea slosh over the stones of the crumbled mole, foaming over them like shampoo on a bumpy scalp, slicking them down as it slid away. Beyond the mole, out toward the horizon, three gunboats moved north, line astern through the shafts of light that pierced the bruised pillowy clouds. Heading up to Lebanon, she guessed, up to where her son was fighting in Ehud Olmert's summer war against Hezbollah. Sasha, her precious only child, was a young man now, and in Israel young men went to war. It came with the territory.

She lit a cigarette and glanced down the beach again. The SUV was closer and it had several high radio antennas at the back. The kind of vehicle IDF officers rode around in...or the *Shabak*, the security police.

Noa had grown up with the macho-military culture of the country. Guns on every street corner, guns in every home. She'd accepted it, which didn't mean she'd also grown to like it, just that there was little she could do about it. Israel was no promised land for feminists and she did not remember fondly doing her national service in the army, fending off the middle-aged men who revelled in their call-up for reserve duty, men who looked forward to a month away from home to grope a young girl and maybe get laid. Some of them expected to be serviced and later boasted about it. She'd met Rafi Bourla, her future husband and father of Sasha at that time. But Rafi had not been one of those older gropers then – his time would come later. Dashing, with dark curly hair, Rafi had been a gorgeous young paratroop officer who'd seduced her, made her pregnant, married her, and then got on with *his* life, all as easy for him as stripping a Galil sniper rifle and snapping it back together. Always a strong-willed woman, Noa had determined to get on with *her* life too. A brilliant science student, she had been accepted at the Technion in Haifa after her mandatory military service. She deposited her baby boy, Sasha, with her parents on the kibbutz where she had grown up and where the children still lived communally, and then went to university for the next eight years while Rafi made a lot of money in construction and then the arms business and fooled around with other women. When she returned from the United States with her doctorate, she shared with Rafi and their son the big house that Rafi had built in Herzilya, an affluent suburb on the beach north of Tel Aviv. But she did not share his bed, and their marriage continued only because it was difficult to *get* a divorce under the religious laws of Israel. She and Rafi got along amicably enough and her principal concern other than her work was the upbringing of her son.

Noa did not believe that in giving birth to Sasha that she'd made another soldier for the IDF and she'd awaited his time to go in the army with considerable worry. She feared he would be infected by the same macho virus that afflicted her husband and her father, their arrogance and their patronizing attitude towards her when she expressed her concerns. Sasha had laughed at her.

"But I'm not like that Mom. I respect women." He winked at her. He had Rafi's good looks and cavalier attitude. "I just worry I won't find one as smart as you. What'll I do then?"

Had she detected a tiny hint of sarcasm in his voice? And what was wrong with smart?

What had upset her most was Sasha's insistence on going into the tank corps. She had called her father - a retired tank corps general - and railed at him, convinced that Yosef had influenced the boy. Yosef said he was proud that his grandson had chosen tanks and was dismayed with his daughter's lack of patriotism.

"Patriotism for you means brute force," Noa had said. "You think that will solve everything. I didn't bring up Sasha that way."

"The boy is doing his duty," Yosef replied. "Tanks are special in Israel. The man in the tank will be victorious."

The tan SUV kept coming, lurching across the last rocky spur, radio antennas swishing back and forth, moving forward on to the strip of sand and rockslide between the cliff and the sea. The horse raised its head at the sound of crunching tires, impossible to ignore the vehicle now.

Noa had come riding on the beach as a kind of therapy, a favorite spot to relax and calm her nerves about Sasha. The animal had been her one concession to the ostentatious lifestyle displayed by her husband and his *nouveau-riche* crowd in Herzliya-Petuach and Savyon. She preferred to ride up on weekdays when there were fewer people on the beach. When she was working at the Institute in Rehovot she could often manage her weekly visit, but when she was down at Dimona in the desert she rarely finished the long drive home until after dark.

She flipped her cigarette into the sea, the nails of her free hand picking at a seam of white mortar that fitted the blocks of the ancient Crusader ruin together. She'd had nightmares about Crusaders when she was young. Cruel, chain-mailed men in white tunics with blood-red crosses on their chests who would slash down at her as she tried to dodge the flailing hooves of their horses. The cause of the nightmares had been mostly her own doing. She loved to ride out from Kfar Borochov with the boys, thundering across the green hills of the northern Galilee, always led by Gavri Gilboa. They would pretend to be Saladin's horsemen at the Horns of Hittin, a legendary battle site, chopping down the exhausted Crusaders. "What if it is the Arab side?" Gavri had cried. "It's the winning side." After a 25 kilometer overnight hike from their kibbutz to Montfort Castle, perched on a mountaintop in a wild, densely forested area, they would sit around a fire in the ruins and scare each other. It was like telling ghost stories. Shadows flickered on the ancient walls of Starkenberg – they preferred the German name for the castle for its added effect – and there they were, fresh-faced kibbutz children, innocent of the ways of the world outside their commune, giggling and clutching at each other as they told scary fantasies of cold-eyed, Jew-hating, Christian knights. Nazi knights! Later, when she whimpered in her sleep, Gavri was there to hold her hand and stroke her head, his soft brown eyes lustrous in the firelight.

Her father had tried to put a stop in his iron-fisted way to what he called her "wild riding." She was only a girl he shouted, and she hated him for that. But her beloved *Dedi,* her grandfather Sasha, after whom she had named her son, was alive then and Yosef couldn't stand up to him. "Goddammit! She wants to ride like a cossack, let her go," Sasha roared in Russian. And he laughed and slapped her behind, propelling her towards the door, Yosef scowling. Her mother, Anna, old Sasha's daughter, stood behind Yosef where she couldn't be seen, smiling and nodding, giving silent permission for her to bolt to the kibbutz stable, to an impatient Gavri and the other boys, and to the waiting horses.

She sometimes wondered what would have happened if she had married Gavri long ago as he had wanted. Things couldn't have turned out worse than they had with Rafi. She had slept with Gavri once, her first time, and it had been awful. He had never been married, probably never would now. The conventional wisdom at the kibbutz was that he'd seen too much war, too much violence. He'd been traumatized, poor Gavri. Ask what his country had done for him.

The engine sound of the SUV stopped. Very nearby. Noa stared at it, wondering nervously if they had come for her? Why? She didn't like it whatever it was and she felt a flicker of fear. She was startled to see the man she'd been thinking about, Gavri Gilboa, get out on the passenger side. She hadn't seen him in ages. The other man behind the wheel didn't move.

"Gavri! What are you doing here?" she called out.

He didn't seem to hear.

He strode towards her quickly, head down, the bald patch at the center of his closely cropped skull gleaming bronze. He passed the horse, his hands jammed in the pockets of a pair of cargo pants, his wide shoulders swinging and dipping as he found his footing through the ruins. His hands stayed in his pockets when he reached her, his head still down.

Her fear deepened, nearing panic just before he lifted his head and spoke.

"It's Sasha, Noa ... he's been killed..."

His hand came out of his pocket, reaching for her.

"...his tank took a direct hit from a Hezbollah rocket...the whole crew...all of them..."

She heard him suck in breath.

"They thought I should tell you...Rafi being away..."

She saw his lips compress to a grim line, saw the wetness in his soft eyes. His hand was still coming towards her...

Her scream and the echoing skreel of the gulls, their white feath-ered shapes in startled flight against the blue sky, the long frothy line of the surf below, the jerk of her horse's head tossed up at her cry – that instant, that click in time when she learned of her son's death, was etched forever on Noa's soul. And frozen in that frame too was the messenger, Gavri Gilboa, a statue in front of her, his hand out, palm tilted up and facing her, as if trying to stop the sound of her pain.

She turned away from him to the cliff, her fingers digging into her scalp, saw before her eyes the strata pressed down and warped and twisted, as if wringing itself in grief for what it had witnessed in the weary embattled land; heard the rush of her own pulse in her ears and the splash of the sea-swell in the tumbled ruins of Arsuf, the once proud Crusader castle which had been dismembered in death like her son, huge stone chunks of wall and turret tumbled down to the edge of the sea where they lay like battered toy blocks left behind by the children of departed giants.

*

The grass on the lawn at Kfar Borochov was emerald green, even in summer, and the fresh smell of pines filled Noa's nostrils. To the east, looking through the pines, she could see the steep, khaki wall of the Golan heights on the other side of the Hula valley. Far below, the rich farmland was a checkerboard of colors: browns, greens and yellows. The Jordan river, a thin metallic ribbon, writhed down the valley towards the Kinneret, a distant body of blue water that Christians called the Sea of Galilee.

Behind Noa, her father was delivering a eulogy for Sasha to the large crowd of people gathered for the memorial service. Angered by her father's voice, she had held herself back on the fringe of the central lawn of her kibbutz. The place had changed drastically since the time when she had grown up here, just like the country itself had changed. Once a social experiment in communal life and work, the kibbutz was more like a country club now or a New York cooperative. New members bought into it. The living units had been privatized, the common nursery and the children's quarters where she had grown up with Gavri were gone, and the residents worked outside the kibbutz. Her parents were in the kibbutz records – Yosef and Anna Peled – as second generation members and they still lived here. She had refused Yosef's surname when she left the kibbutz to go to the Technion in Haifa. Her first name, Noa, she liked. It meant to tremble or shake in Hebrew and she had shook up her family when, headstrong and self-confident, she chose her grandfather's name, Kagan, as her surname, and had kept it even when she married Rafi Bourla. After their separation she had bought a unit at the kibbutz for nostalgic reasons, and for her son who had liked to visit the place.

She turned and faced her father. She wore the same rumpled riding clothes that she had slept in for several days, her thick black hair unwashed and tangled, her lips colorless and compressed to a thin line. The crowd in front of her contained a few of Sasha's young army comrades who wore the black berets of the Armored Corps, some residents of the kibbutz, a small number of Rafi's friends from the "business world," and a large number of Yosef's – high-ranking military officers, old army cronies come to pay their respects to the grandson of a retired general, and right-wing politicians from Likud and Kadima.

She glared at the man delivering the eulogy to her son – his bronze head with short steely hair, his shirt sleeves rolled up above the elbows and tabbed down military style, thick forearms, thick torso, belligerent jaw thrust forward, one hand clutching a microphone, the other clenched in a fist, his impassioned voice ringing in the air:

"It is up to us to make his sacrifice worthwhile, to make the blood he has shed for us remind us of his valor and that of his comrades in the eternal struggle to keep our country strong."

A burial urn sat on a table in front of Yosef. Young Sasha had requested in his will that he be cremated and Noa, more appalled by the fact of the will itself than by the request – the orthodox Judaic faith did not allow cremation and there were no formal crematories in Israel but the practice did exist among liberals and secular Jews -- had made sure to see that it was fulfilled. She knew that her estranged husband would cause trouble. Rafi would insist that cremation wasn't "proper" for a Jew, insist on a service down on the coast with a Rabbi, sitting *shiva*, and all the rest of it. And all for appearances' sake with *his* friends because he wasn't a religious Jew either. Fortunately, Rafi had been away on one of his "business trips" in Africa or Central America, wherever, and it had taken a few days to track him down. By then the cremation had been done. Which was fine by Noa. Her grandfather had taught her that religious Jews were "throwbacks to an age of superstition." In 1905, after he had watched the battleship Potemkin desert the workers on the shores of Odessa, old Sasha had

not given up his faith in socialism. He'd simply added a new dimen-
sion to it called Zionism and took himself south across the Black Sea
to the Mediterranean to found Kfar Borochov and build his utopian
dream in Palestine. And with him he also took his contempt for rabbis
– "corrupt, decadent men who trap Jews in obscure, ancient rituals" –
and passed it down to his daughter, his grand-daughter, and through
her to his namesake, young Sasha Bourla, whose ashes now rested on
a table that shook under Yosef's pounding fist.

"...and his sacrifice will never be forgotten. He was truly a spiritual
son of Kfar Borochov. Young Sasha followed in the heroic footsteps of
his great-grandfather, and like his great-grandfather he did not fear
the tasks which his country asked of him. He understood that only by
strength, only by putting fear into our enemies will we survive...*and
we will survive.*"

His face flushed, his clenched fist raised above his shoulder, Yosef
abruptly brought his eulogy to an end.

One person clapped, three times rapidly, then stopped.

Noa searched the crowd and saw Rafi lower his hands and look
around, a tight smile on his handsome face, trying to hide his embarrassment. Of course it would be Rafi. The fool! He'd never understood
the kibbutz code about displays of emotion. Neither had her father,
who had not grown up here.

She pushed past some of the black berets, heading toward the dais.
Yosef had supported Olmert and his stupid war in Lebanon out of
loyalty to that monster Arik Sharon, whom he'd idolized all his life.
How dare he claim that Sasha had died only to put fear into others!

People parted to make way for her and when she reached the dais
she snatched up the microphone. The low murmur of conversation
running through the crowd died out. Yosef's back was to her.

"Yosef!" she shrieked.

Her father turned to face her.

"Do you want to know the finest achievement of this kibbutz,
Yosef? This home of social and economic and human justice...and
peace of mind? Do you want to know what its finest product is, Yosef?

Well I'll tell you what it is. We've turned out the best damn combat officers in the world..." She laughed, a strange cackling sound. "The best damn fighters in the world! Isn't that what you wanted, Yosef? Isn't it?"

She pointed a finger at him. "And then what do you do with them ? I'll tell you what you do, Yosef. *You kill them!*"

A murmur of protest rippled through the crowd.

She glared at them. "How many wars will our sons have to fight before they become animals? Tell me! How many?"

She threw down the microphone, turned away and raised her hands to her face. Great heaving sobs shook her body. Slowly, her knees bent and she started to sink to the ground.

Gavri Gilboa was the first to reach her, swiftly striding in from behind to catch her beneath her armpits. Next was her old friend from the Technion, Ofra Gefen. They escorted her to her parent's stuccoed bungalow where her mother waited in the front door. Gavri sat Noa down at the cluttered dining table, Ofra held her hand, and Anna brought her a glass of water. Rafi appeared in the doorway, but Noa ignored him. She pulled her hand away from Ofra and picked up several sheets of paper from the table, holding them gingerly between her fingers and thumbs as if they were dirty. The papers trembled.

"This is his will, Ofra," she hissed. "*His will !* What, in God's name, are we doing? What kind of country have we become when a twenty-year-old feels he has to make a will?"

Ofra shrugged her shoulders, shook her head of tangled curls, scuffed the floor with her foot. "I don't know. Maybe now the army orders them to do it."

Gavri, standing erect, hands in pockets, shook his head, emphatically no.

Noa held the papers in front of her. "Listen to this," she said, and she started to read:

> *"The saying these days that goes 'Everyone look out for himself and if he's all right then everybody will be all right' simp-*

ly doesn't work. We are living in Sodom in case you haven't noticed. I cannot and do not ask for attempts to change the world, but it is our duty to cure our country. In order to do so we must stop being uninterested. I want to see all the people I love, including you Mom, stop complaining about the bad state, the army, the racism etc. and start doing. The fight is not yet lost, but it will be if we do not get up and fight. The power and influence lies in the hands of the politicians. They are bad, cynical, and corrupt. They know they are like that. They love their power. Their way of keeping their power in their own hands is by frightening away good talents, like you see in the army, from getting closer and entering the political field..."

She threw the papers to the floor and turned on her mother.

"Talents?...Like you see in the army?... Do you see what Yosef did to him?" She tore at her hair. "Did you hear him out there? Talking about survival? Whose survival? He ruined your life too, the pig-headed, stupid, old fool. We're committing suicide and he calls it survival. What about Sasha's survival? What does he get?...Oh God!...My poor Sasha!"

She was sobbing convulsively again and Anna quickly embraced her.

"Please, leave us for a while," she said quietly to the others.

Gavri nodded and rose from the table. Ofra said she would wait outside. Rafi, still in the doorway, raised his hands, his shoulders, even his eyebrows in a gesture of helpless appeal. Then Gavri placed a hand on his shoulder and steered him out the door.

Noa lay on her mother's bed, gripping her mother's hand, staring at the ceiling. Their voices murmured quietly in the empty house. Noa sighed now and then, deep, trembling sighs, sucking for air as if she had been winded or was in labor. Her other hand lay flat on herself, palm down, on her stomach.

"I'm so empty, Anna. I feel this hollow inside me and it's like I'm suffocating...and so helpless." Her eyes moved to Anna's face. "You know, as a mother there was always something...I mean I could go in there and take charge, but now..." Her grip tightened on Anna's hand, her other hand moving from her stomach to cover her face. "I feel like such a failure...and I don't know how to live without him..."

Anna smoothed her daughter's brow gently with her free hand, brushing back strands of hair with her fingers. "I know, my dear, I know, but you didn't fail him. There was nothing you could have done, and you were a wonderful mother, you did everything right. Now the doctor says..."

"But how could he do this to me, be in that stupid army..." She pounded the bed with a clenched fist. "...*and in that stupid stupid place up there.*"

"They all have to go in the army,"Anna said quietly, "and you know he wanted to do that, it was his duty."

Noa stared at her mother, hair braided in coils around her head, her kind plain face; she plucked at her brown sack-like dress cinched with an old belt she remembered from childhood. She had tried at one time to do something about Anna's indifference to her own appearance, but she'd always met with a resistance that resembled fear, a fear that she was sure came from Yosef.

She took a deep, shuddering breath. "I know, I know, and I wanted him to do his duty. But to die up there like that, it's so pointless. What are we doing there?" Her head rolled back and forth on the pillow. "I keep remembering when he was little...he was so beautiful..." She took a tissue from Anna and blew her nose. "Do you remember the time he got his nose broken in that fight at school and I was so worried that it wouldn't be straight? But I was so proud of him for standing up for what was right..." She looked away at the ceiling. "You know, back when it started to go bad between Rafi and me, I was so worried about Sasha. I mean about his values, the kind of men he was around. I wanted him to be up here more which is why I got the house, but ..." She turned to her mother. "Oh, Anna, I wanted him to grow up to be like old Sasha but I was afraid of him being around Yosef. I couldn't stand his brutal pig-headedness, the way he treated you when I was growing up. I know I've not been as close to you, but the distance...it was really because of him..."

Anna nodded slowly and stroked her brow. "It's not your fault. You're a brilliant girl and I'm proud of you." She smiled. "And I've envied your busy life. But we can talk about us later. Now you must try and rest. The doctor has given me these sedatives to help."

And soon, drifting away, Noa had an old, familiar dream, one in which her son was falling. In the past, always, he had been falling towards her, turning slowly in the air as she drew him in by some invisible cord. And always she had landed him safely beside her. But in this dream he was falling away from her, untethered, arms and legs spread out, pin-wheeling slowly through space, receding further and further into the void. Feeling desperate, helpless, she could only watch and moan in her sleep.

Many hours later, when she awoke, she felt a dark weight pressing down on her, like the leaden winter sky that could cloak the mountains of the northern Galilee during a storm. She moved over to her own house at Kfar Borochov and resisted Anna's efforts to talk again. In the years since she and Rafi had stopped sleeping together and especially after she had moved into her own condo in Tel Aviv, she'd had a few brief affairs but no serious romantic attachments. She had lived for her son and her work – a senior scientific position at the Weizmann Institute in Rehovot and at the Negev Nuclear Research Center near Dimona. Now she had only her work. Within a week she left the kibbutz and went back to it, hoping that she could keep her mind involved in it. On the day she went back she wrote the first of several letters to Dr. Jerold Raskin, her old professor and mentor at the Massachusetts Institute of Technology in the United States. She was reaching to the outside world for relief from the madhouse, the hateful place, that she felt Israel had become for her. But writing wasn't enough to escape her claustrophobia, and a few weeks later she decided to take some leave and return to New England for a visit. She called Gavri Gilboa and asked him if he would like to travel with her. They had not been close for years, but she felt she needed some reassurance, a reminder maybe of the past and what it was that she had loved in this land. The army had sent Gavri to her as the *notifier* of her son's death. Maybe he could *notify* her when it was time to return, somebody to make sure she came back. To her surprise, Gavri said he was unable to go, but he gave no reason.

As the aircraft lifted off from Ben Gurion airport and crossed over the coast, she looked down at the shoreline, the white line of surf, the western boundary of the state of Israel. *The state that killed my only son,* she thought bitterly, the embers of her anger still burning in her belly. The state had asked for her son and she had let him go. But not as a sacrifice, not the way Abraham had offered up his son Isaac when God had asked for him. Maybe men could do that to their sons without compunction, men like Abraham or her father, Yosef. But the State of Israel was not God and she was not a man. She was a woman, a mother. And if God had come to her and asked for her son as a sacrifice she knew what she would have told him: "Go fuck yourself!"

***

Two

Gavri Gilboa peered at the bus through his binoculars. Framed in an open window, midway down one side, a man's face was clear to him in three-quarter profile. The face had sharp semitic features: large thin nose, bony cheekbones, fierce eyes, scrawny neck with a bulging Adam's apple, beard neatly trimmed. Maybe mid-thirties, a hard-looking man, though the face showed some tension, which could be good...or bad...depending. He could see the man's lips moving as he talked to the Israeli army officer who stood in the roadway below the bus window. That officer's job was to "negotiate," to keep the man talking while they tried to get details - the number of terrorists on board, their locations among the passengers, weapons and explosives, and, if possible, identifications so they would know who and what they were up against.

"Dammit!" Gavri swore. He rubbed his eyes, then peered again. Light wasn't the problem. The red and white Egged bus was sharply illuminated by searchlights, blinding those inside. The problem was that he was coming up empty when he compared the face of the man in the bus window to the dozens of pictures that flipped over in his memory like a visual Rolodex.

"I can't make him," he said, lowering the glasses and shaking his head. He passed the glasses to Benny Brosh, a short wiry man with a thick black brush-cut who was lying beside him.

"You try again."

They were crouching on an embankment overlooking the road about fifty meters from the bus. Behind them it was dark and quiet, except for an occasional burst of radio static and the muted voices that came from a command tent pitched on the stubble of a field between the road and a railway track. The bus, heading south, had been stopped, finally, near an intersection at Bet Qana on the highway to Beer Sheva, about fifty kilometers north of that desert town.

Benny pressed the rubber flanges of the glasses over his eye sockets. After a moment he lowered them. "Shit! He's new to me."

Down below, the negotiating officer, Captain Moshe Elbaz, a Moroccan Jew from military intelligence, turned away from the bus and walked across the floodlit patch of roadway to the embankment and started climbing up to the command tent.

"Looks like this round of chit-chat is over," Gavri said. "Check with Tel Aviv once more then meet me at the tent."

He pushed up from his crouch and walked along the rim of the embankment a little, working the stiffness out of his knees. Order had been restored now within the wide cordon around the hijacked bus. Military police had rounded up the few journalists who'd been alerted by the police radio monitors in their bureaus and who'd made it down here before the army sealed off the area. They stood herded together near the command tent. Hours before when he and Benny arrived it had been a real *balagan* - a madhouse. Beside the journalists, there were settlers, every reservist and off-duty policeman within miles, all with their weapons, the whole lot running around and shouting different stories about who was on the bus, what weapons the terrorists had, and how and where the vehicle had been boarded. That had been well before midnight.

He looked at the luminous dial on his watch. A couple of hours to dawn. They would have to act soon. Nearby, Benny cursed as he talked with Tel Aviv center on the field radio. He was having no luck with the Arab informer network.

Gavri peered up the road in the opposite direction. As his vision adjusted to the darkness he found what he was looking for -- the second Egged bus, identical to the hi-jacked vehicle, the practice bus. Around the dark hulking shape, shadowy figures of the *Sayeret Matkal* rehearsed for the assault. As he watched the men of his old elite commando unit, a wave of feverish heat came over him. His headache had been with him for hours and the fatigue was always there. Never enough sleep, not able to sleep, and then the endless cups of coffee to stay alert during the time at work. But now that telltale fever heat. His jaws were clamped together so tightly the knots of muscle at the hinges hurt. He had palpitations in his chest. They probably wouldn't ask him to do anything this time. But then, they never let you know for certain. If only he'd had the courage to take up Noa's offer to join her for a holiday in the United States he would have been out of Israel now, avoiding all this shit. Why had he lied to her? Pointless question. He knew why. His fucking fear...

A hand touched his shoulder and with animal speed he spun round in a defensive crouch.

"Shit, Benny!...Don't do that! "

Benny waited a moment as if, like an experienced servant, he knew what to expect. "OK now?" he said gently.

Benny had been Gavri's junior partner for several years. They were an odd pair, an *ashkenazi* kibbutznik and a *sephardic* slum kid from south Tel Aviv. They had little in common, but the pairing had been done deliberately. Mixing it up was the way of the future. Gavri'd had no objection. In fact, he liked the combination of Benny's cunning and his own thoughtfulness. He also envied the way Benny and the *sephardim* could come straight out with their feelings. If only they weren't so brutal about the Arabs. But then, they *were* Arabs themselves, they just happened to be Jewish Arabs.

"It's decision time," Benny said. "Moshe's gone in the tent and we don't want to keep that cunt Kessar waiting."

Gavri took several deep, slow breaths. The palpitations had slowed. He felt cooler too. He nodded to Benny. "OK... Let's get in there."

Yacov Kessar was talking when they entered the tent. He was briefing the Defense Minister, Matti Rivlin, who had arrived by helicopter a short time before. Kessar was the deputy head of the *Sherut Bitakhon Klali,* the General Security Service, known as *Shin*

Bet or simply as *Shabak* to Israelis. Originally, it had been part of the *Mossad* organization, its famous cousin now responsible for foreign intelligence operations. But *Shabak* was different, its people came from inside the country, *sabras* only, and it shunned publicity. Aside from security details at embassies and on El Al airlines, *Shabak* was a secret police that worked exclusively inside Israel and the occupied territories and reported directly to the Prime Minister.

Kessar paused and glanced at Gavri and Benny. Gavri shook his head slightly, negatively, and saw a flicker of irritation on Kessar's face before he turned back to Rivlin and went on with his briefing:

"After the old woman in Qiryat Gat ...her name is Levana Mato...told the driver about her suspicions and got off the bus, it became a circus. She was screaming the alarm to everyone in the bus station and the terrorists must have heard the commotion, probably saw it, and they probably panicked...I'm guessing here..."

Rivlin nodded and flicked his fingers impatiently for Kessar to continue.

"Anyway, the bus headed south towards Beer Sheva at high speed and the situation was soon out of control. The police were after it, taking potshots at the tires. Word spread down the road and everybody who had a gun was trying to take out the tires as it passed by. Our first decision was where to stop it. We chose this spot and took out the engine block with a heavy machine gun. Now the situation on board..."

Rivlin, shaking his head slowly with disbelief, interrupted. "Do you know how many of our own people on board we've *killed* so far, Yacov?" He drawled the words in a deep, sarcastic tone and didn't wait for an answer. "It seems to me the only thing we know so far is that they're not suicide bombers...not yet anyway. Other than that do you know how many hostages are on board, Yacov? How many terrorists? What they want? In other words, do we have some *accurate* intelligence yet?" He tapped his watch. "We haven't got all night, you know... what's left of it."

Shabak and Rivlin both reported directly to the Prime Minister and, technically, Rivlin could not pull rank. But Gavri knew that someday Rivlin could get the top job - he wanted it badly enough - and then Kessar would need Rivlin. He wasn't going to face him down now.

"I was about to get to that, Matti," Kessar said. "From our negotiations down on the road and from our own surveillance we're pretty sure that none of the hostages has been injured. There are thirty-eight, by the way. As for the terrorists, we count at least four. Captain Elbaz has been negotiating with them... Moshe?"

"I don't think there's more than four, sir," Elbaz said, "despite what the Mota woman said about six or seven. They say they've got explosives, but I haven't seen any yet. Now they've changed their original demand about shutting down Dimona. Just let them cross the border into Egypt, they say, and they'll release the hostages. I told them..."

"Hold it Captain!" Rivlin interrupted, his hand raised, a questioning frown on his face. He turned on Kessar. "Why didn't you mention this thing about shutting down Dimona before? How long have you known they were headed there?"

Kessar opened his hands in appeal. "You just got here Matti...and besides we've stopped them, whatever plans they had. They're pretty stupid fucking Arabs if they thought they could get inside Dimona and blow it up."

"They didn't have to get in there," Rivlin snapped. "Who else knows about this?"

Kessar looked around the tent, shrugged. "Just the people in here."

Rivlin scanned the faces of the men in the tent, all of them army or *Shabak*. "Let's keep it that way for now. Am I clear?" He grasped the arm of his executive aide in the Ministry, a colonel. "Get me the Prime Minister on a secure line, as fast as you can. Let me know when you've got him." Then he swung on Kessar again.

"And just who are *they?*" he demanded. "Have you got any clue about that?"

Kessar pointed, deflecting Rivlin's attention to the men at the back of the tent. "Gavri? Have you got an answer yet?"

"We don't know," Gavri said.

He walked to the table, took his hands from his pockets and leaned on the surface. He looked steadily into Rivlin's eyes. "There are only four of them, I'm sure. One front, one back, and two in the middle of the bus. I've been down close, on the dark side behind that stone hedge while Moshe was talking to them. I couldn't see any weapons, but there's a couple of kit bags on the floor, the kind that athletes carry. I don't know if they contain explosives. We've photographed with infrared every square centimeter that we can see through the windows and still no weapons in view. We've used directional mikes and planted others on the outside of the bus. No sounds that would indicate anybody was wounded and not much else. They whisper in Arabic when they speak. We can't get much of it, but we've got a few first names. There's a Jemayel, who I think is the leader, probably the one who comes to the window to talk to Moshe. And there's a Raja. They're a pretty disciplined bunch." He shrugged his shoulders. "But that's not much help at all."

He reached his hand out and shuffled some of the dozens of photographs spread out before him on the table, clear shots of the floodlit bus and blurry, infrared close-ups of some faces.

"If we could make an identity on just one of these we could run a background check," he went on. "Get a better idea what we're up against, where they're from, what they might do. We've run the pictures through all our networks and come up with nothing. Neither has the PSS. I talked to Mohammed Dahlan down in Gaza and they're cooperating. But if these guys are Hamas, Dahlan won't be of much help. Moshe took one of our most reliable Gaza informers up to the bus and gave him a look at the one who's doing the talking, but he couldn't make an identity. He thinks they're new and I agree with him. I'm not saying yet that they're from outside the country, but the bus started on the coast in Ashkelon, a regular commercial service to Beer Sheva, and if they got on in Ashkelon how did they get there in the first place? Over the border terrorists usually hit the first thing they see, their nerves give out. These guys maybe tense, but they're pretty cool, well-trained...and one other thing... I thought I detected a Lebanese accent..."

"Hezbollah?" Rivlin said.

Kessar snorted and received a scathing look.

Gavri shrugged. "That would be a first..."

"Dimona is a first," Rivlin replied. "Answer the question, as a probability."

"We have nothing to indicate Hezbollah is operational inside Israel," Kessar said, taking over. "If you're looking at this as something spawned by the war in Lebanon last month I have to ask how they could put four operatives into Ashkelon with explosives...if they have them. We haven't had a sea attack from Lebanon since Fatah tried it in '78. You think they came as far south as Ashkelon in Zodiacs?"

Rivlin looked at Gavri. "What's your answer?"

"It's possible," Gavri said. "But what I don't understand is the bus. The bus is retro. We haven't had a bus incident in years. And the men on board are retro. They don't just find a target, any target, and blow it up like terrorists do these days. That would have happened by now. But what is not retro is Dimona. If Hezbollah is after something that far south then the bus makes sense. They could have been dropped off further out at sea from a bigger ship. We should check the beaches around Ashkelon for inflatables..."

"Do it!" Rivlin said.

"Matti! It's almost dawn!" a deep voice boomed through the tent. A tall, thick-chested officer with a red beret and a General's insignia who had been sprawled in a canvas director's chair with his eyes closed stood up abruptly. "If my boys are going in we've got to get on with it. You're as well informed about this fiasco as you're going to be without talking to one of those bastards down there and we're running out of time."

"Alright! ...Alright!" Rivlin said irritably. "Proceed. I've got to talk to the Prime Minister...and once again," he said, his voice rising to take in everybody in the tent, "not a word outside this tent about Dimona. Understood?"

He stared around at the men in the tent, waiting for their nods of acknowledgment.

"Proceed!" he said, and instantly the men moved and radios crackled, a babble of voices, men on headsets talking. Gavri had turned to head for the exit, thinking about the beach at Ashkelon, about getting some people down there to check for abandoned inflatables, when he heard his name called. He knew the General's deep voice, Chaim Carmon, the Chief of Staff of the IDF, the man in charge of the *Matkal*. He stopped, his stomach muscles clenching, his heart pounding, and he started shaking his head slowly from side to side. They were going to ask him again! They couldn't!

He felt the hand on his shoulder.

"It's alright Gavri," Carmon said. "I want you to go out with Lieutenant Landau here and help him with the boys. Just help him, that's all."

Gavri nodded and looked at the young Lieutenant with the blackened face, dark watch cap, odd bits of uniform that made him look sloppy. He jerked his head at the exit. Outside the tent, he stopped in the dark and took a deep breath. Benny waved Landau away. "Give us a moment," he said. Gavri could hear the voices inside the tent.

Kessar: "What was that all about?"

Carmon: "Nothing..nothing at all. Gavri and I used to be in *Matkal*. He's been through a lot. Saved my life once in Lebanon in '82. Moved like a native among the Arabs."

Kessar: "Sure! But you gotta know them in your gut, grow up with them, like we did in Yemen. Anyway, I think Gavri's getting soft. I hear he's getting religion or something, becoming a fucking *maggid*..."

"Asshole!" Benny said, loud enough for the men inside to hear. Then he linked his arm through Gavri's and pulled him away from the tent towards the waiting figure of Lieutenant Landau.

"We're over there," Landau said, pointing to the dark hulk of the practice bus. On the way they walked past the shadowy corral of journalists and a voice called out in English:

"What's happening?"

"You getting a hard on?" Benny yelled back.

For the next five minutes Gavri watched the final rehearsal for the assault. In teams of three the *Matkal* commandos sprinted at the empty bus, the man in the middle a pace behind the other two and holding a Beretta automatic pistol in his hand – the Beretta was for accuracy, pin-pointing terrorists whereas an Uzi assault gun would spray and possibly hit some passengers. As they came up to the side of the bus the front two each dropped to one knee and formed a step with their linked hands, and, without breaking stride, the middle man went up on the hand-step to the window of the bus with his Beretta pointing inside, all of it in one flowing motion and with startling speed. Another team of three tackled the door, two men prying it open at the rubber seal, the third squeezing through with his Beretta out front. They had been at it, over and over, for hours.

Gavri moved among the men. Blackened faces could not conceal their youth, twenty years old at the most. He had been eighteen himself when he was selected. Like their Lieutenant, the men wore shabby, odd pieces of uniform, running shoes on their feet. Each one of these young, blackened faces, carefully selected and trained, had the speed and reflexes of a panther; could sight the quarry with a keen and eager eye. And kill. They were quiet and confident. They had been told they were the very best and they knew it. They made it seem easy.

If only they knew.

It had been easy for him, too, at the beginning. So easy to be bloodied. Almost natural. There was nothing to it if you were good. And he had been very good and he did it over and over. Until one day the voice that always said to him – *Don't let the others down. If they can take it you can* – that voice had stopped speaking to him. His nervous system rebelled and his heart knew it wasn't natural at all. Anxiety and anger were his only feelings, he had trouble with women and sex, had trouble sleeping, and, what puzzled him most, he didn't have dreams. He'd finally told his superiors that he couldn't do it anymore. And they thanked him for telling them, gave him some tests, and told him to get some rest and get better. What he had not found out since then was what they had meant by getting better.

He turned to Lieutenant Landau. "What's your name?"

"Gadi."

"The timing has to be very precise, Gadi," he said quietly. "To the very slightest fraction of a second if we're going to save lives. That's difficult when it happens because the noise and the light can throw your timing off. Remember that and you'll be alright. Now get me the man you've chosen and I'll go through it with him."

Gavri was stunned by the shock wave of sound -- even though he knew from the countdown in his earpiece that it was coming – the huge percussive slam-bangs of the stun grenades. And then, instantly, the light surrounding the bus went from bright garish yellow to blinding white. Magnesium flares.

"Shoot!"

He barked the word without lowering the glasses he'd trained on the front windscreen of the bus, seventy meters down the road. The 7.62mm Galil sniper rifle held by the *Matkal* kid lying beside him cracked rapidly and he saw a tight cluster of holes appear suddenly in the windscreen of the bus, saw tiny radiating cracks embracing them like wreaths. The head of the terrorist in the driver's seat of the bus snapped back, his face blossoming red with blood. He counted three holes in the windscreen. And he counted seven seconds from the first crack of the Galil rifle beside him to the end of the gunfire at the bus.

"One...dead...terrorist!"

The young *Matkal* commando, cradling his sniper's rifle, spoke the words with an affected nonchalance. But Gavri was already moving, rolling over the edge of the embankment, then up on his feet and sprinting up the road. Benny Brosh was ahead of him and had wedged himself through the broken door of the bus right behind three commandos. More of them were clambering in through the rear window. Gavri tore off half the door, coming in behind Benny. He grabbed the hair on the head of the man his kid had shot and jerked it back. Three small entry wounds, purple holes, one under the right eye and two in the forehead. Still, there was enough left to recognize the face and he didn't. He let go of the hair and the head flopped down on the man's chest, the back of it missing. Medics were trying to get through the door now and Benny kicked at them, yelled at them.

"Not yet! There's a fucking bomb."

A woman's voice shrieked. "That's him. That's the leader."

"Down here!" Benny yelled, and started pushing his way up the aisle with Gavri pushing on his back. Flashlight beams arced and slashed like frenzied laser swordplay through the interior, stabbing into the corners and under the seats. Light splashed on the side of a man's face, twisted in pain. Gavri recognized the man who had talked at the window of the bus.

"That's him! Hold that light!...Gadi? Are you in here? Get your men back!"

Benny reached down, grabbed the terrorist's shoulder, rolled him over. An automatic pistol lay beneath him. Blood was spattered on the front of the man's white shirt. Benny knelt and stuffed the gun in his waistband, clutched the short beard and held the face in the beam of his flashlight. Two dark, defiant eyes stared at him.

"He's alive!" Benny yelled over his shoulder. Then he dropped his light and slapped the man's face hard. "Where's the bomb?" he yelled in Arabic. He pulled a switch blade from his pocket and slit the man's nostril. "Your throat is next! Where is it?"

Gavri saw a black canvas duffle bag in the aisle and another man crawling crabwise towards it on his side, his stomach a bloody mess. The man groaned as he reached out for the bag and Gavri stepped on his arm, pinning it to the floor. "Don't touch it!" he said in Arabic. He swung to Benny. "Not a another move Benny! Understand?" There was a sharp tone of command in his voice and Benny nodded quickly, his fingers still clutching his man's beard.

"Medic! Medic! In here!" Landau's voice bellowed above the others.

"Gadi!" Gavri yelled. "Hold the medics. We need a minute."

"I can't. It's one of our own. A woman. She's badly wounded."

"Hold it! Just for a minute. That's an order!"

He shone his light in the face of Benny's man. "Are you Jemayel?"

"Jewish dog!" the man spat at him.

He turned and knelt beside the man whose arm he had stepped on. "What's your name?" he asked quietly.

"Jewish pig!" said the man Benny was holding.

Gavri ignored him. "You want something for your pain," he said to his man. "Tell me your name. Tell me what's in the bag."

"Open it and see," said Benny's man.

"Is it booby-trapped?"

"I said, open it and see," said Benny's man again, and Benny slapped him..

"We can wait till you bleed to death," Gavri said to his man. "That's a gut wound. The pain must be awful. Tell me if he is Jemayel."

His man gasped in agony. "He is Jemayel...help me!"

"Your mother's cunt!" the one called Jemayel rasped and Benny slapped him again.

"Something more first," Gavri said, ignoring him. "Your name and what's in the bag?"

"Mustafa...my name is Mustafa. There are explosives in the bag, but they're not booby-trapped... Help me...give me something..."

Gavri decided quickly. He pulled the bag over, unzipped it and shone his flashlight inside. Packs of cemtex taped to a frame, wires and a timing device. But nothing ticking, nothing flashing. They hadn't armed it. He breathed deeply through his nostrils and, for the first time, he was aware of the stench - a mixture of urine, sweat, shit, oil, cordite, and blood. Nothing changed. It was always disgusting. He lifted his head and looked for Gadi Landau, raising his voice.

"Call in your medics, Gadi. It's over."

*

The sky to the east began to brighten. Silhouetted tamarisks swayed in the backwash of the helicopters that came like giant black bugs risen with the dawn. They clattered in and out of the stubbled field behind the command tent, ferrying wounded hostages from the makeshift field hospital in the roadway behind the bus to the modern operating rooms in the cities up the coast. One hostage, a young woman, was not moved from the roadway. Frenzied medics worked on her, their hands flying, probing, swabbing, injecting, pounding on her chest, fighting to save her life under the lamps which were paling rapidly in the new day. Over at the shattered bus, the small platoon of journalists who had been released from their corral scuttled about, the lone camera crew and several still photographers among them. The bodies of two dead terrorists were rolled unceremoniously out the windows and the soundman grimaced when he heard in his headset the thwack of a body hitting the pavement like a sack of wet mud.

Gavri got a medic to bind up the wounds of his two captives. They had selected in advance a mud-brick farmer's hut less than a hundred meters away as a place for interrogation if any of the terrorists survived the attack. As he came out of the bus shoving Jemayel by the elbow a middle-aged man in a Boston Red Sox sweatshirt and journalist's credentials hanging on a chain around his neck stood below the door in the roadway. He was blocking the exit.

"Alan Raskin...Reuters," he said. "Can you tell me what those guys were after?"

"No," Gavri said, pushing the man aside.

"Out of the fucking way!" Benny said, coming behind him.

"Where were they headed? What did they want?" Raskin called after them.

Gavri and Benny ignored him. "We should never let those guys stay and watch," Benny said as they moved off, each of them hauling a prisoner by the arm.

"It's a trade off," Gavri said. The pictures and sounds would be zipping soon via satellite into millions of homes around the world, including the Arab world where the Israelis wanted to send a message. See and learn, the pictures would say, otherwise you too could end up like a piece of dead meat tossed out on a lonely road at dawn. "They want the story out, let people see what happens to the bad guys,"

Raskin was following them now and Gavri located a military policeman nearby, called him over and pointed to the reporter.

"Keep that bastard away from us!"

The last he saw of the journalist the man was arguing, lifting his credentials and shoving them in the face of the policeman. He looked too old to be playing reporter, a children's game in Gavri's view.

Yacov Kessar had a reputation for carrying out brutal interrogations with Arabs. Gavri had seen a few of them and he thought that most of the time Kessar's method was counterproductive. The two prisoners, Jemayel and Mustafa, their hands taped behind their backs, were propped against a wall of the mud-brick hut, their legs sticking out across the floor. Their faces were pulped from pistol whippings and Mustafa, the one with the gut wound, was unconscious. Benny Brosh and another *Shabak* agent had taken turns at the job and sweat had darkened their shirts at the armpits and between their shoulder blades.

Gavri knew he couldn't stop Benny from taking part, even if he'd wanted too. Kessar was giving the orders, and besides, he knew that Benny didn't mind doing this sort of dirty work. Normally he would have stepped outside during the beatings. But this time an inner voice had told him to stay and he had hunkered near the doorway and watched. He was familiar with this mysterious voice. He'd first started hearing it about the time of the *Al Aqsa intifada* in the late summer of 2000. He had never sought professional treatment. Instead, he'd gone where the voice had told him to go, searching for answers in the volumes of Jewish mysticism called the Kaballah. The voice had come to him more frequently over time. Among other things it told him that

his country was going backwards in time. They were no longer fighting
outside enemies, the armies of the Arab nations. Those armies had
been defeated. The wheel had come full circle and they were once
again fighting the people who lived on the land, the Philistines. They
were also fighting among themselves, a struggle fueled by the worship
of the false idols of *Samael,* the agent of Satan. They had retreated to
an ancient tribalism where suspicion, fear, even hatred of the outsider
was the bond and military strength was the only guarantor of respect.
The sands were shifting and the fragile roots of the culture that they
had brought with them and transplanted here, a morality from
another continent, were not strong enough to hold. The old ways, the
brutal savage ways of the ancient land, sharp as a knife-edge and hard
as flint, those ways formed the bedrock that had been swept bare and
exposed for those who had eyes to see.

Among wolves, be a wolf!

He looked over at Benny, resting on his haunches, his elbows on
his knees, smoking a cigarette, chatting and laughing. Benny was in
his element here. He understood fear and hatred. He was a wolf. He
belonged here. And the voice said to him:

As does the Blind Dragon if you will let him.

Gavri shook off the spell of the voice, got up from his crouch near
the doorway and went outside. He wanted to get away from the hut for
a moment and he walked back to the bus, thinking to look for
anything they might have missed. There was a press briefing going on
in the roadway and he saw the journalist from Reuters, Alan Raskin,
standing with the other "children." Raskin had grey hair, definitely too
old for this game. Gavri listened for a few minutes and marveled at
how glibly the military press briefer lied. The terrorists, the reporters
were told, were from Hamas and they wanted the release of Hamas
prisoners held by Israel in return for the hostages. Where did they
originate? Gaza, the officer replied, with complete assurance.

Back at the hut, Gavri went to the *Shabak* officer who sat with a note-pad at the table with the radio. Beside him lay three hand guns, two black duffle bags and their contents: a Swiss Army knife, blocks of cemtex, timers, detonators, an open carton of Marlboro cigarettes, and a Koran. Nothing else, nothing that could help identify the men, who they were, where they had come from. Gavri asked to see the officer's notes. There was little written down from the interrogation itself. When they stormed the bus he'd confirmed a Lebanese accent in the speech of the gut-wounded man. But Kessar wouldn't allow him to explore that line of questioning. It was so simple. The man Mustafa – if that was his real name – was in great pain already, so why inflict more? Use his condition against him. Instead they had beat him so that he was unconscious.

Now, Kessar himself took over. He stepped between Jemayel's legs and kicked him viciously in the crotch. Jemayel's body doubled over from the waist and he retched, thick gobs of blood and saliva dribbling from his mangled lips.

"*Allah o'Akbar*" he gurgled.

Kessar grabbed his hair and slammed his head back against the wall. "So God is great, hey!" he shouted. "You little piece of shit!" And he started beating the man's head against the wall in time to his own words. "You big...tough...little...piece ...of shit!" He stopped and stooped to look in Jemayel's face. "You'll be sorry you ever left your mother's cunt."

Bursts of static and crackling voices came from the radio pack in one corner of the room. A message for Gavri Gilboa. He listened to the radio and learned that an inflatable and an outboard motor had been found, hidden at the back of the beach just north of Ashkelon. He looked over at Kessar.

"I think they're Hezbollah. Let me try to talk to them for a minute."

Kessar shrugged. "Go ahead."

He went to the one called Mustafa, his best bet. He bent over and patted the man's face. No response. Still unconscious. He knew Kessar wouldn't give him time to revive him. He rose and went over to Jemayel.

"Jemayel?"

At the sound of his name the man opened his eyes and stared at him.

"Are you from Beirut or from the south?"

The man's eyes flashed with defiance. His face twisted with pain and he gurgled two words.

"Jewish filth!"

The radio crackled again. A message for Yacov Kessar and all police commanders. The voice said that one of the hostages, a young Israeli woman named Gony Padeh, had just died at the field hospital in the road behind the bus. Gunshot wound. Ballistics check to follow. Investigation to start immediately.

Gavri had closed his eyes somewhere in the middle of this message. He opened them in time to see Kessar punch the wall in rage. Everyone in the hut was watching the chief now, waiting for his reaction to the news of Gony Padeh's death. Cradling his injured hand, Kessar looked wildly around the room. Then he strode to a corner, picked up a heavy rusted spanner and returned to the two Arabs sprawled against the bloody wall. He pushed Gavri aside and stood over the one called Jemayel, gripped the wrench with both hands, raised it over his head and smashed it down on the Arab's skull.

Once. Twice. Three times.

When he finished he turned and held the bloody spanner out to Benny Brosh. Benny glanced at Gavri, hesitated, but only for a second. Then he took the spanner and with two swift, one-handed blows he crushed Mustafa's skull.

***

Three

On his first week in Israel, Alan Raskin had wandered through the old English churchyard in Jerusalem looking for his father's grave. The cemetery lay on the terraced slope of Mount Zion overlooking the Hinnom valley, the valley of Hell where idolatrous Israelites of old had sacrificed their children to Moloch and Baal. It was here that the consuls of the British Empire had tried to make a proper churchyard far from their precious sceptered isle. They'd had to do without oaks and elms – the trees were tamarisks, cedars, a scattered palm. They'd also had to do without grass. The four-footed caretakers, a herd of shaggy brown goats, had seen to that. Only minutes after Alan found his father's headstone, they came clambering up over the terraces, swarming over the graves, showing an amazing acrobatic skill as they balanced on their hind legs on the tops of the tombstones and nibbled at the low hanging branches of the trees. The flowers he'd brought were gone in a minute or two and he was left to stare at the inscription on the plain, flat stone:

THOMAS PENROSE
1916 – 1948

That was all there was to it. No epitaph, no loving care, no beloved father of so and so. Nothing but the name and the numbers. The last date, the date of Penrose's death, was also the year of the birth of the State of Israel and of Alan, himself, a son who not only had never known the man buried here but who also hadn't known until recently that the man was his father. Now, he wanted to know more about him, much more.

He felt at this moment no sense of loss, felt nothing but a lingering resentment with his mother for having withheld this information from him until she had died. He'd been based at Reuters headquarters in London when that happened and he'd had to hurry home within three days to Massachusetts for her funeral. Six months ago, winter in New England, the oaks and maples stripped to bare black sticks at the Jewish cemetery in the Everett suburb of Boston. That cemetery was somber and depressing, the uniformly sized headstones packed in tight stacks, reminding him of the stark Potsdammerplatz memorial to the holocaust in Berlin. Some twenty or thirty people gathered at the gravesite, mostly the same people who had been at the synagogue service in Cambridge.

It all had come as a surprise for Alan. His parents, Jerold and Ruth Raskin, had never been religious Jews, nor were they pro-Zionist, especially not his mother, even though she had been born in Israel. The day he arrived in Cambridge his father, an *emeritus* MIT scientist and an atheist, told him there would be a funeral service at Temple Beth Shalom.

"The old Tremont Street Shul? You must be kidding?" Alan exclaimed. "Ruth wouldn't be caught dead in..." He stopped himself, lowered his voice. "What happened to you two?"

"I know, I know, I can understand your surprise," Jerold said, nodding his head, clearly uncomfortable with the question. "In the last few years Ruth began to get interested in Judaism, in the religion. I told her it was because of her age, that she was facing death, and she replied '*Exactly.*'" He shrugged. "You know your mother. I went along with her to keep her company. They have a lot of young people at the temple and there's a lot of singing, guitar music...it's not too bad as religions go."

Alan snorted. "Charismatic Judaism!"

It was not until after the cemetery when he and Jerold were back in the big wooden frame house on Ellery Street where Alan had grown up that Jerold said that he had something important to tell him. Just between the two of them, he said, and he ushered Alan solemnly by the elbow into his study and closed the door, even though there was nobody else in the house.

Bemused, yet politely patient, Alan sat down in front of his father's desk. Jerold stayed on his feet behind the desk, shuffling back and forth, his hands fidgety. His father was pushing eighty, a stooped, white-haired, fragile figure.

"You're making me nervous Dad...Please sit down!"

Jerold shook his head but he stopped shuffling, leaned with his hands on his desk and faced Alan.

"A long time ago your mother swore me to secrecy about something that could not be revealed to you until after her death. I kept my word to her, although there were many times when I wished I hadn't because I didn't think it was fair to you...that she was being selfish." He paused and stared at Alan for a moment. Then he gave up the protection of the desk, came around it and when Alan turned in his chair Jerold placed his hands on his son's shoulders as if to hold him down. "You have been my son for many years," he said, "and this is the hardest thing I've ever done in my life..." His voice broke and his eyes teared-up. "I have to tell you that I am not your true father."

"Oh come on!"

"It's true Alan, believe me. I wish it wasn't so, but it's true."

"Stop it Dad! This is not funny."

But Jerold wasn't a joker and he could feel his heart pounding in his chest. Over his years as a journalist he'd learned to keep emotion at a distance, but that wasn't working now. *This* man in front of him was his father, he loved *this* man who had his hands on his shoulders, but what *this* man was saying frightened him. He wanted to shake him, hit him, make him stop. Jerold had frightened him only once before, long ago, when he was six years old and they'd played a game where his father pretended his boy had disappeared after he'd eaten some magic cabbage. "Where's Alan, Ruthie?" Jerold said. "I can't see him anywhere. Where's my Alan?" At first, enjoying this, the boy had grinned and said "I'm here." But when Jerold persisted, when he kept saying "Where's Alan? I can't see him," he had panicked and started screaming "I'm here! I'm here! Why can't you see me? I'm here!" Now, he wanted to shout – *I'm not somebody else's son! I'm your son! I'm here!* But that urge to shout was drowned in a flood of icy anger that he felt surging up inside him and carrying with it the awful realization that this was no game.

He shoved Jerold's hands from his shoulders. "And just *who* is my real father supposed to be?"

"Alan please!...Hit me if you want to, but don't freeze me out. I'm only telling you what I think is owed to you, what has been hidden from you for so long."

Hidden? The story that he'd grown up with had been pretty straight forward: his mother's parents, Benjamin and Helga Stahlmann, German Jewish immigrants to Palestine in the 1920's, had been killed by Arabs a month before the Jewish declaration of the State of Israel in 1948; Ruth, eighteen years old at the time and their only child, had been brought to Canada by a relative and in a very short time she had met and married Jerold Raskin, a young science student at the University of Toronto.

"Why did she want it hidden?"

Jerold sighed. "For reasons of shame, I think."

"*Who is he?*"

"His name was Thomas Penrose, an Englishman, a lawyer with the British civil administration in Palestine. He was the victim of a hit-and-run accident on a Jerusalem street in 1948, a month before the British Mandate expired. The car was driven by a couple of Irgun terrorists who had just robbed a bank."

"Where's the shame in that?"

Jerold shrugged. "That's the story your mother told me. The shame, I suppose, was in the fact that you were conceived out of wedlock. Penrose was dead and couldn't marry her. Remember, this was just after the war and morals were different then. She was pregnant when I met her, but she never tried to hide it." He paused, his eyes welling with tears. "Her story was so tragic and I loved her so much, we just said the baby was premature. But she made me vow that I would never tell you. Please forgive me."

Still angry with disbelief, Alan shook his head slowly and Jerold, apparently misreading him, kept on talking, filling an unbearable vacuum.

"I'm sorry, but maybe with some time you'll come to understand. Anyway, she never went back to Israel. Wouldn't step foot in it. I went once by myself to have a look. Nineteen eighty-two, remember? You were up in Beirut then and one day I was standing on the beach in Tel Aviv when some fighter jets flew overhead heading north and the people next to me cheered. I thought I didn't belong there and I went back to the hotel and packed and came home."

But Alan wasn't listening.

In the following days, he visited Temple Beth Shalom on Tremont Street, a squat yellow brick building with a triple arched doorway and stained glass windows, a building which seemed oddly out of place among the wood-framed houses that lined the quiet street. He questioned the young Rabbi about Ruth – "a charming, lovely woman who came to us late in her life," the Rabbi said – but he learned nothing new about her past. The lobby of the Temple was plastered with posters advertising forthcoming family events: songfests, children's games, country hikes, talks about support for Israel, Hebrew lessons. Alan found it hard to imagine Ruth and Jerold amongst all that. He could remember friends who had gone to Hebrew school at the Tremont Street Shul, but he had not been among them. He had followed in the footsteps of his God-free parents and, like them, he'd never been a Zionist. He was suspicious of identity politics in all forms. Even during the hysterical excitement among American Jews at the time of the miraculous Six Day War in 1967, a time when pride and testosterone fired up many young Jewish males and made them fierce *macho* warriors who vowed to go fight for Israel, he was not moved. In fact, throughout many years of foreign reporting he had avoided Israel altogether, didn't want to go there, for reasons he had never fully explored. Some Jewish friends joked that he was a self-hating Jew, and some of them, he felt, were not really joking at all. But now, in the light of this startling news about Thomas Penrose, he became curious about Israel and the cause of his father's death.

On returning to London he searched in the Colonial Office records on His Majesty's Mandatory Administration for Palestine,1920-1948, and discovered that Thomas Penrose was not just a lawyer for the civil administration. He was a prosecutor of Jewish terrorists. And the transcripts of his trials revealed an undercurrent of anti-semitism in his words that ran through page after page in the cases he prosecuted: *You can't expect anything different from this kind of people, your Honour.* A few months later, when the bureau chief's job in the Reuters bureau in Tel Aviv became available, he used his seniority to abbreviate the selection process and to take the position. He was a professional and he would see to it that he did the job properly, but he was also in Israel because of his curiosity – he wanted to find out as much as he could about what had happened to the man named Thomas Penrose.

In the week after he discovered his father's grave, Alan found the police report on his death in the Public Records Office in Jerusalem. The accident in 1948 was described as a hit-and-run on the Jaffa Road, just below the Law Courts in the Russian Compound. Hit-and-run, pure and simple. No bank robbery, no Irgun. He then placed an advertisement in the personal columns of Israel's leading newspapers requesting that anybody who had known or had information about a Thomas Penrose, an English lawyer with His Majesty's Mandatory Administration for Palestine, 1944-48, who had been killed in a traffic accident on April 17th, 1948, in Jerusalem to please contact him. He gave his name and the phone and address for the Reuters Bureau in Tel Aviv.

The day after his advertisement appeared in the papers, he dropped by the CBS News bureau to pick up Frank Harris, the American TV bureau chief, before going to lunch. CBS was a client of

Reuters, the bureaus were in the same building on Hamasger Street in Tel Aviv, the same floor, and there was an easy flow of staff and information back and forth between them. While he was waiting for Harris, Ofra Gefen, an Israeli who managed the CBS office staff, sidled up to him.

"I don't mean to pry Alan," she said, "but I saw your advertisement and I wondered if the person who was killed in Jerusalem was a relative."

Ofra was good at her job, Harris had said, fast and efficient, "if only she didn't always look as if she'd just rolled out of bed." Harris was right. Ofra had no make up, tangled hair, torn jeans that looked unwashed, and one ever-so-slightly skewed eye. A strabismus, Alan thought it was called. Or more crudely, a walleye. Maybe she didn't think she was attractive because of that eye.

"No, just a friend of the family," he replied. "And you're not prying. I placed the ad in the papers."

"I'm sorry," Ofra said. "A close friend?"

Alan let this sit for a minute. When he'd first met her he'd thought that Ofra was rather gentle and sweet, but that was only until he heard her bossing the other Israelis in her bureau. She could be *sabra* rude and tough. According to Harris she was also incurably nosy.

"No need to be sorry," he said. "I'm just doing it as a favor. I thought I might take advantage of my assignment and poke about a bit."

"Well, it's a small place," Ofra said. "Everybody knows everybody so something should turn up pretty quickly. Let me know if you need any help."

She smiled at him, and in that moment she gave Alan the distinct impression that she already knew something. But whether she did or not, she was right about one thing – something did turn up pretty quickly.

Three days after the ad appeared he received a phone call at his bureau from a man who said his name was Yitzhak. He was calling about the ad. When Alan asked him for his second name he replied,

"Yitzhak will do." Pretty quick and pretty mysterious. Yitzhak wanted to meet that night at the bar in the King David hotel in Jerusalem. When Alan asked how they would recognize each other Yitzhak said not to worry, he would find him.

Alan drove up to Jerusalem that evening and sat in the King David bar for fifteen minutes listening to some loud Americans. They were arguing about what the Israelis should do to Hezbollah which had attacked an Israeli border patrol that morning, seizing two Israeli soldiers and taking them back into Lebanon. Earlier in the day, Alan had sent one of the three reporters in the Reuters bureau north to cover the story. The consensus among the Americans at the bar was that "we" should bomb Hezbollah in Lebanon the way Bush had bombed the Taliban in Afghanistan.

"Flush 'em out!"

Alan felt a hand on his shoulder, a voice with a thick Hebrew accent in his ear: "You demean yourself, Mr. Raskin, listening to this trash. Why are you American Jews so very gung-ho about Israel's wars?"

He turned and saw an old man with dentures smiling at him. But it was not a sincere smile. Yitzhak, if this was indeed him, was seventy at a minimum and he looked like a diplomat: dark lightweight suit, crisp white shirt, striped tie, neatly brushed white hair, a trim mustache, and a deep tan. Not many Israelis dressed like that.

"May I have a word with you? Outside where it is quiet. I suggest the terrace."

"Hot out there," Alan said. "You're Yitzhak I assume?"

"Of course."

"Of course! You obviously know who I am, so do you mind telling me who you are?"

Yitzhak smiled again, a rictus that disappeared as quickly as it came. He looked impatient, like he wanted to get on with it.

"Yitzhak will do."

Same as on the telephone, which was like saying "Bill" in Israel. He held out his hand, playing along for the moment. "Alan Raskin," he said, and Yitzhak gave him a limp shake, then pointed to the terrace.

"Shall we go outside?"

The terrace overlooked the floodlit Ottoman battlements of the Old City. The night air was fetid and filled with diesel exhaust. Yitzhak brushed off one of the white lawn chairs, sat down, and got down to business.

"What is it you are looking for about Thomas Penrose?"

Alan thought that he was the one who should be asking the questions. "Did you know him?"

Yitzhak smiled. "Only indirectly, many years ago. You know, the English have a piece of good advice. Let sleeping dogs lie. I think you should follow that advice. There is nothing to be gained by digging up the past now. Those were passionate times, ugly times in many ways, best forgotten. England and Israel have made, shall we say, an accommodation over the years since then and we get along with each other quite satisfactorily now."

"I don't understand what you're saying.," Alan said. The man was talking like a diplomat and it annoyed him. "Thomas Penrose was my father and I'm an American. I don't care about your relations with Great Britain."

"Your father?" Yitzhak seemed taken aback. "Really? Why have you left it so long to come here and ask about him?"

"Because I only found out recently that I was his son. And who the hell are you to tell me I shouldn't ask questions about my father? Do you know who murdered him?"

Yitzhak crossed his legs and sighed. "You've looked at the British police records?"

Alan nodded.

"There's nothing in those records about murder," Yitzak said. "It was recorded as a hit-and-run accident. Right? That was the conclusion of the British police. And now I will tell you why I have come to you." He leaned forward with his elbows resting on the arms of his chair. "They did not want to push the investigation further on the public record because Thomas Penrose was working with them. The Special Branch and the Secret Service. As I said, those were passionate times, ugly times. Let me explain."

Alan took out a notebook. "Do you mind?"

"Please," Yitzhak replied, and he sat back and continued:

In 1944, he said, the country was in great turmoil. The war against the Nazis was almost over and the Jews were looking to the future, a future that would be determined by what the British would do with their Mandate. Menachem Begin's Irgun and the Stern Gang were striking at the British with terrorist attacks. The Haganah, the military arm of the Jewish Agency which had 30,000 members fighting with the British against Hitler, bitterly opposed this policy of the Irgun and the Sternists. In their view nothing should be done to damage the effort to win the war as quickly as possible and save the Jews in the death camps. Then, to bring things to a boil, in November 1944, Lord Moyne, the British Minister of State in Cairo, was murdered in the street by two members of the Stern Gang. This maddened the British and the police in Palestine struck hard, rounding up scores of Irgun and Stern Gang followers and deporting them. The job of Thomas Penrose was processing the potential deportees. Over the next few years he had the power to decide who could stay in Palestine and who would go. He worked in secret, using police dossiers, and his decisions were final.

Yitzak lifted a finger, pointing at Alan. "You must try to imagine what his power meant to the Jews. Many of them had escaped the horrors of the extermination camps in Europe. They had managed with great difficulty to get to Palestine. And here sits this man who can decide in a moment that they can be deported. Sent away from their homeland! To where? The whole world was a hostile place for us then." He paused, agitated by his own story and sweating in the heat. He took out a clean white handkerchief and mopped his brow, tucked the handkerchief away, and went on. "So Thomas Penrose was bound to be hated, even if he'd been devoted to the English virtue of fair play in his adminstration of justice. But Penrose wasn't that kind of man. If you've looked at the court records of the cases your father prosecuted, you must know that he was a vicious anti-semite. He was able to use his power indiscriminately, without being questioned. For us the last straw came when he started working with some anti-Zionist British Secret Service officers to select Haganah men, not just Irgun and Stern, for deportation." He paused again, shaking his head slowly, as if looking back in the past. "Valuable men," he said. "Men we needed against the Arabs."

There were angry exchanges in the higher councils of the Haganah, Yitzhak went on. The Rama, the chief himself, was involved. Some were for a presentation of the evidence to the British High Commissioner, Sir Alan Cunningham, appealing to the British sense of fair play. Others scoffed at the naivete of such an appeal.

"Then, on the night of April 17th, 1948," Yitzhak said, "three men took the law into their own hands. They sat in a truck on the Jaffa Road near the the Russian Compound. It was the British Security headquarters then. They waited for Penrose and when he came out they ran him down and killed him."

He peered at Alan, waiting for a reaction.

"Were you one of the three men in the truck?"

That startled Yitzak for a moment. Then he shook his head and smiled as if the question were naughty. "No. One of the men is dead now. He died over thirty years ago. I'm not going to say who the other two were except to tell you this. The Haganah held its own courtmartial and they were punished. Today, they are highly respected citizens of Israel who have served the State well and it would do no good for anyone to dredge up the past. I have come to tell you this story to satisfy your curiosity about this man Penrose, a natural if rather belated curiosity, I might say, if he was indeed your father."

Alan bristled. "Are you saying that you doubt he was my father?"

"Not at all. I take your word for that. But you see, given the time that has elapsed, you could not have learned any of this in London or anywhere else. May I hope that you are satisfied?"

"Sounds like these guys might be important men who don't want the stink of a murderous past washing over them. Who *are* you?"

"And why am I doing this? I forget you are a journalist, Mr. Raskin." He paused. "Let's just say that I think it only fair that you should know the truth about your father and his death. That it's better to do it discreetly rather than have you poking blindly into old wounds that may not have healed fully."

"I see. Well thank you, but you still haven't answered my question."

Yitzak laughed, that was all. Alan didn't know what was funny. Then Yitzak stood up, pulled down his jacket.

"I must go now. Goodbye Mr. Raskin."

"How can I find you?"

But he was off, out through the lobby to the street and back into the night from which he had come so mysteriously. Alan flipped through his notes. He'd been presented with a very neat package on Thomas Penrose, one designed to stop him probing further. Who were these two men? These *highly respected citizens of Israel who had served the state well.*

He bit his lip and tapped his pen on his notebook. "Shit!" He'd forgotten to ask about the women in Thomas Penrose's life, specifically a woman named Ruth Stahlmann, his mother. Did Yitzhak know her?

*

The opulent villa in Herzyliya where the pool party took place was built in the style of a Spanish *hacienda*. Red-tiled roofs framed a spacious courtyard open at one end to a wide marble terrace and a turquoise swimming pool, all of it aglow in flickering torchlight. Purple bougainvillea climbed the white walls, palms swayed on the terrace, a fountain splashed in the courtyard, and a combo of musicians thumped a beat in the evening air. Waiters with drinks and canapes glided among dozens of guests. The host was Rafi Bourla. "An arms dealer or something mysterious like that," Frank Harris had said when he'd invited Alan to accompany him and his wife. "He likes to throw pool parties and invite the foreign press. Bring anybody he said, so I guess that includes an old hack like you."

Harris liked to kid Alan about his age, and lately Alan had wondered about it himself. Maybe foreign reporting really was a young man's game. It had been over three months since the night he'd met the mysterious Yitzhak at the King David Hotel in Jerusalem and he'd not had a moment's rest. The very next day Hezbollah had hit Haifa with rockets and what the Israelis called the Second Lebanon War was on. Alan had left one man in the bureau and gone north with the rest of his staff to cover the war. For a month, he'd lived amidst a daily barrage of rockets. He had covered the first war in 1982 from the Lebanese side in Beirut and he knew the IDF could inflict far harsher punishment than it received. Still, each individual loss of life in the small country of Israel was painful. The IDF had not been ready for this war and had suffered relatively heavy casualties. The commanders had miscalculated badly and now the Olmert government and the army were being heavily criticized by an angry population. An investigation by a judicial commission was underway, and as Alan circulated through the guests at this party he eavesdropped enough to know that the conduct of the war was still a popular topic of conversation. That and the recent bus highjacking down in the southern desert.

Alan heard whoops and splashes from the pool beyond the courtyard, some of the guests already at play. Harris had told him that the host, Rafi Bourla, had lost a son in the war and that this party was a signal to his friends that it was time to move on. Obviously, Mr. Bourla didn't believe in observing *shanna*, the twelve month period of mourning kept by religious Jews, a time when entertainment and social activities were prohibited.

Alan lifted a glass of champagne from a tray, nodded to some of the foreign newspapermen he knew, all younger men who worked for the dailies. He knew how they viewed him. Over the years, he'd been asked a number of times why he'd stuck with a wire service like

Reuters for so long. The normal career trajectory for American print journalists was to start with the wires, graduate to the dailies, and then, if you had the ambition and the talent, you climbed on up to the pinnacle at one of the great papers such as the New York Times or the Washington Post. He didn't have an answer for the question, certainly not a satisfactory one. It wouldn't sound right to say that maybe he wasn't ambitious, that maybe he wasn't competitive. Or that maybe he didn't have kids to put through college, even though he'd been married long ago for half a dozen years, care-taking a woman who had the same bipolar condition as his mother. Maybe he was too easy-going, had grown too fond of the well-worn ruts of a wire service career. The truth was that he just didn't care. He had his comforts and his pleasures. The reputation of a journeyman hacker was good enough for him.

He strolled out on the terrace. A faint sunset afterglow along the sea's horizon. Nice view. Nice breeze. He could be in southern California...or Ibiza. He had a lovely old *finca* on that Spanish island, a holiday hideaway, almost 2000 miles straight west down the Mediterranean from where he was standing. Not bad for an aging hack.

"Alan! How did you get here?"

Ofra Gefen, tactless as usual, stood five feet away with some other guests. She looked different. For one thing, she was wearing a dress and some makeup, had brushed her hair. She was not unattractive.

"Do you know Rafi?"she asked.

A fit-looking, well-bronzed man in his forties was standing with her.

"No, I don't," he replied and held out his hand to the man. "Nice to meet you. Nice place you've got here." Should he say something about the son?

Ofra laughed. "He's not Rafi. This is Gavri Gilboa, a friend of the family like me."

Gavri Gilboa didn't hold out his hand, didn't smile. He nodded to Alan, his dark eyes steady, unblinking. And in a fraction of a second Alan knew where he had seen those eyes before – three weeks ago at the door of a high-jacked bus in the desert north of Beer Sheva. He'd been lucky to get there. He'd been in the Reuters bureau late that night when Shlomo Weiss, one of his Israeli staff, had monitored a police broadcast. They had barreled south through the night, Shlomo driving the bureau's Land Rover like it was the Humvee he drove when he was called up to the army. Alan had watched open-mouthed at the ruthless efficiency of the *Matkal* – "I'm not supposed to tell you their name," Shlomo had said – when they stormed the bus. He had run down to the roadway when the few journalists who had got through the cordon were allowed to go closer. And it was at the doorway to the bus that he had met this man Gavri with his steady unblinking eyes, pushing a wounded Arab terrorist out on to the road.

Alan dropped his hand. "We've met before," he said.

"And where was that?" Gavri asked.

"On the highway down near Beer Sheva. Bus high-jacking. What happened to those two Arabs you guys were hauling off that bus?"

Gavri stared at him. "I don't know what you're talking about," he said, and he muttered something in Hebrew to Ofra and walked away.

"Touchy guy," Alan said to Ofra.

"Gavri's with the security services. They don't like to be questioned." She smiled and cocked her head, her skewed eye seeming to look over his shoulder. "Any luck with Thomas Penrose?"

She asked this question regularly now and he'd decided from the beginning not to tell her about Yitzak. "No, nothing yet. How do you know Rafi?"

Ofra searched among the other guests. "His wife Noa is a good friend of mine. I don't see her yet, but she said she'd drop by this evening." That knowing smile again. "She's not really his wife anymore. They separated a few years ago. She's a smart woman. I'll introduce you when she comes. You'll like her."

"Was it her son who was killed in the war recently?"

Ofra nodded. "Sasha, yes. She's taken it badly, but she said she'd come by, so that's a good sign. Did you bring a bathing suit? Rafi's got lots if you didn't."

He begged off, not wanting to display his aging body among the taut and tanned flesh that was on show in the pool. Instead, he wandered among the guests for a while, drinking champagne, until finally Harris introduced him to his host, a handsome man ten years younger than himself.

Rafi Bourla was wearing a lightweight navy blazer, a white shirt and red-striped ascot, white pants, and he had dark hair that could have been dyed. Very debonair.

"How do you like Israel?" Bourla asked.

Alan had been asked that question a number of times in the months that he'd been in Israel. It seemed to him that the natives asked it with a sort of pent up anxiety or uncertainty about the place they called home and that they needed some affirmation that they had made something worthwhile, something to be praised.

"Too soon to tell," he said, knowing it was not what his host wanted to hear.

"But Frank tells me you've worked all over the Middle East."

"Oh, you mean what do I think by comparison. That's easy. This is like living in southern California. High tech, all the mod cons, clean streets, beautiful women, the only democracy in the Middle East. What more could you ask?"

Rafi smiled. "You're Jewish aren't you? You should feel right at home."

The second most popular question for visitors: Are you Jewish?...or...Aren't you Jewish? If you were Jewish you felt warmly embraced, immediately included. But at the same time you were made to feel guilty because your answer to the often unasked follow-up question – Why aren't you living here? – would be unsatisfactory whatever reason you gave.

"Oh I do, I do," Alan said. "Although I could live without a war every few years..." He caught himself. "I'm sorry, I didn't mean to be flippant. I understand you recently lost a son up in Lebanon. I'm deeply sorry."

Rafi nodded solemnly. "Thank you, and please don't feel badly. We have accepted our loss and we are moving on now." He swept an arm around the courtyard and the terrace. "Please enjoy my home and all that we have to offer, and now excuse me, I must see to my guests."

Graciously dismissed, Alan thought, and despite regretting his insensitive comment about wars, he felt a little annoyed once again with what he called *The Jewish Question*. He'd been debating it with himself ever since he'd been in the country. Why had he avoided having anything to do with the *Jewish Homeland* for so long? Part of his reason lay in Rafi's assumption - *You should feel right at home here*. As far as he was concerned he'd felt right at home growing up in America. He didn't think of himself as a Jew who happened to live in America but as an American who happened to be Jewish. America was his homeland. Perhaps it was his parents' example that had reinforced this notion. His only boyhood experience of anti-semitism had come when he was an eleven year-old walking home from Cambridge Rindge & Latin school with his friend Joey De Luca. Another boy, one who had taunted him before about being Jewish, came up to them and asked him what the difference was between a Jew and a pizza. When he shrugged the boy said, "A pizza doesn't scream when you put it in the oven." Without a word, Joey De Luca stepped up and cold-cocked the boy. Joey was an American who happened to be Italian.

At the buffet, Alan filled a plate with food and sat with Harris, his wife, Sadie, and Daniel Bergmann, an Israeli journalist with the newspaper *Ha'aretz*. He had met Bergmann that summer at a hotel up in Nahariya during the Lebanon war. They enjoyed sharing one thing over the other reporters – their age. Bergmann was sixty-three and he was fifty-seven. Other than one of the commanding generals, they were the two oldest men involved in the war on the Israeli side. He had quickly learned to value Bergmann for his knowledge and wisdom about matters Israeli and he had later offered to put him on a retainer as a "consultant" for Reuters, a practice followed by all the big foreign news bureaus. Israel was a talkative country, a place in continual debate with itself, and the government leaked like a sieve. These journalist "consultants" knew from their Israeli sources what had happened in cabinet meetings within minutes after they were over. An outsider could never get that close. But there was one drawback: the "consultants" were also patriotic Israelis and when the order came from on high to shut up about a particular subject, not a word was heard. All things nuclear, for example, were strictly taboo. Bergmann had said he already had a "consultant" role for Fox News which both amused him and paid him very well. But if that didn't bother Alan then he could always use the money and double up.

"Tell me about Rafi Bourla...all this." Alan asked him now, sweeping his arm like Rafi to take in the extravagant scene. "Where does the money come from?"

"He started with settlement construction in the administrative territories, what you call the West Bank," Bergmann replied. "Those settlements are built to military specifications and he got some of the contracts. He was young then, former paratrooper, good contacts with the military. He became a successful businessman using those contacts. Then he got into the arms trade and the really big money. He and his wife Noa were a smart couple, very social, she's one of our best scientists and he's very rich."

"*Were* a couple? What happened?"

Bergmann shrugged. "Who knows? Their politics are miles apart. She's pretty left and Rafi was in with Sharon and Likud for some time, went over to the Kadima Party with him and now he supports Olmert. Whatever's good for business I guess. " He pointed across the courtyard. "Well, well, speaking of the devil, there's the lovely Noa herself! That's surprising."

Alan looked to where Bergmann was pointing and saw a beautiful slender woman, could still be in her thirties he guessed, dark hair swept back in a sleek chignon. She wore a black tunic over slim black pants, a purple scarf and purple shoes with two inch heels. A severe yet striking image.

"Ahhh, so that's Noa," he murmured, and he gulped at his wine, staring at her.

Bergmann smiled. "Do you want to keep staring at her or would you like to meet her?

***

Four

When she had been living with him it was not so much Rafi's parties that Noa had disliked but his compulsive need to show off. He liked to have the media around, especially the foreign media, above all the Americans. The New York Times man was a prize catch, also the Washington Post, correspondents from the big American TV networks. Entertaining them in his house made him feel important. It had made her feel like she was living in a fish bowl. She had come to this evening's pool party only to stop the nagging of Ofra Gefen and other friends who'd told her she had to stop being a recluse, hiding away from the world. After her return from Boston three weeks earlier, she had holed up in her condo in Neve Tzedek. She didn't feel she was hiding. She just couldn't tolerate company, or the chatter in cafes and restaurants, the voices of people going on about the ordinary business of their lives in this country. Not without screaming at them.

She had given herself one hour at Rafi's pool party, but minutes after arriving she wasn't sure she could last. Rafi had rushed up to her, his unctuous self, inquiring about her trip to the United States. That wasn't so bad. It was when she *shalomed* and air-kissed her way through the crowd and heard *yet again* condolences for Sasha and *yet again* the criticism about the dreadful conduct of the war. Talk, talk, talk! And none of it would do any good. Finally she spotted Gavri Gilboa and made a bee line for him.

"Hold my hand," she said, and he did so without a word. She let go reluctantly to light a cigarette and Gavri frowned. "I started again in the States," she said. "Stupid me. You can get arrested for lighting up on a street corner in Cambridge." She took another puff and threw the cigarette down and stepped on it. To hell with Rafi's marble floors.

"I shouldn't have come, " she said.

"It's good that you came," Gavri replied. "You can't hole up by yourself."

"Look who's talking. The prince of isolation. Why didn't you come with me to America? I needed you."

"I got caught up in that bus hi-jacking down in the Negev, and now there's an investigation..."

"But that happened after I left," Noa said. She tugged on Gavri's arm, smiling seductively at him. "Were you trying to avoid me?"

Gavri blushed, but before he could reply Ofra Gefen interrupted them.

"Noa! I'm so happy you came!" she cried, leaning in to kiss cheeks. Unlike most others, Ofra was still bearable for Noa. Ofra wasn't sappy when it came to understanding loss, and she could be scarifying when it came to mocking those who were. Noa had talked to her on the telephone since her return, but she had hedged when Ofra asked if she was happy to be back. She didn't want to say *No* and hurt Ofra's feelings. Instead, she'd told her how much relief she'd felt to be anonymous in America, to be in a country where nobody said how sorry they were at every turn.

"Not bad for a grieving mother," Ofra said, stepping back to size her up. "Your trip did you some good."

Noa laughed. Only Ofra could get away with something like that.

"New England in the fall is sad and glorious," she said. "Sad because everything is dying, yet glorious because it does so with so much beauty..." She stopped and gritted her teeth. Grief still swelled up without warning, sudden waves of sadness. A *tsunami* had swept over her a month ago when she was standing on the side of a mountain road in New Hampshire viewing the fall colors. She had cried then and Jerold Raskin, her old MIT mentor, had put his arm around her shoulders to comfort her. She controlled herself now.

"I understand there's a new Bureau chief here for Reuters," she said. "Alan Raskin. You must know him."

"Certainly," Ofra replied. "He's here tonight. How do you know him?"

"I don't. I know his father."

"Would you like to meet him?"

"I'd like to say hello." She looked at Gavri. "Do you mind?"

Gavri shrugged and Ofra spun around and was off across the terrace. In a minute she was back with two men. Noa knew Daniel Bergmann. The other one had to be Raskin.

"Alan Raskin...this is Noa Kagan," Ofra said. "She knows your father."

Raskin frowned, looking puzzled.

"I studied under him at MIT some years ago," Noa said quickly. "I was with him just a few weeks ago in Cambridge and he told me you'd taken on the Reuters job here."

"Oh, I see," Raskin said, relaxing. He pushed his hand through a mop of greying curly hair and smiled, a boyish smile, friendly blue eyes. "Did he tell you to look me up? Or was he keeping you all to himself."

Noa smiled, accepting the compliment. Alan Raskin didn't look much like his father. Jerold Raskin was stooped and tentative, courteous to a fault, patient, brilliant. His son was tall, forthright, an American transparency about him. She'd been told by his father that he was unambitious and easy-going, though inquisitive and restless, unlucky in love, but a good man at heart. Jerold clearly loved his son, and indeed had urged her to look him up when she returned to Israel.

"No," she said, "or yes...I mean he did tell me to look you up. But here you are."

"You know Dan Bergmann?" Alan said.

"Everybody knows Dan," Ofra chipped in.

"And this is Gavri Gilboa," Noa said. "Gavri is *hayalim kedoshim*, one of our holy soldiers, who try to protect us from bad things." She patted Gavri's cheek. "But it doesn't always work, does it my *tateleh* ?"

"Noa!" Ofra exclaimed, and there was an awkward silence while Gavri looked at his feet.

"We've already met," Alan said quickly.

"I was sorry to hear about your mother's death," Noa said. "I knew her a little."

And before Alan could answer or say something in return about her son she hooked her arm through his and tugged him away from the others.

"Your father has told me a lot about you. Where are you living? Tel Aviv or Jerusalem?"

She'd decided that if she was to stay any longer it would be safer to spend her time talking to an outsider, a complete stranger.

"Tel Aviv," Raskin said. "The bureau is..."

"Excuse us," she said, smiling to the group, and then to Gavri.

"I'll be in touch soon...and hope for better luck."

*

"How are you coping with it?" Gavri asked.

Noa swirled the wine in her glass and frowned as she pondered his question. They sat in the Café del Mar in Jaffa where she liked to go and watch the sunset. Twilight had launched a thousand starlings, chirping and swirling around the bell-tower of St. Peter's Monastery; in the harbor below a couple of sailboats were heading in for the docks. A week after she had seen him at Rafi's pool party, she'd called Gavri and apologized for her abrupt exit. She asked him if they could get together, suggesting her favorite café.

"You know I can't believe that I'll never see him again," she said. "That's the hardest thing to live with. I'll see something that reminds me of him or I'll recall something he said and all of a sudden I get this horrible sensation in the pit of my stomach and ...*Voom*! The bottom drops out of everything and I'm falling and nothing will stop me..."

She looked up at Gavri, grimacing. Then she passed her hand over her face as if she were wiping off whatever showed. It was a gesture they used to make when they were children on their kibbutz and Gavri smiled.

"I didn't mean to bring it all back," he said. "I only asked because I didn't get much chance to talk to you at Rafi's."

"It's OK for you to ask. You're a special friend, but I'm not very good yet in company. I'm not the only one who's lost a son, I know that. I mean others have got through it and I guess I'll get by too..." She tried a smile. "How does the song go? With a little help from my friends?" Then, without calculation, she dropped the smile. Her moods shifted uncontrollably. "But sometimes I think I'm just going to blow up," she said fiercely. "I want to hurt them, punish them for taking Sasha from me. And now they're building a wall around us...A wall! The symbol of the ghetto! Everybody must see what's happening but nobody says anything. I have a job I can't talk about. You have a job you can't talk about. Security is a sacred cow, no choice is the only answer we're ever given. I hate this stupid government, people like Olmert and Rivlin."

"Rivlin might not be around much longer," Gavri said. "There's an investigation into the deaths of the two terrorists we captured in that bus highjacking. " He leaned forward, lowering his voice. "You know, what they really wanted had nothing to do with the release of Hamas prisoners. They wanted to shut down your nuclear facility in Dimona."

Noa scoffed: "Shut it down? That's crazy!"

Gavri nodded. "Obviously it never got out to the media." He shifted his chair closer to the table. "But what's worse is that before we had a real chance to interrogate the two guys that we captured alive, Yacov Kessar killed them. Went berserk when he heard a young woman hostage had died and bludgeoned each of them with a spanner. We said they died of wounds inflicted when we stormed the bus. If the truth comes out it could cost Kessar his job and probably Rivlin too. He was in charge of the operation." He smiled at Noa. "See? I'm talking about my job. It's not so bad."

"God!" Noa exclaimed. "Strange way to cheer someone up! You were there?"

Gavri nodded. "I'll probably have to testify and Kessar will want to kill me. But you don't have to be brave if it's all kept in the dark."

She smiled and picked up his hand. "You were always brave Gavri. Especially in the dark."

When they were in their teens, rock music played softly at night in the darkened dormitories at Kfar Borochov. In the West it was called the era of sex, drugs, and rock and roll, but while drugs were totally taboo on the kibbutz, sex was not illicit at all and she remembered now the night she had lost her virginity with Gavri. Brave he had been when he'd crept across to her bunk, his young muscled body hot in her eager, welcoming hands. Neither of them knew what to do and they fumbled and groped quickly and Gavri gushed on her belly before he could enter her. He kept whispering how sorry he was and she shushed him and stroked him and calmed him down until she felt him hardening again against her thigh. She wanted him inside her then, wanted to know how it felt, and she stifled her cry when he succeeded in pushing into her. But again it was too fast for her to feel any real pleasure and when she told him so afterwards he did not take it kindly. Thereafter, he became angry and possessive and jealous when she retreated from him. He fought with other young men and had to be disciplined.

"That guy Raskin, the journalist you met at Rafi's," Gavri said. "Did you really study with his father at MIT?"

"Of course! Did you think I made it up?"

"Are you going to see him again?"

"Gavri! I just met him!"

She paused. He was still jealous and this excited her. It had been a long time since their first attempt at sex and he must be more experienced now. When he had left the kibbutz to do his military service he'd written often to her. But then he was selected for the *Sayaret Matkal* and indoctrinated into the cult of toughness and killing. He wrote less and less. When she married Rafi, he remained silent and for a number of years they didn't see much of each other. They met again when she started coming back to the kibbutz and bought a house there. He had changed. He was quiet, withdrawn, sad. He never made any advances toward her and she treated him like a long-lost brother. It was a platonic friendship and one that she needed only now and then. But since that moment on the beach when he had been the *notifier* of Sasha's death something had changed. She felt herself pulled closer to him, felt safe with him and she needed him, wanted something more from him, which was why she had asked him to travel with her.

Gavri was looking down now, tapping the table lightly with his fingers. He stopped and inhaled deeply through his nostrils, let the air out and looked up at her. "Did you ever think of me when you decided to marry Rafi?"

There was silence between them. Then he groaned and put his head down. "I'm sorry. It's none of my business. I shouldn't have..."

She took his hand again. "It's all right. Look at me."

A warm southern breeze floated through the café with the dying sun and she raised her free hand to brush back her hair from the side of her face. She peered into his sad dark eyes.

"How long have you wanted to ask that?" she said softly.

She sat up in bed holding a sheet to her breasts with one hand, a cigarette in the other. A light breeze from the window wafted the curl of smoke up towards the high ceiling. She was alone in her bedroom now, alone and helpless and increasingly angry. It couldn't be all her fault, his impotence, he must have known. But how was she to get out of this situation now without hurting Gavri more than he must already feel.

She listened for sounds from the bathroom. He had taken his clothes in there with him so he was probably getting dressed in there. Why had he let her lead him on if he knew it wouldn't work? But maybe she was being unfair. Maybe he didn't know. Maybe he hoped it would this time. She remembered now his awkwardness at the café when she suggested they go to her condo in Neve Tzedek, only a short distanec away. He had looked at his watch. Then he'd mentioned another cup of coffee – he'd already had three – but the café owner said he was closing. Perhaps she should have paid more attention to his reluctance then, but she had charged ahead as she always had with him, treating him once again as the playmate she had grown up with. His nervousness she attributed to pent up desire. He said her image had been with him for years and that had excited her and made her feel sexier and gayer. And she had giggled when he finally shrugged in his calm but tough *bli panika* way and said, "Why not?"

"Dammit!" she muttered, stubbing her cigarette in an ashtray. Had she been too aggressive? He had been curiously passive, letting her lead him to her bed and take his clothes off. When she saw the scars on his wiry body she cried out in pity, "What have they done to you?"

He smiled and lay back on the bed and she moved her hands gently over his flesh, brushing his limp penis with her fingertips.

"Just go slow," he said.

And she did. She went very slow. She lay full length beside him and moved her body on his, lifting her leg across him. He didn't move and she felt nothing stirring under her leg. But when she tried to slide her hand down to hold his genitals he grasped her wrist and stopped her.

"Wait a while," he said.

And again she did. But what was he waiting for? He still didn't touch her and after some minutes had passed she got up on her knees and looked down at him, his eyes closed. She lowered her head and brought her mouth down on him and suddenly his body jack-knifed up and he pushed her roughly away.

"Don't," he rasped. "It's no use."

Gavri opened the bathroom door and came into bedroom fully dressed. He stood in the shadow outside the fall of light from the bedside lamp.

"Come and sit here," she said, patting the bed beside her.

He didn't move or say anything.

"These things happen, you know," she said, paused, and then, "It's not the end of the world."

Stupid thing to say. Shut up!

He turned away to the window. "Why don't we change the subject."

God! He's being impossible!

"I'm sorry...but what are we going to talk about? Nuclear weapons?"

He swung on her with a fierceness that frightened her. "How about killing? I'm pretty good at that!"

Tears welled in her eyes. He didn't have to attack her. What had they done to him? "Please come and sit," she pleaded. "I need to talk to you."

He just stared at the foot of the bed, his fists clenched at his sides.

"Please!...Gavri?"

Slowly, he came over and sat down at the end of the bed.

"I want to answer your question," she said. "I want to tell you why I married Rafi."

And when he didn't say anything she started talking, filling the awkward space between them with words. It had been her rebellious nature, she explained. When Rafi made her pregnant her father wanted her to have an abortion instead of marrying him. He told her she was ruining a brilliant career by passing up the Technion. But Anna, for once, had stood firmly against Yosef's demand and told Noa to make her own decision. And she did. She decided to have her baby and her career, too.

"I was going to show them all," she said, "and I did, didn't I? Just look at me! A failed marriage...a failed mother...I should never have put Sasha up on that kibbutz with his grandparents. In a way I used Rafi, I suppose. But he's had his revenge." She reached out and took his hand. "Oh, Gavri! We were so naive about the world, sitting up in those mountains on our little kibbutz, dreaming. It all seemed so perfect then. So ideal!"

Gavri didn't move. "No need to be so hard on yourself," he said. "Many of the things we've had to do in our lives we've had no choice. It's just that things haven't always turned out the way we expected them to. And they never taught us that."

She squeezed his hand. At least she had got him back from that place of black fury. Then Gavri looked at his watch again and she felt hurt, and stupid. She should have paid closer attention back at the café.

"I've got work to do tonight," he said, pulling his hand loose.

She nodded. "I understand," she said. But she didn't. She felt betrayed and abandoned.

*

"You know, there are two Israels for me now," Jacob Meisel said, ushering Noa into a cluttered room that appeared to be his den. "One is an awesome military machine and the other lives only in my memory. I presume from your telephone call that it's my memory you're interested in?" He gestured to a leather sofa for her to sit. "I know there are some others who feel like me so I suppose there are two kinds of Israelis also." Still standing, he held up two fingers. "First, there are the hard-minded people who revel in this mightiness, and then there are those, a diminishing breed, I think, who are saddened by it." He paused and smiled. "But we must not despair...there's always hope."

Noa had not met Meisel before and she felt relieved by the direct yet tactful way he had broached the subject she had mentioned in her phone call when she made this appointment.

"Maybe three kinds," she said. "You forget those who have left the country. My husband has an old army friend, an ex-paratrooper like himself, who lives in Los Angeles now. Every year this friend comes back with his wife and children to visit. Each time he picks one morning when he gets up hours before dawn and drives to Masada. He wears his old paratrooper fatigues and when he gets there he climbs

up that cliff in time to watch the sunrise. I asked his wife if they were
going to leave Los Angeles soon and come home to Israel and she said:
'Well, Amnon's doing really well in California.' It turns out they have
no *immediate* plans for coming back. And here was her clinching line -
'Our children really *love* Los Angeles, you know.'"

Meisel laughed. A big, balding man with a hearty laugh. He had
seated himself in a matching leather chair facing the sofa. "That's a
form of tenacity, I suppose. Your husband's friend is hanging on to
something." He shook his head as if in wonderment. "Masada!...Of all
the places to choose."

"Two of Olmert's sons live in New York," Noa said.

"Yes. I read with some astonishment our Prime Minister's opinion
that there were only some 400,000 Israelis that really mattered. A
business, scientific, cultural elite, leaders who were important to keep
here. Otherwise all is lost. That's a very bleak view."

Meisel's manner was an odd combination, both formal yet relaxed.
When he'd greeted her at the door of his apartment in the Rehavia
district of Jerusalem he was wearing a tweed jacket, shirt and tie. He
had introduced her formally to his wife, Eva, and then had set about
putting her at ease, even though he knew she had asked to meet with
him to discuss what must have been a very distressing time in his life.

The question that had brought her here had first been raised not
long before at a luncheon in Cambridge in Massachusetts. Jerold
Raskin, the host, had brought together some of her former MIT
colleagues and professors. The discussion turned to an inflammatory
article by two distinguished American academics about the Israel
lobby in the United States. The authors claimed to show that the lobby
and its principal arm, AIPAC or the American Israel Public Affairs
Committee, were instrumental in pushing the United States into pre-
emptive war with Iraq, even when there was no evidence of nuclear
weapons there. Next it was going to be Iran, someone said. "The same
people who were behind the invasion of Iraq now claim that the
Iranians are developing a nuclear bomb, and if we don't take it out the
Israelis will." As she was the only Israeli at the table, attention focused

on her and she was asked a question: "Don't you think that Israel's nuclear weapons are a spur to others in the Middle East to get a bomb of their own?" She would never face such a question in Israel, but she knew the stock reply and she gave it: "Israel will never be the first country to introduce nuclear weapons in the Middle East." She knew that those at the table had heard this before and she waited as they smiled and chuckled at its meaningless sophistry. Then she told them a story about Prime Minister Eshkol who had once asked the diplomat Abba Eban what "introduce" meant in this context – to use the bomb or to manufacture it. And Eban had replied that it meant that something that didn't exist, *suddenly,* did exist. That got her a round of laughter, and it also got her off the hook. But the question had stayed with her. This was her life's work. Were Israel's weapons really part of the problem? How did it start? So when she returned to Israel she did some research and discovered a large advertisement in the newspaper *Ha'aretz* in July 1966 *protesting* "the introduction of nuclear weapons into the Middle East." The protest had been signed by a number of Israeli university professors, among them a scientist named Jacob Meisel.

"I can hear she's been making you laugh," Eva Meisel said, coming through the door with coffee and pastries on a silver tray. "That's a good sign."

Eva wore an elegant silk blouse and a skirt of fine, expensive wool. Noa guessed that she had probably dressed up for the occasion. Although her aging body looked fragile, she had a proud aristocratic bearing. The skin on her cheeks was still tight and her eyes were direct, bright, inquisitive.

"He doesn't laugh much, my Jacob," she said. "But then we don't get many visitors now that he's retired from the university." She stood with the tray for a moment and looked at her husband, her head tilted to one side as if she were appraising him. Then she turned to the guest. "But then we have each other. He's from Vienna and I'm from Budapest so we're a bit like the old Austro-Hungarian empire. God knows we've lasted as long."

Noa laughed and Jacob looked pleased. Eva set the tray on a low table and started to pour. The morning sun slanted through arched windows adding to the warmth Noa already felt in this place. An antique desk sat opposite the windows, the wall behind filled from ceiling to floor with books. Original paintings by Israeli artists and several European reproductions hung on the two side walls. A low, glass case with a modest collection of antique vases and oil lamps sat beneath the window ledge. There were carafes of fresh flowers on the ledge, the coffee table, and the desk. The place, and the couple, charmed Noa, and she felt Eva and Jacob had planned carefully so she would be comfortable.

Eva finished pouring the coffee and looked up at Noa. "We hear you're very brilliant, my dear. Do you have your mother's spirit?"

"You know my mother?"

"Oh, she's probably never mentioned me," Eva said. "Anna and I knew each other briefly when we were girls in Haifa. Anna Kagan from Odessa and me, Eva Szeckely, from Budapest. We were free spirits then and much sought after, if I may say so."

"I find it hard to think of my mother as a free spirit," Noa said.

"She was, she was," Eva replied. "And beautiful and brilliant too... and so lively! We would go to the old Bat Galim Casino and dance all night. Your mother had the whole town catching its breath, especially the British officers. There was one I remember, a handsome one. What was his name? Anyway, your mother, you know, she could have been a professional concert pianist. She had so much talent. But then... Poof! She just up and disappeared, back off to that kibbutz. What is its name?"

"Kfar Borochov," Noa said. "I grew up there."

"We were sorry to hear about your son," Eva went on. "We read about it in the papers. I don't know if I would have been able to handle it here if I'd had a son. You must be very brave."

Noa lowered her head. "Thank you."

Jacob shifted in his chair. "Pass the coffee now, Eva, before it gets cold."

"Jacob tells me you have something important to talk about," Eva said, passing the coffee, "and since I wouldn't understand a word of what you two wizards were saying I'll leave you to it. Perhaps we can have a little chat after you've finished."

"Of course," Noa said. The couple had such dignity, a politeness and forthrightness that one didn't encounter anymore. They were so beautifully old together. And when Eva left the room Noa suddenly felt a strange melancholy, a sense of loss for something she had never had. She looked up at Jacob and saw that he was watching her. Could he sense her emptiness? Then he smiled and nodded as if to encourage her. He was waiting for her to begin.

She put her cup down, clasped her fingers together and went straight to the point. "I'm interested in the history of our nuclear program. I wanted to talk to you about Dimona in the early days and, well, I suppose, some of the questions that arose then about...what should I call it..."

"Let me help you, Dr. Kagan," Meisel interrupted, suddenly formal. "You want to know why I resigned. Correct?"

Noa nodded. "Thank you...yes, the answer is yes. You and the others. I only know the rumors, and my reason...well, let's just say I find I have a need to know. Is that a problem?"

"No, no," Meisel said with a wave of his hand. "I understand. Give me a moment."

He closed his eyes and stroked his temples with his fingers. After a few moments he suddenly dropped his hands, opened his eyes. "We're going back over half a century, but I suppose the short answer to your question is that we didn't want our country to have nuclear weapons."

Not only had his tone changed, but also his demeanor. Gone was his kindly, avuncular expression. His eyes were sharp, challenging. His speech brisk and precise. "We resigned, foolishly so hindsight tells me, because we thought we might stop Ben-Gurion from pushing ahead with the nuclear option. We were working on simple fission weapons right from the beginning at the Weizmann. We became very good with heavy water. It was exciting. Like a game. Just to see if we

could do it. But our own aggression in the Suez war in '56 frightened us. Ben-Gurion hooked up with our French ally to build the reactor at Dimona for plutonium separation. Then it became a serious, and a very secret, business. So...our resignation, mine and my colleagues I mean, was supposed to stop that. We wanted to strip away the secrecy and take the issue to the public. Needless to say, it didn't work. We just lost our jobs and became pariahs. A few years later some of my colleagues formed the Committee for the De-nuclearization of the Israeli-Arab Conflict. We opposed the introduction of atomic bombs into the Middle East. Nobody wanted to listen and it just fizzled out."
He lifted both his hands from his stomach, palms up in the air, and smiled. The kindly uncle had come back. "So here I am. A retired professor of nuclear physics."

"It was pointless then, your resignation, and that of the others."

Meisel nodded. "Ben-Gurion was determined to have the nuclear option and we stood in his way. Looking back now, I can see we were naive. Only an outside force, a superior force like the United States for example, could have stopped him, and we hid everything from them. Once started this kind of thing takes on a life of its own. It breeds...like a reactor." He stopped, and suddenly he looked weary and sad. "When did you come in?"

"Nineteen eighty-seven."

"Twenty years after the real decision. The 1967 war changed everything. The public celebrated Israel's invincibility but the leaders developed a different view. They saw themselves surrounded by implacable enemies with very few friends other than the Americans, and as I said we deceived them." He waved his arm towards the window. "You know I often think the true symbol of the decision to make the leap from experimentation to actually building the bomb lies just a few miles from here, over at Yad Vashem. It was the Holocaust syndrome. It's a fascinating paradox, really. As our military power and our territory grew we were supposed to be more secure, whereas, in reality, we became more insecure. In the isolation created by that war in 1967, the Holocaust became a vivid nightmare for the leadership.

There was an intense secret debate. It went on for days. Eshkol, the Prime minister, and Golda and Allon, all vetoed the construction of a plutonium separation plant. That should have killed it. However, Dayan secretly ordered the start of construction. Interesting, eh? The westerners are all against it, but it's the sabra, Dayan, the wily soldier born in the Middle East who wants it. When Eshkol and the others found out they just gave in. Just shrugged it off. They saw it as a project already underway. Nothing they could do about it, they said, so they rubber-stamped it." He shook his head slowly. "Dayan...and his minion Peres. That was the time when we started making international heroes of our generals. They lapped it up and moved into politics. The Kirya down in Tel Aviv rivaled the Knesset and there was an infusion of military thinking into political life. The military became a shadow government. Here in Israel, among the tribe, everyone knows who we are and what we are. We tear each other down pretty quickly. What became important then was one's fame abroad, in America. It became theater, and still is. The darkest day in the life of our Israeli leaders will be when they no longer appear in the New York Times or the Washington Post or on the American networks."

Noa smiled. He was right about the importance of the United States to Israel. She wished he wasn't.

"Anyway," he went on, "until that time the bomb was still an option, a possibility. It was like a letter you write but don't mail. Dayan mailed it. And you, Dr. Kagan, you know more about what's happened since then than I do. I hear some rumors that you've done great work with lasers." He quickly held up a hand. "But don't tell me."

"I won't, I promise," Noa said, forcing herself to smile. She looked down at her hands, clenched in her lap. "But tell me, what do you think about the program now? What you know of it?"

There was a long silence. Meisel looked off towards the windows. Then he uncrossed his legs and leaned forward, his hands resting on his thighs.

"Forgive me, Dr. Kagan, but you seem to be troubled about something which is probably none of my business. For what it's worth I still think it was a mistake. It's a Golem, a modern day Golem. In the legend, the medieval Rabbi, the kabbalist, the man with secret knowledge, creates a Golem, a giant made from clay to aid the Jews in their times of persecution and need. Then the Rabbi abuses his holy instructions and loses control over the Golem. It becomes a dangerous monster which threatens the Jews themselves. We scientists have no control over what we've created and the public here certainly doesn't, not after the way the Holocaust has been used by Begin and his successors. You know, any horrific tragedy like that, any collapse of humanity, can be used for a long time afterwards by a wilful government to frighten a population into blind obedience."

He sat back and again there was silence. The knuckles of her clenched hands had whitened. She stared intensely at Meisel. "Do you think, now, that you should have stayed in the program?"

He tilted his head to one side, appraising her. "You shouldn't ask me for advice, Dr. Kagan. But the answer is yes. Probably. I should have stayed."

"And what would you have done?"

"Worked from the inside, I suppose. Tried to limit the growth, the expansion, the variety of weapons. I don't know what's there now, but I have some suspicion it's probably far more than we need. If we have to have it, try to keep it simple. Most likely that wouldn't work with the military or the government though. There's no public pressure at all in this country, and the politicians only seem to bend to leverage from the outside." He shrugged. "I hope I'm not rude, but I don't envy you, you know."

"You're not rude. But we all seem so..." She fluttered her hands.

"Helpless? Don't let my generation depress you, Dr. Kagan. If I understand your concern correctly, I encourage you not to give up."

*

Yad Vashem, the Memorial Hall to the six million victims of the Holocaust, was a building which brooded on death, as it was meant to.

Constructed with huge boulders, it resembled a giant, truncated cairn hunkering on a hilltop overlooking the Jerusalem forest. It was a symbol, Jacob Meisel had said, a place to understand not only the past but the future.

Noa drove straight over from the Meisel flat in Rehavia. She had been there before, many years ago on a school trip organised by her kibbutz. Once inside, the sound of her heels on the stone floor echoed through the low, windowless chamber. She walked slowly, her arms folded tightly across her chest, circling an eternal flame which flickered in the center of the room. The flame was fenced around with blackened iron spikes. It cast shadows, including her own, which fluttered on the bare, stone walls. Tongues of firelight illuminated the names of the death camps inlaid on the floor: Belzec, Majdanek, Sobibor, Auschwitz, Chelmno, Treblinka...on and on. As a schoolgirl, she had shuddered in this place. She had wanted to get out and back to the open spaces of the Galilee. There, on the kibbutz, Holocaust Day had been honored with a moment of silence at noon, then it was back to work. Later, in the city, it was a day-long affair. She hated the wailing siren, the empty squares, the closed cafes.

She stared at the flame. The whole subject, the obsession with the terrible past, depressed her. But for the government it had a practical purpose: to "educate" schoolchildren. With what? It had frightened young Sasha on his school trip, and others too, she'd heard from some mothers. What they really meant to instill was fear of the past repeating itself. But that was the future and, thanks to the State that had created this monument to the Holocaust, her Sasha had no future.

Still staring into the flame, she saw in her mind's eye a shiny piece of machined metal shaped like a discus. She was standing over it like a priestess before a sacred object laid on an altar. Only she was not in a temple. She was in MM2, the metallurgy section on underground Level 5, Machon 2, at Dimona. She was standing in one of the box-like rooms with the lathes, looking down at a U-235 warhead. She heard snatches of her own voice addressing the men who stood around her, reverently beholding her work: "The disc-like shape channels the destructive force into two opposite-directed cones of energy. The destruction is not widespread but focused on a specific target. It is a nuclear rifle." Under their admiring gaze, the solitary discus gleamed in the harsh fluorescent light. It looked menacing, weighty and dense, immensely compacted and powerful. She had created it. Brought it forth from the natural uranium clay with her lasers. Two things she had created in her life – a boy and a tactical nuclear weapon. And the boy had been taken from her by the same people who employed her to make that weapon.

For some time she continued to stand and stare into the eternal flame, her arms folded and clutching her elbows, holding herself together. Others who entered the chamber veered away from her as they passed by, keeping a respectful distance from a solitary woman who appeared to be lost in memory. But the memory she focused on now was barely an hour old: a phrase that Jacob Meisel had used just before she left him.

They only seem to bend to leverage from the outside.

***

Five

Alan Raskin pulled open the door of the *Relaxe* bar and the canned music that hit him was deafening – *When you grow up son you gotta be a man.* Some of the customers, including American journalists who Alan knew, drunkenly bellowed the words, led by Zev Tamari, an American-Israeli habitue of the bar who had worked in Beit Agron for Netanyahu's old Likud government.

"Crikey!" Nigel Gort yelled, wincing at the noise. "The Soviets did this because they didn't want to be overheard. What's the excuse here?"

"Argumentative country," Alan yelled back. "They practice shouting over noise. I'll get Shimi to turn it down....Beer OK?"

Gort said jolly good and Alan headed for the bar.

It was Gort's first time at *Relaxe,* a Jerusalem hangout for the media tucked away in a warren of alleys behind Beit Agron, the GPO or Government Press Office where foreign correspondents got credentialed and were issued the censor's rules for reporting in Israel. The owners of the place catered to the foreign press. A stand up Victorian bar was said to have had its original home in Fleet Street. The walls were covered with an odd collection of newspaper mastheads – *Svenska Dagblat;* magazine covers – *The New Yorker;* and front page stories – *The Washington Post,* March 27th, 1979: BEGIN AND SADAT SIGN TREATY.

Alan brought back two pint jugs and he and Gort settled at a stained wooden table. The volume of the music had been lowered over Zev Tamari's protests.

"Cheers!" Alan said, lifting his jug. Nigel Gort, a British diplomat posted in Moscow in the late 1980's when Alan befriended him, was now the British Consul in Jerusalem. A week ago Alan had asked him as a favor to look into any connections between Thomas Penrose and the British Secret Service during the Mandate period in Palestine.

"Cheers!" Gort replied. He took a swig and set his jug down. "Well now, it seems your man Yitzhak, whoever he is, is a teller of tall tales about Thomas Penrose."

"How so?"

"I had a friend in the FO in London look at the old Colonial Office records and Thomas Penrose was never anything more than a crown prosecutor in His Majesty's Mandatory Government."

Alan was disappointed. He'd searched the same records himself and he knew this already. He'd been hoping for something more.

Gort went on: "The records mention nothing about the Secret Service or the Special Branch. The part about the hit-and-run accident is true, though, and the investigation was closed, marked unsolved when we pulled out of Palestine in '48."

Alan drank some beer, wiped his lips with his hand. "But if Thomas Penrose was working with the Secret Service wouldn't that be unlikely to appear in the official records of the Colonial Office?"

"Precisely so," Gort said, holding up a finger and tapping his nose. "And just to make sure, my friend had a friend over in the world of shadows and whispers zip through the old MI6 computer. Absolutely nothing. Thomas Penrose never did any work for the dark side. Period. He's absolutely clean, so whoever this Yitzhak is who's feeding you this rubbish, he's having you on."

So that was that. Did Yitzhak think that if he could make Penrose appear sinister as well as anti-semitic then he, Alan, would indeed let the sleeping dog lie? Stop asking questions? But there was no chance of that now. The day before meeting Gort, Alan had driven up the coast road to Haifa and paid a visit to City Hall. Since he'd been stymied in his inquiry into the death of Thomas Penrose – nobody else had answered his ad – he'd decided to check out another part of his mother's story. At the office of records on births and deaths he looked up the names of Ruth's parents, Benjamin and Helga Stahlmann. He discovered that Benjamin had died in 1974, Helga in 1980. In his mother's story they had been killed in 1948. Another lie. Why? He called his father in Cambridge that night and asked him the same question. Jerold was shocked and perplexed.

"Honestly, I have no idea why she would lie about that Alan."

"Could she have been protecting somebody here in Israel? Was she in touch with anybody?"

"Yes, she had some correspondence, with a friend she said. But she never showed me the letters and she always dismissed the place and its violence. Nothing ever changed, she used to say."

"Do the letters still exist?"

"I don't know, but I'll look for them and let you know if I find anything."

At the end of their conversation Alan told his father that he had met one of his former students, Noa Kagan, and that she was quite beautiful.

"She's also very clever," Jerold said. "I was her thesis supervisor. A brilliant piece of work. She doesn't talk about her job much, but I understand she's very important in their nuclear weapons program."

"Nobody talks about nuclear weapons here," Alan said. But he didn't tell Jerold that her work wasn't the part of Noa Kagan that interested him. She was a very attractive woman, and there was also something else, something unfathomably tragic about her that intrigued him. He felt drawn to her and he just needed to find the courage to *act...Soon!*

Shimi had been persauded to turn up the volume again and *Moonlight in Vermont* boomed through *La Relaxe*. A maudlin sing-along started up.

"Good Lord!" Gort exclaimed as he and Alan turned to watch. A couple of the men were mumbling the words, slack faces, eyes staring off into space, seemingly lost in some dream of a distant snow-filled land. Alan was glad he worked for an English agency. The men who worked for the American news services, wires, newspapers, magazines, or electronic media, could have a rough time here, especially if they were not viewed as "friends of Israel." Neutrality or "objectivity" was not an easy option for them. And it was not so much the Israelis who made it this way -- they were often their own best critics – but Jewish groups and lobbies back in the United States who went directly to editors, publishers, and the top network executives to protest any report they thought was critical of Israel. American reporters in Israel had to watch their backs. Frank Harris had told him that AIPAC once tried to get his correspondent removed after a piece that was critical of the IDF and its disregard for collateral damage, i.e. civilian casualties. "The piece was fair," Harris said, "and much softer than one that *Ha'aretz* published on the same subject."

Dan Bergmann drifted in with Susan Miller, an American-Israeli who was part owner of a small advertising company in Jerusalem. Susan had done *aliyeh*, emigrated to Israel, five years ago. She was a plumpish blond news junkie from New Jersey, mid-thirties, who liked to hang out at *Relaxe* and drink with the hacks – something she had in common with Nigel Gort, Alan had observed. He'd met Gort in Moscow because the English diplomat liked to hang out late at night in the compounds where the media lived and worked. He had more fun there, he said, better than being bored at Embassy dinner parties. Gort also liked to trade bits of information, which made Alan and others think he might be a spook.

Gort now went to work on Bergmann, fishing for information about what the Olmert government was going to do with the growing tension in Gaza between Hamas and Fatah.

"Why don't you ask Alan these questions?" Bergmann parried. "He's your friend."

"He never knows anything," Gort said. "He just scalps your paper and puts it on the wire."

Alan could feel Susan's hand on his thigh. "That's right," he said. "We're humble translators not journalists." He put his hand down on

Susan's and squeezed. Sex had not been difficult for him to find in secular Israel. Susan and he had gotten a little drunk together the first night they met and subsequently fell into bed. Now it was simply something they did on occasion. Recreational sex, Susan called it. Good for the nerves. Nothing serious. Alan was sure he wasn't the only man who enjoyed Susan's appetite for sex and that didn't bother him at all.

"Naughty, naughty," Zev Tamari said, wagging a finger at Susan as he stood over the table. "You know, I've never had sex with an Arab woman. They just won't let it happen and that's a true sign of racism. Plain sex, I mean. Nothing kinky like Susan here. I don't want to tie her up or anything..." He dodged the lit cigarette that Susan flicked at him. "...or do it up the ass. Just plain sex. I've never had it. Not even a hand job!"

"Who's the vulgar chappy with the foul mouth?" Gort asked in a clearly audible voice.

"Billy Feigenbaum," Alan said. "A loud mouth from Cleveland who changed his name and became self-important over here."

Tamari gave him a finger. "Fuck you Raskin, you self-hating Jew!"

"Fuck off Zev!" Susan said, then turned to Alan and simpered with a *faux* southern accent."Thank you for defending my honor sir. What are we drinking?"

"Tamari means figtree in Hebrew," Bergmann explained to Gort. "Feigenbaum translates from German as figtree. Now how do you translate the kind of sky you have at this time of the year?"

"Oh wild west wind thou breath of autumn's being," Gort recited.

"Close," Bergmann said, smiling. "You asked what's going to go down in Gaza? That's a clue."

*

The IDF slugged it *Operation Autumn Clouds*, a combined force of infantry, engineering, and armored troops pushing into Beit Hanum in northern Gaza. Sderot, an Israeli town close to the Gaza border, had been hammered by rockets fired from the area around Beit Hanum and there had been mounting civilian casualties in the town, children among them. The IDF had had enough. The generals didn't care if the rockets came from Hamas fighters or from Fatah's Al Aksa Martyrs brigade. Only weeks before those two Palestinian factions had fought a pitched battle for control of Gaza with machine guns and RPGs in the crowded streets. The fight was still unresolved.

"The IDF would love it if they killed each other off," Dan Bergmann said to Alan who was sitting in the driver's seat of the Reuters Land Rover. They were moving slowly through traffic in Gaza City, south of Beit Hanum, having crossed the border point at Erez ahead of the Israeli thrust that morning. Handprinted signs – SAHAFI : PRESS – were taped to the windows of the wagon. Alan could hear the dull thump of artillery explosions to the north. The Israeli attack was underway. Driving was close to bumper-cars and he eased carefully through the intersections, dodging ambulances and pick-up trucks careening around the corners. Sharon had been able to withdraw Israeli forces from Gaza over a year before by bucking his own Likud party with what Israelis called the "Big Bang" – the formation of Kadima, a new political party. But the Israeli government and the Bush administration were stunned a few weeks later when Hamas won the Palestinian elections.

"Free elections don't always bring you the democracy you want," Bergmann told Alan. "They *can* bring chaos like this."

Hamas had refused to recognize the State of Israel and was termed a terrorist organization by the United States. All international aid to the Palestinians was cut off. Gaza, the Hamas stronghold, was isolated, but home-made rockets continued to rain down on Sderot. The IDF was sensitive to criticism about the number of civilians it was killing in retaliation, especially women and children. Bergmann had been tipped off that they were using a new technology to cut down collateral damage and he wanted to check it out. Alan had accepted Dan's offer to share the story, and on the drive down from Tel Aviv he'd decided to tell Bergmann about Thomas Penrose and Yitzhak. If anybody could help find out something about the mystery man, he thought it might be Dan.

"So, it seems everybody is lying in this affair," Bergmann had said after hearing a summary to date. "Both your deceased mother and the elusive Yitzhak. The question is what are they trying to hide." He was silent for a moment. "You know, our new historians are just getting into archives that have been closed for decades. They've been turning over a lot of national myths, shoveling out a lot of stables on stuff that went on back in 1948 and before. You might want to consider talking to some of them." He then made Alan repeat his description of Yitzhak several times, concentrating on how fastidious the man seemed to be, both in his manner and his appearance.

Their destination was the Shuhada Al-Aqsa hospital and in the corridors inside they found an abattoir. Slabs of bloody human bodies lay along the walls, parts of them bound with dirty bandages. Everybody was shouting, a deafening clamor, while several blood-stained doctors attempted to do triage. Alan had seen a lot of war and gore and death. He'd learned not to stare at the carnage, to keep it in his peripheral vision. Think about something else as he waited patiently for Bergmann to track down his contact.

The man's name was Dr. Raja al-Rashid and he took them to a quieter ward at the back of the hospital where wounded patients lay in rows of beds. Al-Rashid was a solemn man with soft brown eyes and a neat moustache. He did not smile.

"It started this past summer," he said. "I have never seen anything like these kinds of injuries. There are burns, mutilated limbs, but no shrapnel."

He took them to one of the beds and flipped back the sheet covering a man's legs. The patient, watching them with frightened eyes, said nothing. There was only one leg, the other was amputated above the knee. The stump was covered with small black spots. "They call it black dust," the doctor said, "and some of them fear it will cause cancer, which is nonsense. There are plenty of rumors but also a few facts."

"Such as?" Bergmann asked.

Al-Rashid told them that the non-profit group Physicians for Human Rights was convinced that the Israeli army was using an ammunition called D.I.M.E. The initials stood for Dense Inert Metal Explosive. "The blast area is small and there's almost no shrapnel," he said. "It's supposed to reduce collateral damage. But it is a very hot and powerful explosive. You can never find a clear wound or any shrapnel, but you get severe mutilation. Many of my patients do not survive."

Outside the hospital, Alan asked Bergmann where he was going to go with the story now.

"Back to Tel Aviv and the Kirya," Bergmann replied. The Kirya was the Defense Ministry, a complex that remained down on the coast when the Israelis claimed Jerusalem as their capital. "Could be interesting for you."

"How's that?"

"Possibly a happy coincidence," Dan replied. "If the IDF is using this D.I.M.E. stuff, then the man I have to get to for confirmation is the civilian Deputy Minister for weapons procurement. He's an old Irgun warhorse, buddy of Begin and Sharon, named Yitzhak Gavish. He fits the description of your Yitzhak very well."

"Jesus!" Alan exclaimed. "Just like that! You're a walking wonder."

Bergmann grinned. "It's a small country. I'm sure you've heard that."

The bulldozer driver was having trouble maneuvering. He rammed the heavy machine backwards into the hovel opposite the one he was trying to demolish. The Arab women who had been standing outside, clutching their children and watching the demolition of their neighbor's house across the way, started wailing and shrieking. The driver, ignoring them, changed gears. The bulldozer growled and charged forward, its tracks chewing through the open sewer that ran down the middle of the lane, its wide blade smashing through the mud-brick facade of the targeted house, pushing on across the floor to the back wall. When the driver backed away for another run, splinters of wood and bits of colored cloth protruded from the pile of rubble that tumbled down behind the retreating blade.

The main road back to the Erez crossing had been blocked and Alan and Dan had tried a quick bypass through the outskirts of the Jabaliyah refugee camp. Now they were blocked again by an Israeli armored patrol that had penetrated the camp accompanied by a demolition team with a dozer. A solitary Arab woman stood closer to the house being demolished with a paratrooper beside her.

"That's her family's house," Bergmann said. "They make her stand and watch." He pointed to a pile of belongings that lay in the mud beside her. "That's as much as she could get out of the house in the fifteen minutes they gave her. We inherited the tactic from the British. Unpleasant business. I didn't know the army was still doing it here since the withdrawal. Usually it's air strikes now, but that brings more collateral damage. Maybe that's the reason for this ground incursion."

"How do they know they've got the right house?"

Bergmann pointed down the lane to a tan SUV bristling with antennas sitting beside an APC. Two men in plain clothes were leaning against it, one of them smoking. Alan recognized them. The hard-assed pair from the bus, and one of them, Gavri something, he'd also met at Rafi Bourla's pool party.

"*Shabak*," Dan said. "They're the bloodhounds. Very little moves here or in the West Bank that they don't know about. They capture some guy with explosives or a rocket and they lead the army straight to his house."

Something clanged on the yellow metal roof of the bulldozer's cab, bounced, then came down in the muck with a plop not more than three meters from the Land Rover. Alan looked out the open window at a piece of white limestone, angular, half the size of a man's fist. He looked up and saw that the woman was staring at the stone, too, a faint smile spreading on her face. A second stone smacked into the

muck at the woman's feet, splattering mud on her dress. The paratrooper moved back against a wall. The woman didn't move. A third
stone smashed into the windscreen of the Land Rover. Then came the
rattle of automatic weapons.

"Back up!" Bergmann yelled.

The street was clearing rapidly, women herding small children
into doorways. Alan twisted in his seat, steering back down the lane.
He heard a horn blasting furiously and when he glanced to the front
he saw that the SUV was coming head on, its heavy welded grill
practically pushing against him. At the first intersection the SUV
pulled alongside and the man called Gavri yelled across:

"Follow us!"

For the next few minutes they charged through the camp behind
the SUV, sticking to one of the broad swaths that had been bulldozed
by Sharon for riot control in the old days before the pull-out. Alan
heard more gunfire, but nothing hit them. And then, suddenly, they
were out in the open and on the main highway heading north. Ahead
of them a cluster of Israeli armored vehicles. The SUV slowed and
pulled to the side. Alan came up alongside and Bergmann exchanged
some words in Hebrew with the two *Shabak* men.

"Let's go!" he said, closing his window. .

"What did they say?" Alan asked.

Bergmann shrugged. "Keep your dumb ass out of our business,
what else."

"What about my windscreen?"

*

When Alan called Noa Kagan for a "date" she told him that she was
going out in his neighborhood on Friday night with Ofra Gefen and
maybe he would like to join them. Not exactly what he had in mind,
but he accepted. His neighborhood was a trendy area called *Shenkin*
where he'd rented an apartment from which he could walk to work.
He knew the place where she said to meet – a bar called The Jackpot –

but he'd never been inside. When he pushed through the swinging doors just after nine o'clock he was jolted into another world.

Russia!... A chorus of voices singing Russian cossack songs!

The place was crammed with tables filled with men and women, but it was mostly the men who were doing the singing. They wore shirts with rolled sleeves or polo shirts, tanned arms and faces, fit-looking, solidly built men, most of them in early middle age. The walls were filled with photographs of more of them, except they were younger and in uniform. A soldiers reunion? What had Noa brought him to?

The singing stopped and the men raised their glasses, shouted a toast in Hebrew, and knocked back a clear transparent liquid. Vodka? It was after sundown on *Shabbat,* party night in secular Tel Aviv. But Alan had never seen anything quite like this since the vodka busts in the old Soviet Union. He looked around for Noa and then heard his name. Ofra Gefen was over by the bar, waving her hand. *Two's company, three's a crowd* – his thought immediately when Noa had asked him to join them. But he wanted to see Noa and if Ofra was what he had to put up with, so be it.

He sidled through the crowded tables to the bar, bumping against some of the men on his way, solid men, like nudging telephone poles. Shaded poker lamps hung suspended over the tables, the lamplight thick with cigarette smoke. It was hard to breathe, maybe because the ceiling fans weren't working. The bar was long and curved with a footrail, a large mirror behind – Wyatt Earp would feel at home.

"Hi there!" Ofra cried and flung out her arm, pointing across the room. "We're over there. Get yourself a drink and join us." She turned back to the bar and rapped her knuckles. "Zee Zee! How about some service!"

Alan leaned in. "Who are these people?'

Ofra grinned. "Aren't they great. It's a hangout for Golani veterans...and paratroopers...elite brigades. Zee Zee! Meet Alan Raskin from Reuters. He used to live in Moscow."

On the other side of the bar stood a broad-shouldered man with a shaved head and a wide grin. "Oh yeah? *Vui gavariti pa Russki ?*"

Alan held up his hand, a small space between his forefinger and thumb."*Chou chou.*"

"*Spetznaz,*" Zee Zee said, holding out his hand, still grinning.

Was he kidding? *Spetznaz?* The old Soviet special forces? He took Zee Zee's hand and shook it.

"Navy Seals," he said.

Zee Zee slapped the bar and roared, flashing a row of large white teeth. "You are welcome Navy Seal. I have *Moskovskaya*, best vodka in town. You will try?"

Before Alan could reply, Zee Zee placed two shot glasses on the bar and poured the vodka. "*Dadna!*" he cried, throwing the shot back. Alan winced, then threw his back and winced even more. The trick back in Russia had been to get soda water in your glass and down it before anyone noticed the bubbles.

Ofra got a pack of cigarettes and then led him to a table where her CBS boss, Frank Harris, and his wife Sadie sat with Noa. A bottle of *Moskovskaya* sat on the table, a third empty. They'd been into it a bit.

"Come sit beside me," Noa said.

"Never been here before," Frank said. "They're quite a bunch when they get going with these songs."

"Men celebrating war?" Noa said. "It's disgusting."

Alan pulled out the chair beside Noa and sat down. He could feel the single shot of vodka, it made him a little light-headed. "Guy behind the bar says he's *spetznaz*, Russian special forces. Or used to be. I told him I was a Navy Seal. How did you get in?"

Frank laughed. "I said I was from Soldier of Fortune magazine..."

"No you didn't," Sadie said. "We came with Ofra."

"Right," Frank said. "Nobody stops her. Right Ofra?"

Ofra raised a fist. "Right on!"

Alan turned to Noa. "And you? What are your qualifications for entry?"

"I've got a bomb."

"You mean you're a little bombed," Ofra said quickly.

Noa smiled, an indifferent smile. "Whatever."

Alan was surprised. She was a little drunk, he was sure. "I talked to my father recently," he said. "He passed on his regards."

"You don't have any children do you?" Noa said. "You told me that already."

"That's right."

He waited, not knowing exactly where she was going with this. Nowhere it seemed. Frank picked up the bottle and went around the table, pausing before each person for a nod before pouring a refill. Sadie passed, as did Ofra, but Noa took some and Alan kept her company. Then she linked her arm through his Russian style and he looked into her eyes. Her dark blue irises had shiny flecks of steel.

"*Dadna!*" she said and tilted her head back and swallowed the vodka. He did the same. She wanted to get drunk? Fine! He would get drunk with her.

Ofra had come around the table and leaned into his ear on the side away from Noa. "She never drinks like this," she whispered harshly. "You have to do something."

"*Ischo raz!*" Noa said, asking in Russian for a refill. Alan glanced at Ofra, shrugged, and then picked up the *Moskovskaya* bottle and filled both their glasses. Again Sadie declined and this time Frank did too. He and Noa drank again. He didn't notice that Ofra had slipped away from the table until she returned now with two men.

"Noa! Look who I found!"

Alan recognized the same two men who had rescued him in Gaza.

Noa reached for her glass and raised it. "To the finest killer of them all! Gavri Gilboa!"

She started to drink the vodka when Gilboa reached in and slapped the glass from her hand. The glass bounced on the table, the liquor flying in a stream over Sadie's blouse.

"*Eizel!*" Noa said, hissing the word at Gavri through her bared teeth.

Frank jumped to his feet and grabbed Gilboa's shirtfront. "Whadda think you're doing?"

In a blur of movement Gilboa had Frank's arm locked in a painful grip. Men jumped in from the surrounding tables to separate them. Alan tried to rise but found a hand on his shoulder pressing him down in his chair. It was Gilboa's wiry partner.

Noa was on her feet now, swaying against the table, laughing, an ugly laugh. "Why don't we all sing another war song?" she cried.

Gilboa said something harshly in Hebrew and Noa shook her head vehemently, reached down and took Alan's hand.

"Take me home," she said.

Alan took Noa to his nearby apartment, keeping her steady on her feet by holding her close to him with his arm around her waist. It was the first time he'd seen an Israeli drunk, a woman at that. And from the number of people who turned and stared at them on the street he assumed it was a novelty for them too. Several asked if she was ill. Did he need any help?

Inside his apartment Noa seemed amused and acted coy. "I asked you to take me to my home," she said, "and here I am in yours. Are you trying to seduce me?" She tried to piroutte in the middle of the living room floor and fell on the sofa. She sat up and patted the sofa beside her. He sat down.

"You like Israeli women?" she asked.

"I like you," he said.

She looked at him with a drunken intensity. "Gavri doesn't like you. He's jealous of anybody who pays attention to me."

"He's a pretty tough customer. I saw him at work in Gaza, and down at that bus high-jacking in the desert."

"Brutal! Stupid brutal men!"

"I was there. We got through before they could cordon off the area."

"They murdered two men."

"Killed them, you mean. Yeah...and they got two alive. I saw Gavri and his partner take them off the bus. They say they died later of wounds."

"That's a lie!" Noa snapped. "I meant murdered... by Yacov Kessar. He went crazy... killed them with a wrench or a spanner or some tool like that. Gavri told me. There's a secret investigation, but it won't do any good... Savages."

Alan was speechless for a moment. "And you got this from Gavri Gilboa?"

"Stupid fools!" Noa scoffed. "They were Hezbollah and they were trying to get to Dimona, shut it down. Could never do that. I know the security there."

"Did Gavri tell you that too?"

"Screw Gavri!" she said loudly. "Why do you go on about Gavri? Forget about him."

She stared at him, her face slackened, eyes glazed, dilated pupils. He looked away.

"Don't do that! Here, look at me!"

And she took his chin and lifted up her mouth and kissed him. Her breath was fuggy, a dank earthy taste. He put his arm around her and she nestled her face into the hollow between his neck and his shoulder. He could feel her warm breath on his skin, the rhythm slowing and deepening. In a minute she was fast asleep.

*

The following morning Alan found a note in his kitchen.

Thank you for the sofa and for saving my honor. Today is the anniversary of the assassination of Yitzhak Rabin and there will be a big memorial service in Rabin Square this evening. I'm sure you will be covering it and I would like it if you could take me with you. Please let me know.

Noa

The night before, after Noa had passed out, he didn't think he would be able to carry her to the bedroom and put her to bed. Instead he'd brought some blankets and a pillow to the sofa and tucked her in. Drinking his coffee now he went over the few lines of her note several times. *She wanted to see him again.* So it wasn't just the booze acting last night. That part pleased him. On the other hand, she had let something slip that maybe she hadn't intended to.

He mulled this over while he walked over to the Reuters bureau on Hamasger Street. *What to do?* He'd never had a "big" story, the kind that journalists were supposed to dream about. None had ever come his way and he had never gone looking for one. But this one had fallen into his lap! He'd seen journalists turn into monsters when they had a "big" story, adrenaline surging through their bodies, like warriors going into battle. He felt none of that. In fact he felt a little frightened by what he knew he could do, or what other reporters would do with what he had been given.

Come on! he urged himself. *To hell with caution! Man up! Go for it!* And turning the corner into Hamasger Street he picked up his pace.

When he'd arrived in Israel to take over the Reuters Bureau, he'd learned from his predecessor that their communications were probably monitored by Israeli security, to be careful on the phone. Later he'd also been cautioned about this by Dan Bergmann, who'd mentioned his home phone too. Now, in his office, he picked up the phone on his desk and punched Bergmann's cell number.

"Dan...You going to the Rabin Memorial Service tonight?"

"I'm in Jerusalem. I hadn't intended to why?"

"I've got something that I'd like to confirm with you before filing it on the wire."

"What's it about?"

"Remember the bus that was hi-jacked down in the desert near Dimona?"

There was silence for a moment before Bergmann spoke. "Say no more. I'll drive down and see you there, in the press section. About nine o'clock?"

That night more than 100,000 people jammed into the square facing Tel Aviv's City Hall. The air was warm and tee-shirted activists from Peace Now draped their banners over the crowd control barriers. Rabin's assassination anniversary had become an annual event for left-of-center factions to protest against right wing governments. Peace Now placards read OLMERT AND PERETZ – YOU ABANDONED HIS PATH. Other left-wing activists chanted slogans against the IDF operations in Gaza. One group of women held up a broad banner that read WAKING UP ON TIME and Alan felt Noa tug his arm. She wanted to speak to the women. He waited patiently and when she returned he asked who they were.

"It's based on the Four Mother's movement against the occupation in Lebanon six years ago," Noa said. "They're very brave. It's not easy to stand on the street with a sign and have people drive by and spit at you. Sharon claimed they were destroying morale, weakening the home front. I admire them."

Alan did not like to get caught up in the middle of a large crowd. It could become uncontrollable, a beast which acted independently of the thousands of souls who formed it. Years before in Iran, during the overthrow of the Shah, he had been nearly smothered by a friendly mob in a Teheran cemetery eager to show him the bodies of young men tortured to death by Savak, the Shah's secret police. Now he worked his way around the edges of the crowd, holding Noa's hand. At the area for the press beside the stage, he showed his pass to the police and Noa showed something too before they went inside the barrier. Alan recognized the big name politicians up on the stage – Ehud Olmert, Shimon Peres, Ehud Barak – and Noa pointed out a writer, David Grossman, who was to be a featured speaker.

"He lost a son in Lebanon this summer too," she said.

"Is that why you're here?"

"Partly."

Alan was curious. "What did you show the police?"

"My security clearance."

"I'm impressed."

"Don't be. It means nothing."

She'd been tersely remote, acerbic and cool, ever since he'd arrived at her place in Neve Tzedek to pick her up. At first he thought she might be embarrassed because of the previous night. When he tried to bring it up, she brushed him aside. "I'm part Russian. Vodka is in our blood."

Alan found his translator, Shlomo Weiss, and discovered that copies of the speeches had been translated in advance for the foreign press. He looked around for Dan Bergmann, but the *Ha'aretz* man was nowhere in sight. It was still early. Then the writer went to the podium and a hush fell over the crowd.

The man's voice was soft, barely audible even when amplified. Alan glanced down at the transcript Shlomo had given him...

This year, it is not easy to look at ourselves...

Alan looked out over the crowd. They were riveted, hanging on every word. So was Noa. He glanced down at the transcript again, scanned down the page...

For me, the establishment and very existence of the state of Israel is something of a miracle that happened to us as a people – a political, national, human miracle. I never forget that, even for a single moment...

But look what happened...Look at those who lead us...When was the last time that the Prime Minister suggested or made a move that could open a single new horizon for Israelis? A better future?...

Alan looked at the row of men seated behind the writer. He watched Olmert's face. Impassive, stony-eyed, his bony features rigid. The writer had guts. He looked at the transcript again.

Mr. Prime Minister, I do not say these things out of anger or vengeance. You cannot dismiss my words tonight by saying a man should not be held to what he says when he is in mourning. Of course I am in mourning. But more than that I am in pain, I hurt. This country, and what you and your colleagues are doing to it, pains me...

Alan felt a grip on his shoulder, turned to see Dan Bergmann. Dan pointed up to the writer at the podium and raised his eyebrows. Alan nodded. Neither of them spoke. A palpable tension had gripped the crowd. The soft-voiced writer went on, caressing his language now, feathering the harsh Hebrew gutturals...

...Yitzhak Rabin turned to the path of peace with Palestinians not because he was fond of them or their leaders...Rabin decided to act because he detected, with great astuteness, that Israeli society could not long continue in a state of unresolved conflict...

Alan looked for Noa, located her nearby. A tear trickled on her cheek. He went over to her and took her hand. She squeezed his hand hard, but her eyes never left the prematurely aged face of the writer.

...He understood, before many people understood, that life in a constant climate of violence, of occupation, of terror and fear and hopelessness, comes at a price that Israel cannot afford to pay...

He felt Noa shudder. She released his hand and put both of hers to her face, hiding her tears. He put his arm around her trembling shoulders.

From where I stand at this moment, I request, call out to all those listening...Ask yourselves if the time has not arrived for us to come to our senses, to break out of our paralysis, to demand for ourselves, finally, the lives that we deserve to live.

The writer folded his text and turned away. The square erupted in a roar, tens of thousands of voices shouting their acclaim.

Alan turned Noa by her shoulders so she was facing him. She pushed his hands away, found a tissue and blew her nose. She drew in a deep breath through her nostrils, wiped her eyes, then looked at him fiercely.

"I'm fine,"she said. "Got carried away for a minute."

"That's OK. I've got to talk to Bergmann. I won't be long. Can you wait?"

Noa nodded. "Like I said, I'll be fine."

When Alan first put Bergmann under contract as a "consultant" the *Ha'aretz* reporter had explained to him the conditions of the deal. Among them was the fact that there were some kinds of information that Israeli journalists were privy to but that they could never publish. However, if a foreign news service published that information independently then the Israeli press was free to follow and publish as well, claiming that they were only reporting on what had already been reported abroad. Also, if a foreign journalist came by some information independently, an Israeli colleague might be able to confirm it, even though he, himself, couldn't publish it.

He found Bergmann now and they moved to the side of the stage, a vacant space in the press area where they were alone. "I've got a good source on this," Alan said. "The two terrorists taken alive on that bus were murdered later by a *Shabak* officer in a fit of rage. His name is Yacov Kessar, and there's an official investigation, very secret."

Bergmann nodded. "Anything else?"

"I never believed they died of wounds received in the attack because I saw them when they were taken off the bus. They were injured, yes, but they were walking fine. My source also tells me that their target was Dimona, to shut it down, not the release of Palestinian prisoners. And finally, they could have been Hezbollah, a long way from Lebanon and a disturbing sign that they may be hooking up with

Hamas. North and south. Shi'ite and Sunni in common cause sort of thing."

"The enemy of my enemy is my friend?" Bergmann said. He looked over at Noa. "You're getting along very well with our lovely lady scientist, it seems."

Alan smiled, shaking his head. "It's not her. Can you confirm any of this?"

"All of it," Bergmann said, "but obviously I can't publish. When are you putting it on the wire?"

"How much time do you need to get your follow up story ready?"

"You run it tomorrow night and I'll be fine," Bergmann said. "We'll have it in Monday's paper."

*

Noa's place in Neve Tzedek was a spacious condo in a re-modeled 19th century mansion. The job had been done beautifully, tastefully, expensively. The architects had kept what was good about the old - high ceilings and decorative plasterwork, ogees and rosettes - and knocked down some walls to provide new open areas. Enlarged windows made it feel even more open, the dark night breeze floating the curtains out from the walls. Noa Kagan was a very neat and orderly woman, Alan judged, her space uncluttered and with a rather stark aesthetic feel to it. White walls in the living room, abstract Israeli photo art on the walls, mostly black and whites. The color in the room came from the flowers in two vases. The bedroom was done in the same manner, and Alan got there more quickly than he hoped he might.

They'd been in the flat barely more than a few minutes when Noa placed her arms on his shoulders. "Would you like to stay?" she said. "Last night couldn't have been much fun for you."

What bothered him was that she said this so coolly, as if she *didn't care* whether he accepted the offer or not. Even made it sound like a favor. And while he was still searching for a way to say yes with some dignified independence, she led him into the bedroom where he discovered that she *did care* about her pleasure and that she was a practiced lover in making sure she achieved it. Not that he suffered in the process. Eventually they separated, their slippery bodies lying side by side, cooling on the tangled sheets. And as much as he wanted to think they'd been making love, he knew they'd been making sex. Or having it. Fucking, it was called, plain and simple. Good fucking.

He had wanted to make it more than that, but Noa didn't give him a chance. She lit up a cigarette and said that his father had told her that he, Alan, had been in Iraq. What did he think of the Bush war?

"A colossal strategic blunder," he said. "Anybody who lived or worked in the Middle East could have told them that."

"We didn't. What if Saddam had weapons of mass destruction?"

"But he didn't."

"And Iran? Ahmadinejad says that Israel should be wiped off the map."

"How're they going to do that? Iran hasn't got any nukes and Israel is the sixth largest nuclear power in the world."

"How do you know that?" she said, laughing. "Did your father tell you that?"

She was teasing him.

"Of course not. He doesn't know, but you should."

"Israel will never be the first country to introduce nuclear arms into the Middle East," she intoned with a mock seriousness.

"God! This *is* romantic," he said.

She stubbed out her cigarette and climbed on top of him.

"You mean we should make love not war?"

Much later that night, he asked her about the story she had told him the night before about a man called Yacov Kessar and the murder of two Arabs. Did she remember that?

"Yes. Gavri told me that story. It's brutal. We've become like the people who hate us."

"I was there. I saw the two men come off that bus alive. I'm thinking about writing a story about what you told me. Of course I won't use your name. Do you mind?"

"Are you a friend of Israel?"

Teasing again?

"Of course. I'm Jewish aren't I?"

"Do it!" she said fiercely, spitting out the two words. "I want you to do it. Serves him right."

Serves who right? Alan wondered. Hot, then cold, mood shifts in nano-seconds. He couldn't make her out.

At the Reuters bureau the following morning, he settled in to write the story of the murder of two Arab terrorists by a *Shin Bet* officer. He had promised Dan Bergmann that he would put in on the wire that evening. The sourcing of the story bothered him a bit, but he knew that if he tried to contact Gavri Gilboa directly he'd get nowhere. On the other hand he convinced himself that he had every right to go ahead. He'd been at the scene and had seen the two men alive with his own eyes. And since Bergmann had confirmed his version of events, then Bergmann must have got the story elsewhere, probably from official sources, even though he couldn't publish it.

He had finished a draft and was editing it when Ian Munro called in from Jerusalem. Munro was the bureau staffer who'd been assigned to cover the regular Sunday morning cabinet meeting.

"I'll be filing a flash in a few minutes," Munro said. "The government has announced that a *Shabak* officer named Yacov Kessar has been removed from his duties. He was involved in that bus hijacking..."

"I know about the hijacking," Alan interrupted. "Did they say why?"

"Yeah. There's going to be an investigation into the deaths of two of the terrorists. They were taken alive and later ended up dead during interrogation. Kessar could be charged with murder."

Alan's mind raced over the possibilities. The timing of the announcement was too neat to be a coincidence. They must have been tipped off.

"What do you want me to do?" Munro asked.

"Go ahead and file it."

Alan hung up. He stared at the printed draft of the story he'd been working on for several hours. He'd been scooped by a government. No choice but to spike his version.

"Fuck it!"

He scrunched the paper sheets in a ball and threw them into a waste bin. Then he picked up the phone and punched Dan Bergmann's cell number.

"I'm in the bureau," he said when Bergmann answered. "Pretty nice timing on the Kessar story from the cabinet this morning."

"Yeah, remarkable, isn't it," Bergmann replied.

"Coincidence you mean?"

"What else?"

"Oh well, I guess that's how it goes sometimes."

"Win some lose some."

"Yeah...well...let me know when you set something up with old Yitzhak Gavish in the Kirya."

"I'm working on it."

Alan hung up and stared at his wastebasket, then picked up his phone and called Munro in Jerusalem. "Was there any mention in the press briefing of a target or objective that the terrorists had?"

"Target? You mean the release of Palestinan prisoners?"

"Was that what they said?"

"Yeah, that hasn't changed."

"OK. Go ahead and file. I'll probably add something to it that I picked up down here."

He hung up and retrieved his copy from the wastebasket. He would add that the terrorists were trying to get to Dimona and blow it up. Put a nuclear angle on the story. That should give Bergmann something to chew over.

*

The rendezvous in Haifa that Ofra Gefen had arranged was in a cafe off Herzl Street near the Technion. From the street, cheap patterned curtains shut out any view inside. When he opened the door Alan heard popular music which turned out to be from a radio tuned to the Jordanian English service. Dirty globe lights hung in clusters from the ceiling, a chipped formica counter held a plastic lion with plastic whiskers quaffing a mug of beer. The only customer was a chain-smoking old man with arthritic hands and hooded eyes. A slovenly waitress asked them what they wanted and Alan ordered a Maccabee beer, Ofra said tea.

"I feel like a spy in some clandestine meeting," Alan said.

Ofra shrugged. "This is where she said she wanted to meet us."

Ofra had come to him in his office and said that she'd heard from a woman she knew who had seen the ad about Thomas Penrose in the papers. The woman's name was Anna Peled. She lived north of Haifa in the Galilee where she was a music teacher. She thought she might be able to help.

The door opened and Alan looked up to see four young men. They looked like Arabs and one of them said in bad English that they were lost. The old man erupted in Hebrew, spewing a torrent of words that sounded to Alan a lot like the swear words Susan Harris had been teaching him. The men left in a hurry. A song called "Just Two Of Us" started on the radio and Alan tried to joke with Ofra.

"Oh, she'll come," Ofra said confidently.

A few minutes later the door opened and a woman came in. She looked old-fashioned: greying hair in a crown of braids, no make-up, not even lipstick, a shapeless brown dress. But she had a remarkably youthful face. She glanced quickly around the cafe, taking in the old man and the waitress. Then she saw Ofra and smiled.

"Come and sit down Anna," Ofra said in English. "Meet Alan Raskin."

Alan stood up, held out his hand.

"Yes," the woman said, coming forward. "Forgive me, but I was trying to remember... it was so long ago." She barely touched his hand, then reached again and took it and held it while she looked into his face. "Anna Peled," she said.

"Please sit down," Alan said. "Would you like to order something?"

She looked around the cafe again, at the old man, the waitress. "Whatever you're having," she said, fluttering her hands.

"I'm not sure you want beer," Alan said, trying to make a joke.

But Anna just stared at him helplessly until Ofra took over, ordered some more tea and got her settled.

"You said you were trying to remember something," Alan said. "What was it?"

"Thomas Penrose," she said, almost in a whisper, hunching forward. "You want to know about him, don't you? That's what Ofra said." She looked quickly to Ofra as if for confirmation, said something in Hebrew. Ofra nodded.

"Yes, that's correct," Alan said.

She leaned back in her chair and stared again.

"You knew him?" he prompted.

"Was he a relative?"she asked. "I mean he wasn't Jewish, and the paper didn't say anything about why you wanted to know about Thomas Penrose..."

"He was a close friend of my father. Did you know him?"

She took what seemed an eternity to answer. She looked at the old man and the waitress again. Pearl Jam was on the radio now - *World Wide Suicide*, the President of the U.S. *writin' checks that others pay* - and Anna appeared to listen for a moment before she hitched her chair closer to the table, leaned forward and started to talk rapidly.

"I had a friend many years ago named Rachel. We were students together at the music conservatory here. Her family lived in Haifa where her father owned a machine shop. I was a boarder in the city with another family. It was near the end of the world war and Haifa was a mad place. Jews and Arabs were fighting each other and both of them were fighting the British. Haifa was the main British port, also the place where refugees from Europe were trying to get into the country. I cannot describe how crazy it was. Everyone was giddy that everything was going to change but nobody knew for sure how. It was hysteria. People did crazy things without a thought for tomorrow. My parents were very concerned about me. I was two years younger than Rachel but she was always after me to go out dancing with her at the Bat Galim Casino...."

She paused and looked at Ofra, as if checking on how she was doing. Ofra nodded and she went on.

"The Bat Galim Casino...it means Daughter of the Waves and it was the most popular night spot in town. Down on the shore under Mount Carmel, near where the Rambam Hospital is today. People would come from all over, even from Beirut in those days. It was very elegant, very sophisticated. It was open to the ocean in summer and there were sea captains, and officers in splendid uniforms, and gentlemen in white suits. They used to play cricket outside on Sundays..."

She was smiling at her own recollection.

"...Rachel met Thomas Penrose there. He was a lawyer in the civil administration in Jerusalem. But he came to Haifa often on business, and when he did he took Rachel dancing at the Bat Galim. She told me about him, but I only met him once. It was at the Bat Galim and I danced with him. He was very handsome and dashing. When I first came in here and saw you I was trying to remember what he looked like. Now I do and I think you look a bit like him...."

She smiled at Alan, and it gave him a creepy feeling.

"...Rachel said that Thomas Penrose was married but she didn't care. She was fun-loving and caught up in the devil-may-care atmosphere of the times. Then her father found out about him and she was put in quarantine. Not allowed out of her house except to go to school. Her father blamed her friends, even me, and she wasn't allowed to see me after school. A month or so later I read in the newspapers that Thomas Penrose had been killed in a traffic accident in Jerusalem."

She leaned back, finished it seemed and waiting for reaction.

"What was Rachel's last name?"

Anna stared at him for a long time. "I'm trying to remember. She was German and I believe it was Eisen ...Eisen something...Eisener? Yes, that was it, Eisener. I don't know what became of her. When I saw your advertisement I remembered the name Penrose and those days here in Haifa and I knew that Ofra worked with the foreign journalists so I called her. I hope you don't mind."

"No, no, not at all. To the contrary, I want to thank you. Do you know anything about the accident? Or Rachel's father's first name?"

Anna was silent for a moment, frowning. "No, but let me think a minute. It's the accident you're interested in, is it? You don't think her father had anything to do with it, do you?"

Alan decided that if he opened up a bit he might be able to get Anna to do the same. He was sure she wasn't telling him all she knew.

"Another person has answered my ad," he said. "I only know his first name...Yitzhak, and he told me that Thomas Penrose was killed because he was an anti-semitic prosecutor working with some elements of the British secret service who were hostile to the Zionist cause. He told me two of the men who killed him are still alive, men who have served this country well."

All this did for Anna was to make her frown deepen. But Ofra was all ears now and she asked him to describe Yitzhak. He did so but said nothing about Yitzhak Gavish, the man Dan Bergmann had fingered.

Ofra shook her head. "I don't think I know him."

"I would appreciate it," Alan said to Anna, "if you could try to help me find Rachel Eisener, if she's still alive."

Anna nodded, eyes wide. "I don't know," she said.

Alan stood up, certain he wasn't going to get anymore at this time. Anna, perhaps startled by his movement, got up too, tipping over her chair. Ofra picked it up, helped her straighten herself out.

"How do I find you again?" Alan asked. "Can you give me a telephone number?"

Anna looked at Ofra and said something in Hebrew.

Ofra replied in Hebrew, then turned to Alan. "I can reach her whenever you want."

When Alan opened the door to the street, Anna let Ofra go through first then turned and grasped his arm.

"You be careful with people like that Yitzhak," she whispered.

***

Six

Tel Aviv's rush hour traffic started early on Friday afternoons, soon after business and government shut down for *Shabbat,* the weekly religious holiday. Gavri Gilboa had come to his curiosity about the Jewish religion only in recent years, being more inclined to the occult than to the orthodox. He was standing at a window in the *Shin Bet* headquarters looking down at the slow crawl of cars on King Saul Boulevard when Daniel Zentler, an older officer who was replacing Yacov Kessar, limped over to join him.

"They live in an oxygen tent," Gavri said.

"Who?"

"The people in those cars down there. I doubt if they've ever seen a goat, let alone an Arab. They don't live in the Middle East. Not in their heads. They're in a bubble."

Zentler peered at the traffic for a moment. "They have a right to live in the safe haven we've built," he said quietly. "We owe them that, don't we?"

Gavri glanced at the older man, his large shaggy head, the benign intelligent eyes peering at him through thick horn-rimmed glasses. He didn't have a reply.

"That's why we do what we have to do," Zentler went on. "So the people in those cars down there can sleep nights and not worry."

Gavri nodded politely. Zentler was not a sabra like himself. He was a survivor from the death camps in Europe and those people had a different view of Israel. This safe haven business, for example. Gavri had never thought of the country that way. For him Israel didn't exist to provide shelter from a hostile world. He had grown up believing that this was his land, his birthplace, a country in which to grow and flourish, to go out from and come back to as a citizen not only of Israel but of the world -- not that he personally had been given much chance to do that. Zentler, on the other hand, had grown up learning to survive. He was a *yekke*, a German Jew, who had come over from Mossad years before and had a reputation as a brainy, meticulous professional. To Gavri, Zentler was too cultivated for *Shabak*. But he did admire the calm control that the man brought to the job compared to Kessar. Before he had retired, Zentler's main responsibility had been security for the Prime Minister's Office. He'd been brought back temporarily to replace Kessar after the *balagan* with the bus terrorists down in the desert.

"Any luck so far?" Zentler asked. "Anything I should know?"

Gavri, still staring down at the traffic, thought he recognized Noa Kagan's Peugeot heading out towards the Haifa highway. He had a sudden impulse to go down and follow the car. Stop it and ask her straight out – Why? Then perhaps it wasn't Noa's car. How many tan-colored Peugeots were there in Tel Aviv, anyway? He turned to deal with Zentler. The *yekke* was persistent, nagging every day. Perhaps it was something he'd learned as a child in the death camps. Not giving up. And because he was a survivor he felt a special responsibility to prevent any of his people from being taken like cattle to the slaughter ever again? Gavri found this creepy. Who would dare try?

"No...not yet," he said, shaking his head.

"You've placed the taps and the surveillance?"

"We already had taps on the foreign bureaus..."

"Oh...of course...I should have remembered that," Zentler said. "And the surveillance?"

"As of Monday."

The order had come directly from the Prime Minister's office to *Shabak* : find out who had leaked the information about Yacov Kessar and the murder of two terrorists *and* the fact that they were Hezbollah and had wanted to set off their bomb in Dimona. The government had pre-empted the breaking of the story in the press about Kessar's murders by getting ahead of the foreign media and releasing the information itself. But the Reuters report the same Sunday *after* the government release contained extra details about Hezbollah and Dimona that weren't in the briefing. So Reuters became the prime suspect as the recipient of the leak. But who was the source? That was what the Prime Minister's office wanted to know.

Gavri thought he already knew.

There had been no byline on the Reuters story, not unusual for a wire service. He had checked the telephone taps on the Bureau on Hamasger Street, and then made sure that the home phones of Alan Raskin and the three other Reuters reporters were tapped. Zentler had been told that the government had been tipped off by Daniel Berg- mann at *Ha'aretz* that a foreign news service was about to break the story. "Bergmann would probably deal only with Raskin at Reuters," Zentler had said in his briefing to Gavri and Benny Brosh, "so he is our primary target to lead us to the leaker."

Zentler also said that he hoped he didn't have to remind them that busting heads with the press was not the way things were done in Israel's democracy. Besides, the point was to discover the leaker and not the purveyor of the leak.

Gavri had called in the Tel Aviv police crime units to help with the surveillance. They used their *LATAM* undercover agents who had the city in a grid, connected by radios and cameras, and as of the past Monday they were watching Raskin's every move. But Zentler did not stop there. He had used his old Mossad contacts to come up with the name of a useful *Sayan*. A *Sayan* was a Jew who lived in the diaspora that Mossad recruited as a willing helper who could do specific tasks without ever having to know the purpose. In any country where Mossad operated, especially in Europe and the United States, it had thousands of *Sayanim* to call on. Although she lived in Israel, Mossad had Susan Miller, an American, on their books as a volunteer and she had provided information on what the foreign press corps in Israel was interested in, what they were thinking and talking about in private. She had given Mossad the name of Alan Raskin as one of her "recruits" and a Mossad friend had given her name to Daniel Zentler.

"Get in touch with this Miller woman in Jerusalem," Zentler told Gavri. "See what she can do to help us with Raskin."

In the parlance of the Israeli military Gavri Giboa was *elite*: former paratrooper, *ex-matkal* commando, present day *shabak* officer. He was highly qualified to join the men who celebrated weekly with a noisy party at The Jackpot. It was a Friday afternoon tradition, and as the hours went by the nostalgia could become maudlin. Former paratroopers, aging tank commanders and over-the-hill commandos...all *elites* and all gathered with their latest wives or newest girlfriends to drink and sing the old songs of war and the Zionist dream.

Gavri and Benny Brosh wedged their way through the crowd of newcomers, many of them nervous young women, bunched up at the door and hoping for a table. The place was jammed, sweltering, noisy.

"Gavri! Over here!" Zvi Zaslavsky shouted through the din, beckoning from a table near the bar. Zee-Zee was the owner of the Jackpot, a former paratrooper, burly, balding, with mischievous blue eyes set in a broad slavic face. The Jackpot served as an unofficial information agency for its *elite* patrons and Zee-Zee relished his role at the center. He called for more chairs and Gavri and Benny squeezed into the table beside him, shaking hands all around.

"*Moskovskaya?*" Zee-Zee asked. "I just got some in. Good stuff!"

Gavri smiled at his exuberance. "*Konyeshna!*"

"*Khorasho!...Khorasho!*"

Zee-Zee poured glasses of chilled vodka and pushed them across the table. "I heard you were becoming a rabbi or something, studying the Torah or the Kabbalah all the time."

Gavri made a face. "Who me?" He raised his glass. "*Lo'chaim!*"

"*Lo'chaim!*" Zee-Zee responded. They drank and then Zee-Zee leaned in close to Gavri's ear. "What the hell's going on? Kessar out on his ass because of a couple of dead ragheads off that bus down near Dimona? Some kind of screw up? What in hell happened?"

At that moment the piano player banged out the opening chords of the *Internationale* and Zee-Zee cursed. A chorus of voices started bellowing a Hebrew version of the anthem. Arms around each other, some customers swayed back and forth and sang in unison, others held glasses and beer steins aloft. There were catcalls and whistles.

Gavri looked at Zee-Zee and shrugged. He knew that for Zee-Zee he was a top quality source for gossip -- he was still "operational." The noise allowed him to ignore the question. He threw back the shot of icy-cold vodka and pushed the glass across to Zee-Zee for more. Then he started humming along, remembering some of the words he had learned as a boy in *Ha'shomer Ha'tzair,* the Marxist-Zionist youth movement. What idealists his parents had been! Joey and Eva Gilboa, migrating to Palestine from Canada via Spain at the end of the Spanish Civil War, their ongoing search for a socialist utopia bringing them into the welcoming embrace of Sasha Kagan and the kibbutz he had founded in the hills of the Galilee. Eva had given birth to him there and Joey had idolized Sasha Kagan, held him up as a model. When he'd grown older he'd idolized Sasha too, and his main rival for the old man's attention had been a girl, Sasha's grandaughter Noa.

Damn Noa! What has she done to me?

He gulped some vodka. The people who had been swaying at the tables were on their feet now, bawling out the closing words of the Internationale. Cheers and laughter cascaded around him at the finish. He gulped some more vodka, closing his eyes as he swallowed. The song was an amusement now, something to be sung when having a good time on a Friday afternoon at The Jackpot. The words he had just mouthed meant nothing. Its message was sentimentalized, disconnected from the ideals of the past and from the grubby reality of life that went on outside the open windows. Behind his closed eyes he saw the window of the bus, heard himself say *Shoot!* He could feel, in himself, the kick of the rifle fired by the young man next to him who had killed with such an icy, matter-of-fact skill. They were all that way now, including Noa's son Sasha before he was killed. Noa would deny that. But she was a hypocrite. Some years ago when a pop song called *"Shooting and Crying"* had been banned by Israeli radio because it was a send up of the myth of the sensitive *sabra* soldier, tough and coarse on the outside but a good soft heart within, he remembered her scoffing: "This beautiful innocent youth who's forced to shoot to kill by day and agonizes about it while reading poetry at night?... Bullshit! The kids aren't buying that anymore." But Sasha did, and Noa knew it.

He dribbled some vodka on his lips, licked it, his eyes still closed.

Noa...Noa...Noa! Goddamn Noa! What to do with her?

He had not shown Zentler one of the *LATAM* surveillance reports on Alan Raskin, a report which was locked in his desk at *Shabak* headquarters. On Wednesday evening the undercover agents had followed Raskin to an address in Neve Tzedek where he had stayed the night. It was Noa's address.

Now, he could feel the heat of the vodka in his body, his mind spinning. He knew he was getting drunk. He wanted to. He had been struggling with his anger and his embarrassment about Noa for days and he wanted to drown it. He cursed himself. First for allowing her to try to make love to him and second for telling her about Kessar. Now he was cursing her too.

The bitch has made a fool of me...but she couldn't have done it alone...she's being used by that bastard Raskin!

"Gavri? How are you?"

He opened his eyes and saw a young woman's face. She had olive skin, thick black hair, and she looked concerned. He knew the face, remembered the failure with her, but he couldn't remember her name. The vodka didn't help. He was a little drunk now and the longer he stared the more he saw Noa's face when she was younger, pleading with him to go to Safed and search for mysteries. He closed his eyes and remembered the dark nights outside the synagogues in that ancient hilltop town, black-hatted men moving into the light that spilled from the doors. They pretended those old men had secrets, the mysteries of the Kabbalah, and they were going to discover them. They hadn't then, but now he had. He'd looked deep into the Kabbalah and discovered the *Shekhinah*, a feminine power in the world of the divine. She was the closest to the sufferings of the people of Israel, like Noa, who had lost her son. *Shekhinah* was Noa's role, but she didn't know that yet.

"Delectable!" Zee-Zee hissed, and Gavri opened his eyes again.

"Come and sit on Gavri's lap, my beauty," Zee-Zee said to the girl. "I've got no more chairs. Have some vodka."

The young woman waved Zee-Zee off. "Just thought I'd say hello, Gavri. Hope you're well. Don't want to bother you." And she was gone into the milling crowd.

"A real beauty," Zee-Zee said. Then, faking a hoarseness in his voice. "My God! I've got a hard on...I'm going to come in my pants."

"Think about doing it with Golda Meir," Gavri said. "Stops me from coming too quick. Works every time."

"Golda?" Zee-Zee tilted his head back and roared. "*Golda Meir?*" He slapped Gavri on the back. "You old bastard! And you couldn't even remember that girl's name, you whoremaster. I suppose she wanted to marry you, too. Did you see that sad look on her face? Talk to me. Tell me what's going on."

"More Vodka!" Gavri said.

Zee-Zee emptied the bottle in his glass and headed behind the bar to get another. The crowd was three deep. Gavri heard a woman's voice shriek. "*Golda Meir?*...Zee-Zee! That's disgusting!" There was a burst of raucous laughter, then Zee-Zee was back, grinning, another bottle in his hand, a small ring of ice still circling its neck. He stood at the table scanning the crowd as he worked at the bottle cap. Suddenly, he froze and scowled.

"It's the Navy Seal, that American journalist you had trouble with. He's just come in with that other American cunt, Susan Miller." He spat at the floor. "Foreigners! I shouldn't allow them in on Friday afternoons."

Gavri looked over his shoulder. As if she had been waiting for him to turn, Susan Miller lifted her hand a little and wiggled her fingers, a surreptitious sign of greeting. He had followed Zentler's instruction, contacted the *sayan,* and driven up to Jerusalem to meet with her. Miller's eager excitement at the prospect of really working for Israeli counter- intelligence – which was what he had told her she might be doing – had led him to doubt her usefulness. Then, after seeing the *LATAM* report on Raskin's overnight visit to Neve Tzedek, he'd changed his mind. Fuck Zentler! He'd talked to Benny and then he called Susan Miller and instructed her to try to bring the American journalist, Alan Raskin, to The Jackpot on Friday afternoon. She said she knew the place and that morning she had phoned and informed him that "all systems are go."

All systems are go? Zhonah! What did she think she was? Mata Hari?

He nodded slightly to her, acknowledging her signal. Then he reached out and grasped Zee-Zee's arm. *"Tovarich!* I have a favor to ask."

"Welcome Navy Seal!" Zee-Zee bellowed.

Gavri watched the giant Zavslavsky bull his way through the crowded tables to greet Alan Raskin and Susan Miller and steer them back to his table. Zee-Zee had cleared off all his guests except for himself and Benny Brosh. When Raskin reached their table he held out his hand.

"We meet again."

Gavri forced a smile, shook his hand, introduced Benny. "I believe you know him."

"Indeed I do," Raskin said, and he shook hands with Benny. "Still holding down the fort?"

Benny grinned and grunted some response and Raskin turned to introduce them to Susan Miller.

"We already know each other," she said. "Hi Gavri!"

Raskin showed a *How come?* look of surprise, but said nothing. Then the five of them sat with the freshly opened *Moskovskaya* on the table between them, condensation glistening on the bottle. Zee-Zee filled their glasses. *"Lo'chaim,"* he yelled, raising his glass, and they all did the same.

"How's my lovely Susan?"

"Oh Zee-Zee!" she exclaimed, laying her hand on his arm. "You're such a flirt."

Zee-Zee had placed himself between the couple. He turned now and punched Raskin on the arm. "I really like this woman. She's got guts... and you know what else?"

"What?"

"She's a *chestnaya davalka*...Right?"

Gavri watched Raskin closely. He knew the Reuters man had lived in Moscow, but how good was his Russian? Zee-Zee had just said that the Miller woman really enjoyed fucking.

"What's that mean?" Susan asked.

"Peace!" Raskin said, raising his glass.

Deflection! Very cool fucker so far! Gavri observed. He sat back to watch how Zee-Zee and Benny played out their roles. "He's calling me a piece?" Susan cried.

"No...Peace!...like in Peace Now," Raskin said.

"Peace Now?" Zee-Zee roared. "Arabs can't have a Peace Now movement. How can you have peace with Arabs? "

"Why not?" Susan said.

"Because it is not in their character, my dear," Zee-Zee replied. "It's not their character."

"But that's racist."

"No, it's realistic. You're an American. You have a problem, you must have a solution, the quicker the better. You don't belong here. In a very involved situation like this there cannot be instant remedies. There can be transitional periods. There can be non-satisfactory solutions, and more than anything else, we will probably have to live with a reality, which for a long time, the foreseeable future, will not be safe in absolute terms."

"No Palestinian state?" Alan said.

"No Palestinian state," Zee-Zee replied, shaking his head.

"What about demographics?" Susan said. "The Arabs are breeding like minks."

"So do our sephardim," said Zee-Zee. "Have you tried one yet?"

Susan blushed. "Fuck you!"

Zee-Zee roared with laughter. "Just teasing. But who in this part of the world is happy with the demography and the borders. Is Syria happy with Lebanon? Is Lebanon happy with Hezbollah? Are the Kurds happy in Iraq...well maybe they are now it's such a fucking mess, thanks to you Americans. And is anybody happy with Iran? They want to wipe us off the map. The whole region may be old historically but it is very young in modern political terms, with the exception of Israel. So to create here a political garden of Eden? To create here a Shangri-la of co-existence? Well, either it's not possible, or it will take quite a long time. So why have these Hollywood hopes with the pop music behind them and on and on. Build your expectations on the short term and you'll fall on your face. No quick solutions. Only those who will not expect something in the next year, the next five years, the next fifty years, only those shall inherit the land. The others will mentally disintegrate." He leered at Susan. "You'll leave, just wait and see. A bottle of *Moskovskaya* says you won't last."

Susan glared at him, fury in her eyes.

"Sounds like a form of Trotskyism to me," Raskin interjected before she could speak. "Permanent war instead of permanent revolution."

At that moment, for some reason unknown to Gavri, perhaps a request, the piano player started banging out the Marseillaise and people started singing. Zee-Zee, ever resourceful, punched Raskin on the arm.

"Up the revolution!" he cried. "Here, have some more vodka!"

Quickly, he poured more shots and raised his glass. "*Na zdroveyeh!*" he said, and threw the vodka against the back of his throat. He gasped, slammed the glass on the table, and wiped his eyes with his thumb and fingers. He grasped Raskin's arm and thrust his face up close.

"My friend," he said. "Every country has its hard men. You've been around long enough to know that. Here, they are the *Shabak* and you know that, too, like my two friends here." He paused. Then his broad, slavic face split into a wide grin. "But I don't allow them in my place. Never! They always cause trouble."

Benny took his cue, leaned into Susan Miller and whispered in Hebrew. Zee-Zee, sweating heavily, reached for the *Moskovskaya* bottle.

"You filthy little bastard!" Susan cried.

She tried to strike Benny, but he caught her hand and twisted her arm.

"*Zhonah!*" he hissed, and she cried out in pain.

"Hey! What's going on?" Raskin yelled.

Benny gave him a nasty, challenging grin. "I called her a fucking whore," he said in heavily accented English.

Susan threw her vodka in Benny's face and he slapped her hard.

Raskin jumped up and stepped behind Zee-Zee and Susan to get to Benny. As he came around their chairs Benny hit him with two Karate blows before he could get his hands up, one in the ribs and one in the mouth. Raskin went to the floor, his mouth a bloody pulp. Susan screamed and dropped to her knees beside him.

Gavri got up and walked around to Raskin. He pushed Susan aside with his knee, hunkered down and slapped the journalist's face lightly until Raskin opened his eyes.

"Stay away from Noa Kagan," he slurred in English. "Try again and it'll be worse, much worse."

Then he stood and looked down at Susan Miller.

"Good job," he said in Hebrew. "*Shalom.*"

And Zentler's so-called *Sayan*, looking bewildered, started to cry.

***

Seven

A blood-red ball boiled up over the edge of the desert in front of Noa Kagan. The sun, rippling with fiery heat, spread its inflammation like lava along the rim of the Judean hills. Arrows of ultraviolet light streaked across the desert floor, flashing pinpoint signals from the silica crystals fused in the ancient rock. To Noa, it was a huge, red sphere of nuclear fusion that was about to cauterize the desert once again. She didn't like the desert. The distances disturbed her, pulled at her, defying gravity. She had a sense of the earth turning and of herself clinging to it. She shivered behind the wheel of the speeding Peugeot and sipped from the muddy black coffee she had picked up in Beer Sheva. Off in the southeast, she could see the white dome of the reactor poking above the Negev floor and catching the flat rays of the sun.

Dimona. Her destination.

She had not thought of Sasha in the last few days, maybe not for a week. But he had been in her dream the night before. They stood side by side, holding hands, in a ruined roofless synagogue. Old Sasha, her grandfather, dressed like a rabbi of all things, was standing in front of them. The synagogue was at Kfar Borochov, on the edge of the precipice overlooking the Jordan valley. Old Sasha held a thick tome which he raised up, intoning, "While we read history we make history!" He held out the tome towards them. Solemnly, she and her son each laid a hand on it and there was a great whoosh and the flames of an immense inferno swept up around them. They were inside the walls of hell, great swirling sheets of red fire streaked with black smoke. Somehow, she knew the firestorm was infinite, that it was the conflagration at the end of the world. And somehow, she knew too that it was a nuclear holocaust caused by war and that Israel had been consumed instantly. She and her son stood frozen to the spot, terrified as the flames roared around them. But why was there no heat? And why did they have air? She looked up and saw that they were standing in a cool, slim, transparent cylinder, fire raging all around them on the outside, and far away, up at the top, she could see a small circle of blue sky ringed with yellow flames. At that moment in the dream, in spite of her fear, she had a powerful sense of certainty that she could stop this and they would survive. They were chosen and she was invincible.

She had come out of the dream with a jolt, looking for Sasha, expecting to find him in her room. She pressed her hands to her face and in a while it all came clear. Jacob Miesel's words came back to her: *Work from the inside.*

It had been well before dawn when she drove under the white, four-posted arch over the gate of the Weizmann Institute in Rehovot and stopped at the red and white pole barrier. She had sped by darkened houses and apartments in the densely populated coastal plain, sickly yellow light from the street lamps splashing on her windscreen. The people behind those shuttered windows were fools. Stupid sleeping sheep! They had abandoned themselves to a system in which they accepted the condition of being ignorant. They were as obedient as lambs when the words *national security* were uttered. They lived with an opaque nuclear culture, never questioning their nuclear weapons. Only their leaders knew what was going on. The people had stuck their heads in the sand. They had to be awakened.

Light from the Weizmann's guardhouse door spilled along the red and white finger of the barrier. She beeped her horn and a sleepy-eyed guard raised the barrier and waved her through. She drove down a tree-lined roadway and parked in front of the accelerator laboratory, futuristic floodlit towers thrusting into the inky sky.

In her office she went straight to the safe. She took out a number of documents with the Weizmann security mark stamped on the outside of their bindings and brought them to her desk. She didn't bother to open any of them, but simply measured them for thickness and tested the bindings by removing them and putting them back on. Finally, she selected two of the documents and put them in her briefcase. Then she leaned with her hands on her desk and stared at a framed scroll hanging on the wall. It was a quotation from Chaim Weizmann:

You see, the Jews are a small people,
a very small people quantitatively,
but also a great people that builds and destroys.
A people of genius and, at the same time,
a people of enormous stupidity.

Old Sasha had given her the scroll many years ago when she was heading off to America and MIT, no doubt meaning to warn her about her overbearing confidence in her own cleverness.

The first Dimona checkpoint came just after the turnoff from the main highway. Noa held her KMG pass up to the windscreen and a military policeman waved her through. *Kirya-le-Mehekar Gariny* - the Negev Nuclear Research Center - was operated nominally by the Israeli Atomic Energy Authority but was in fact controlled by the Defense Ministry. Two miles further along the desert road she came to an electrified fence and another checkpoint. Observation towers sat on the low hills nearby. The hills also contained missile batteries where they had standing orders to shoot down any unauthorized aircraft that strayed into the airspace overhead. During the Six Day War, nervous that the Egyptians would go after their nascent nuclear program, they had shot down one of their own fighters. Later, a Libyan passenger jet had also been shot down when it strayed off course, drifting up from the Sinai desert, and more than a hundred people on board had died. Dimona was Israel's most secret place.

"Good morning! You're early today, Dr. Kagan." The soldier greeting her was leaning over to look in the car window.

She smiled at him, held out her pass. He took the pass and went to the guardhouse. It was routine to record her entry to the facility. A moment later he returned, leaned down, and gave her the pass. He didn't ask to look in the shoulder bag on the seat beside her or in the trunk of her car. Nobody, not even the top scientists and officials, was ever given complete briefcase clearance, the uninspected freedom to take documents in and out as they wished. That inspection would come later.

Inside, she parked in her slot near the library, then walked with her briefcase along a palm-lined pathway which angled through a maze of buildings to the reactor dome at the far end of the compound. Beside the reactor sat a two-storied, windowless building that looked like a warehouse. It was called Machon 2, a self-contained production unit. It was the bomb factory where she worked.

A line of men filed out through a door in the blank wall. A shift was finishing. She passed by, saying good morning to some of the men. Inside, she stepped into an elevator. There were six levels indicated beneath the illuminated ground floor button. She pressed Level 2 and the elevator descended. When the door slid open she was facing a *Shabak* security officer sitting behind a desk.

"Good morning, Dr. Kagan."

She nodded, placed her bag on the desk and opened it.

The *Shabak* officer looked inside and probed with his hands. He took out the two bound documents, but didn't open them He looked at the security classification of the Weizmann Institute stamped on the covers, made an entry in his log, then placed the documents back in the briefcase. He also made a note of her lap top computer– a Dell XPS M1530 – switched it on and saw her desktop background, a picture of her son, Sasha, beneath a bunch of icons. He closed the computer and said thank you.

Noa picked up her bag and walked by the glass windows of the main control room. Several men sat monitoring the plutonium separation process. The only sound was that of her heels echoing on the metal floor. She passed by a balcony overlooking the huge, cavernous production hall which dropped through to the bottom of Level 4 where, inside heavily insulated hot tanks and pipes, the actual separation of plutonium 239 and its concentration to fissionable, weapons grade material took place. It was for the large implosion warheads, the city killers, truly the weapons of last resort and Israel had few of them.

She came to her office, went inside, and closed the door. She took the Weizmann documents from her briefcase, laid them on her desk, then went to her safe and retrieved another document. This one had a Dimona security clearance stamped on the cover. All scientific work was written in English for technical reasons. She opened it to the title page:

LASER ISOTOPE SEPARATION (LIS) TECHNIQUE
(Extraction of U 235 by Tunable Dye Lasers)
Drs. Noa Kagan and Chaim Nebenzahl

She had helped to create this prized technique. It was hers, the jewel in her career. LIS produced an extraction of such purity that it had opened the door to a simpler miniaturization program for penetration weapons. Also lasers required less space and money than the huge centrifuge operations most commonly used for producing weapons grade uranium. Eighty feet below her, at this very moment, thin beams of light from the tunable dye lasers she had designed were forming an eerie lattice of colored lines in a darkened chamber. Green and orange, yellow and red, the lines looked tangible, strung in taut orderly rows like a network of gaudy clotheslines. They were pencil thin, unerring in their penetration of the uranium. Hour by hour, the alchemy of the lasers worked on the substance. Enrichment was the secret. Purity the goal. Weapons grade U 235 the stone the soldiers sought.

And she had found that stone for them and then tooled it into a warhead.

She started turning the pages slowly. They were filled with formulas, arcane signs that marched across the paper like hieroglyphs, signs that could lead a knowledgeable explorer to hidden treasure. But she was seeing more than the formulas. She was looking behind them to a story of herself that was not printed there. For her, the LIS treatise read like a diary. It was all that she had left to show after so many years, and when she had awakened from her dream that morning she had determined to go for it.

LIS belonged to her! It was *her* property! Not that of the state, or the *nachalniks*, the big self-important men of the IDF and the Government, the men who had so heedlessly killed her Sasha. They had taken him from her, but they would not have this. It was hers and she would take it back.

She removed one of the Weizmann documents she had brought in with her from its folder, then did the same with her LIS treatise. She switched the documents so that LIS was now in a folder with the Weizmann security stamp on its spine. But she was not finished yet. There was another document she had written by herself that was sitting in the archive vault. She was determined to have it too. But that would not be so easy. Any document checked out of the vault could not be taken from the premises, although she could keep it in her office for a considerable time. She picked up the LIS Dimona folder, now with the Weizmann document inside, went out the door of her office and down the corridor on Level 2, Machon 2, towards the vault. Her heartbeat quickened as she drew near.

The office door next to the vault was open. It was Zev Rozow's office, the *Shabak* security chief at Dimona. She glanced inside. Rozow wasn't behind his desk and she felt relieved. She wasn't used to being furtive.

She entered the vault.

"Good morning Dr. Kagan. What can I do for you?"

Shlomo Eventov, a *Shabak* officer and the chief file clerk, sat at a check-out counter just inside the door of the vault. He was fat and always pleasant. She looked at his round, smiling face, cheerful eyes behind round granny glasses. Shlomo was the most unlikely *Shabak* officer she had ever known. Completely harmless. Yet her hands were shaking and she had to clasp them in front of her.

"I need to see my file case, Shlomo. Sorry, but I have to...you know..." She was stumbling and she caught herself and stopped. "I just need to see it."

Shlomo shrugged, a little surprised maybe by her unnecessary explanation. "Sure. I'll have it in a minute." And he went into the stacks behind him and came back shortly with a thick box. He placed it on the counter.

Noa walked her fingers through the tags, selecting a thin document with the heading – NATANZ (Ordnance). She laid it on the counter, measuring its thickness by eye.

"I'm returning this," she said. And she placed the fake LIS document that she had brought with her in the box. Shlomo noted only the Dimona file numbers, both on the LIS document that she had returned and the NATANZ document she had checked out. He didn't check the contents.

"I thought you'd have that stuff memorized by now."

Noa jumped at the sound of Rozow's voice. He was right behind her, looking over her shoulder.

"What's wrong? Did I give you a scare? I thought you kibbutzniks were fearless?"

"Don't sneak up on me like that!" Noa snapped sharply.

Rozow, a chunky, balding man with a wide slavic brow, looked startled at the savagery of her response.

"Sorry," he said. "Just making a joke."

Noa, glaring at him, said nothing. She snatched the NATANZ document from the counter and walked out.

Back in her office she hefted the NATANZ document, it would take up hardly any room in the second Weizmann folder she had brought in. She sat down and leafed through the document. It was just what the tag said – ordnance, meaning tactical nuclear warheads, designed for Natanz, the Iranian nuclear complex. For targeting details and delivery systems she would have to go to the computer. She stood and opened up the second Weizmann folder and instead of removing its contents she placed the pages of NATANZ among them. Then she placed both the Weizmann folders – one with LIS and the other with NATANZ – in her bag.

Next, she sat down again and turned on the office laptop on her desk, a Dell XPS identical to the personal one in her bag, but more powerful. Her office laptop was linked to the main frame at Dimona and security made it impossible to copy on to a disc or a flash drive from either one. But she could copy the other way. She removed a flashdrive from her bag, inserted it into the office laptop and copied to it the photograph of Sasha she used as desktop background on her personal laptop. She then removed her personal laptop from her bag and turned it on.

She sat back and compared the screens on the two laptop computers. Sasha's darling face. The screens looked the same, except that the number of icons over Sasha's face was different. Would a security officer giving it a casual glance notice the difference, especially if she distracted him a little?

She would take the chance.

She unplugged both computers and switched them, putting the Dimona computer in her bag, leaving her personal laptop plugged in on her desk. A few minutes later she checked her bag with the same *Shabak* officer at the entrance to Level 2 and he noted in his log that the two documents she was taking out had the same Weizmann covers and security stamps as those she had brought in. He opened her computer and turned it on and she waited until the screen flickered to life with the picture of her son.

"He's still there," she said in a wistful voice.

The officer looked up from the screen. They all knew she had lost a son up in Lebanon. He nodded and gave her a sympathetic smile. "Yes, he is. Have a good day Dr. Kagan." And he turned off the computer and put it back in her bag.

The elevator carried her up to the surface and she walked out of Machon 2 and over to her car. Nobody stopped her and several hours later she was back in Tel Aviv.

*

The breeze off the Mediterranean felt cool on her skin, her toes tingled pleasurably. They always did after an orgasm. She didn't know a lot about the physics of the body, but she believed the feeling had something to do with proprioceptors or maybe with kinesthetics, she was never sure of the difference.

"Are there muscles in your toes?" she asked, stretching her legs and feet on the bed.

"In your toes?" Alan Raskin repeated, lying beside her. "Damned if I know. Why?"

"Never mind."

Noa got off the bed, wrapped herself in a towel, lit a cigarette from a pack on a bureau against the wall and went to the open balcony door. The smoke she exhaled blew across the vertical shadow line at the door and billowed out into the sunlight, a bluish-white cloud that was snatched by the breeze and whisked back into the room.

"That stuff will kill you," Raskin said from the bed.

She ignored him and looked out across the little harbor to a brown headland, the slope dotted with yellow flowers. White spray shot up over the mole protecting the entrance to the harbor. Inside the enclosed space, gentle blue-green swells of water washed up to the beach beneath her balcony. To her left, high up on the old fortress tower at the foot of the mole, a blue and white Israeli flag snapped in the breeze. And over it all, a clear blue sky. The villa was on the coast in Ceasarea and it belonged to an old friend, a former general turned businessman with whom she'd once had an affair. She had been able to borrow it for the weekend and then she'd called Alan Raskin and asked him what he thought about the idea. His answer lay on the bed behind her.

For a journalist, Noa found Raskin to be quite a modest man. In the past week his Reuter's story on the bus hi-jacking, specifically the facts that the target had been Dimona and the terrorists were Hezbollah, has caused an uproar in the Israeli media. But Raskin had taken no credit. He had not used a by-line and her colleagues at work in Dimona were curious about the Reuter's source for the story. She was not bothered at all that she was the unknown source. To the contrary, the ruckus in the Israeli newspapers had excited her, especially reports about the Government's concern. She enjoyed watching the politicians bluster and pontificate about the danger the story did to Israel. *They deserved it.* Alan Raskin had showed her a way to provoke them, to hurt them, and she knew now that she could use him in the plan that had been evolving in her mind ever since she had come back from Cambridge. *A plan that would cause much more pain than the Dimona story.* The idea of *using* Alan Raskin bothered her only a little. She liked him, liked his gentle, non-aggressive manner, and she didn't want to hurt him. But she felt it was a two way street between them, that he was getting something out of it too – a good story and good sex.

When Raskin picked her up in Neve Zedek for the drive to Cesarea she'd been concerned about his appearance – a bruised mouth and a badly cut lip from which he'd just had ten stitches removed. He didn't want to talk about it and had said something silly about seeing what the other guy looked like. Then, while they were making love, he'd cried out in pain when she embraced him. His ribs had been hurt too.

She turned from the balcony and looked at him. For a man over fifty he was still in pretty good shape, slightly thick at the waist, a little jowly with his chin pushed down on his chest, but well-formed shoulder muscles and pectorals. He lay full length on the sheet, relaxed, naked, his arms flung out to the side like a child.

"Who tried to kill you?"

He raised himself up on an elbow and looked at her. One of his legs was bent at the knee, opening a vee to his crotch where his genitals hung, slack, purplish, fully exposed. It seemed a perfectly natural position for him, not conscious at all of any vulnerability. He was very much like a child with his innocent blue eyes. Deceptive though. She was very clinical about sex and she judged him to be well-hung, as the Americans put it, and a very good lover, not at all shy.

"What do you mean?" he said. "Nobody tried to *kill* me."

"Well they did a good job of hurting you. We don't have street crime in Tel Aviv. Who did it?"

He cocked his head, appraising her.

"Come on! Who did it?"

"Your friend Gavri Gilboa...and his lethal little sidekick. Benny something or other. They were drinking in The Jackpot and picked a fight. He warned me to stay away from you."

"*What?*"

"That's what he said...*Stay away from Noa!*"

"He's a fool," she said. *God! It was like the old days on the kibbutz. So possessive! What had she unleashed in Gavri?*

"Maybe he thinks you told me about Kessar and the bus and Dimona. When I was reprimanded at Beit Agron for publishing the story without clearing it with the censor, they demanded to know who my source was about Dimona and Hezbollah. I told them nothing of course, but if your friend Gavri *does* think it's you it appears he's keeping it to himself."

She frowned at the thought of Gavri, shaking her head. "It's hard to have friends here anymore," she said. "This country has hit a wall."

"What does that mean?"

She turned back to the harbor, ignoring him. Caesarea had been a place of arrivals and departures, of beginnings and endings. The Roman Titus had landed his troops here for the final assault that destroyed Jerusalem and dispersed the Jews to the far reaches of the earth. It had taken two thousand years for them to come back, creeping ashore at night under the bayonets of Imperial Britain, founding a new nation and fighting half-a-dozen wars. And all for what? She believed the Zionist dream had exhausted itself. It had been replaced by a militant religious nationalism. Occupation of the Palestinians had become a permanent condition, a cancer, and there would be no peace. The sanctity of the Holocaust was cheapened by using it to justify everything. The settlers and the religious Jews were messianic, uncompromising, and undemocratic. They would not give up land on the West Bank without a bitter struggle. The secular Jews no longer had the heart for that fight, many of their sons didn't want to live here anymore and they escaped at the first opportunity. Israel was shrinking into its own shell.

"I mean that for the first time ever I've allowed myself to think that Israel may be a passing phenomenon," she said.

She looked back at Raskin. He'd put his arms around his knees and pulled them up, huddling himself in a ball.

"Whoa!" he cried. "Are you serious?"

She nodded. "I don't want to think it but I do."

"But you've managed to survive pretty well for sixty years."

"Oh we can manage any conflict, and we'll probably continue to do that for quite a while yet. We have the weapons. Tell me. Why did you never become a Zionist? Move out here and live among your fellow Jews?"

Raskin shrugged. Obviously he didn't like the question. She'd discovered that few American Jews did. Yet the existence of Israel, and support for it, seemed to be such an integral part of their definition of themselves as Jews, and they were far less critical of the Israeli government than the people of Israel itself or much of its media. The Israeli newspaper *Ha'aretz* made the *The New York Times* look like a pro-zionist propaganda sheet.

"I don't know," Raskin said. "Maybe because of my mother. She was an Israeli, but she never had anything nice to say about the place."

"Wait a moment!" she exclaimed. "Your mother was from Israel?"

"Yeah, but she left when she was eighteen."

"That's a surprise. I was a guest in your house in Cambridge a number of times and she never mentioned that. Neither did your father. I wonder why?"

Raskin shivered and reached down and pulled the sheet over his nakedness. She walked over and sat on the side of the bed.

"Maybe they were being oversensitive," he said. "Afraid of hurting your feelings or insulting you. They were very well-mannered in that way." He shrugged. "Or she could just have been embarrassed when confronted with a real Israeli. I understand that leaving Israel is a bad thing to do. What's it called?"

"What's what called?"

"Going down, away from Israel, the opposite of *aliyeh.*"

"*Yerida.* And it seems it's not so bad anymore. Thousands are doing it. The secular Jews, the educated ones. They can't see their children and grandchildren living here and enduring an endless conflict. There has to be something more to life for them than just survival. Ben-Gurion said that Israel had no foreign policy, only a defense policy. That becomes a self-fulfilling prophecy. We are xenophobic and paranoid. We trust no one and that is not a normal way for a country to behave."

Raskin smiled. "Just because you're paranoid doesn't mean you're wrong."

"Don't be flippant about this."

"Alright. The President of Iran, Mahmoud Ahmadinejad, says that your days are numbered. He promises to wipe Israel off the map. Isn't that a real threat?"

"No! How is he going to do it? He doesn't have nuclear weapons yet and we do. But wouldn't our ability to cope with Iran be easier if we were able to trust the outside world, starting with our neighbors? Wouldn't it be better if we didn't try to deal with the problem on our own but rather as part of the world community, through the United Nations for example."

"You know, I worked in Iran. I covered the revolution there, the overthrow of the Shah and the hostage crisis. They're just as paranoid about you as you say the Israelis are about the world. They see the hand of the United States in their history...the CIA coup in 1953...and they see it in your's too. The fact that you've never signed the Nuclear Nonproliferation Treaty means you should not be eligible for US foreign aid. Yet you receive more than any other country. The only answer could be that you don't have nuclear weapons, but you just said that you did."

"Of course we do. We deceived you in getting them and then Golda Meir made a deal with Nixon that we would keep them out of sight, carry out no tests, and tell our neighbors that we would not be the first to use them if we did have them. That's absurd. Why do you let us get away with it?"

"Now?" He shrugged. "The short answer is politics. You've got to know that criticism of Israel has become a third rail in American politics. The Israel lobby, AIPAC, would be all over anybody who suggested that Israel do a unilateral nuclear disarmament."

"Unilateral?" she scoffed. "How could it not be? We're the only country that has them in the Middle East. What do you think would happen if we came out in the open and offered to give up our nuclear weapons in return for a deal with our neighbors not to pursue them? How can you have a nuclear free Middle East otherwise?"

Raskin smiled, shaking his head. "Some people might think that's pretty naive. Besides, you'd first have to prove to those neighbors that you really did have them in order to give them up. How're you going to do that without a test?"

"Show them some proof."

"Such as?"

She got off the bed and went to her briefcase on the bureau. She withdrew a copy of one of the documents she had taken from Dimona and tossed it in on the bed. She had removed the Weizmann cover she'd used to smuggle it out. Raskin sat up in the bed and picked it up. He couldn't miss the word DIMONA in red letters, the security stamp, and the title:

LASER ISOTOPE SEPARATION (LIS) TECHNIQUE
(Extraction of U 235 by Tunable Dye Lasers)
Drs. Noa Kagan and Chaim Nebenzahl.

She watched him leaf through it, pleased that he was no longer smiling or flippant. He was taking her seriously. After a moment he lowered the document.

"I'm not sure I should be looking at this," he said. "Do you know what you're doing?"

"Oh yes. It's like Schrodinger's Cat," she said. "Did Jerold ever tell you that one?"

He shook his head and she went to the bureau and lit another cigarette. She tightened the towel around her breasts, crossed over to the balcony doorway and leaned against the jamb, looking into the room.

"Just imagine, Schrodinger said, that a cat is sealed in a steel box with a Geiger counter, a small amount of radioactive material, a hammer, and a vial of hydrocyanic acid. The device is arranged so that when one atom of the radioactive substance decays it triggers the hammer which smashes the vial and releases the poison..." She pointed her cigarette at him. "Listen carefully now. The problem is to describe the condition of the cat after one hour has passed *without looking in the box.*" She paused, sucked on her cigarette, blew a burst of smoke out the door. "The solution *seems* obvious. Common sense says the poor cat is either dead or alive, an atom will have decayed or it will not. *But not so* according to quantum theory. It holds that such decays neither take place nor do not take place *until* someone performs a measurement, which in this case means opening the box and examining the cat. Until then the living and the dead are suspended...bleared out...waiting." She moved from the door and stubbed out her cigarette in an ash tray on the bureau. "In other words, Schrodinger's Cat is *both alive and dead* as long as the box remains closed. I am going to open that box and take a chance on life."

She went to the bed, plucked the document out of his hands and tossed it on the floor.

"It's about lasers," she said. "When a particle moves from being excited to being relaxed it gives off light." She pulled the sheet off him, planted her hand on his chest and pressed him back down on the bed.

"I'm serious," he said, resisting her pressure. "I don't think..."

"So am I," she interrupted, climbing on to the bed. "You don't have to read it now. After you've relaxed you'll see the light."

"Very funny."

She smiled at him. "You'll see," she said, and she tugged off her towel and tossed that on the floor too before swinging her leg over him.

***

Eight

Alan was used to phone calls at one in the morning, but not from his father. Jerold Raskin apologized for the hour, then told him that while digging deeper through his wife's things just that afternoon in Cambridge he'd come upon a bundle of letters from a correspondent in Israel and he thought he should call despite the seven hour time difference.

"It's okay," Alan said. "Tell me about them. Who are they from?"

"Oh yes," Jerold said . "I have them here and I've read only a few of them, but it seems the writer was a close friend of Ruth's at one time..."

"A name," Alan interrupted. "Do you have a name?"

"Yes, her name," Jerold said. There was rustle of paper. "Her name is Anna Peled."

Alan was speechless for a moment. "Are you sure."

"Absolutely," Jerold replied. "That's the name on the return address and she signs the letters Anna."

"What's the return address?"

"It looks like something the equivalent of our PO Box...a number and some place called K-F-A-R...I don't how you pronounce it..."

"*Kfar*," Alan said.

"Yes, well...*Kfar Borochov*. Does that mean anything to you?"

"Yes it does. It's a big help." He was over his initial surprise, questions coming up fast. "What did Ruth's father do in Haifa?"

"He had a tool and dye business," Jerold replied. "A machine shop."

"That figures," he said.

He asked some more questions, but his father was fumbling with the letters to search for answers and it was taking too much time. He asked Jerold to fax him the letters and gave him his bureau's fax number.

After he hung up he went to his desk instead of going back to bed. Resting on the surface among some pages of scrawled notes was the LIS document that Noa had given him in Cesarea. A week had passed since then and he was still undecided how to use it for a story, or whether he should use it at all. Her Schrodinger's Cat explanation as a motive for exposing LIS was as incoherent to him as Jerold's attempt to explain Einstein's Theory of Relativity had been when he was much younger – he didn't have Jerold's brains and knew that he'd disappointed both parents when he failed to get into an Ivy League college, settling instead for Boston University and a journalism degree. Noa was eager to know if he had written anything yet and when he told her that he wasn't sure that he had a complete grasp of the material, she prodded him impatiently. "Well ask me some questions !" By now he'd slogged through the document several times, and with the help of online research and Noa's answers to his questions he was gradually developing an understanding of what she had given him. But still he had reservations. Should he write such a story at all? He was already in trouble with the Censor over the bus hi-jacking story and this could cause a bigger fuss. But what would Noa do if he didn't write anything? Would she stop seeing him? Now, he picked up the document and locked it in the drawer of his desk along with his notes. The phone call from his father had been a surprise, but it was also a welcome distraction.

First thing in the morning he stopped by the CBS bureau and told Ofra Gefen that he would like to meet with Anna Peled again and asked if she could she arrange it. Three days later he drove alone up the coast highway to the seaside town of Nahariya, north of Haifa, up near the Lebanon border. He knew the place, having stayed in a hotel there during the border war the past summer. A tidy, tranquil town, the main boulevard running back perpendiclar from the beach and split down the middle by a stream bordered with huge eucalyptus trees, Nahariya had been founded by German Jews and had a European feel to it, neat cafes and restaurants lining the boulevard where you could sit in the shade of the giant trees and watch the gaily decorated horse-drawn cabs go jingling by. He found Anna Peled where Ofra had said she would be at eleven o'clock, sitting at a sidewalk table at the *Hollandische Konditorei*. It was early December, getting cooler, and she wore a rather drab cloth coat, her hair still braided in coils. He pulled out a chair and sat down.

"This must be the kind of place that the old European Jews dreamed they were coming to after the war," he said.

Anna nodded. She did not look happy to see him, but he didn't care. He was impatient to get to it and question her about his mother. But he had to wait when a sturdy, beaming *frau* with a scrubbed face and rosy cheeks bustled out of the café. She spoke to Anna in German and smiled at Alan. Anna started to answer in German, then put her hand to her mouth. "Rosa, forgive me," she said in English, "my tongue is tied this morning for some reason. This is Alan Raskin....he's an American and a friend."

Rosa shook Alan's hand, took their order for tea and pastry, went back inside.

Anna was staring at his face, his bottom lip which still carried the scar of his fight in The Jackpot.

"What happened to your face?"

He touched his mouth. "Oh, just some trouble up on the West Bank with the settlers. A story I was working on. A few stitches. It's nothing"

Anna scoffed. "Those people. They'll be the end of us some day. They're religious fanatics."

"I got a call from my father in Cambridge..."

"Excuse me," Anna interrupted. She was looking over his shoulder. "Here's Rosa with our tea."

Rosa unloaded the tea from her tray and said she'd be right back with the pastry. As soon as she left Alan jumped in:

"As I said I got a call from my father in Cambridge about some correspondence my mother had. She wrote and received letters over a long time with a woman here in Israel named Anna Peled. Is that you?"

Anna stared down at the table, her lips pressed to a slit, rubbing her hands together.

"Her name was Ruth Stahlmann before she married Jerold Raskin," Alan prodded, irritated now with Anna's deliberate stalling. "Did you know her?"

Anna finally nodded and glanced up at him. "Yes...we corresponded for many years. I knew her here in Israel before she left."

But before Alan could ask another question they were interrupted by Rosa again, bearing pastry on her tray. He waited impatiently and when she was gone he went back at Anna.

"You must have been good friends to keep up such a long correspondence."

Anna picked up her fork and played with the strudel on her plate, head down, silent again. *Blood from a stone!* Did he have to wring the information out of her?

"Please! This is very important for me."

Anna took a deep breath and looked up at him. "I wasn't honest with you the last time we spoke. That friend Rachel that I talked about? The one who loved to go dancing at Bat Golim?"

Alan nodded.

"Her real name was Ruth...Ruth Stahlmann. I made up the name Eisener. It comes from iron which is like the steel...stahl in German...Stahlmann."

"Why would you do that?"

Anna sighed. "It was all so long ago. I was trying to find out why you wanted to know about Thomas Pensrose."

It still didn't make any sense to Alan, but he had to keep the conversation going with her before she dried up again. "So Ruth was the one who didn't care if Thomas Penrose was married."

"No, she didn't. She had a passionate affair with him until her father found out."

"And what did he do?"

"That part of the story was true. He broke it off, kept her at home except for school, and then he found out that she was pregnant."

"How?"

"I think she told him...to spite him...and because she really loved Thomas Penrose. I don't know what she thought the Englishman was going to do for her."

"What did her father do?"

Anna hesitated. "I'm not sure. Ruth had a brother and he and her father vowed to get the Englishman. A month or so later he was killed in an accident in Jerusalem. Ruth was hysterical when she first learned of his death. She blamed her father and her brother and vowed to separate from her family forever. And then somehow she arranged a loan from one of the owners at the Bat Golim, a Canadian Jew, and he got her to Toronto." She paused. "I've wanted to ask you...you look to be about the right age. Are you the child that she was a carrying when she left here..."

"I am that child," Alan said.

"So Thomas Penrose...he was your father?"

Alan nodded. "And I'm curious now why you wrote to Ruth so much and how you know so much detail about how she left here, the loan from the Bat Golim Canadian and so on..."

Anna stalled again, slowly shaking her head.

"Please Anna! You have to know how much this means to me."

"Ruth was my sister-in-law," Anna said. "I married her brother, Yosef Peled."

Alan sat back, stunned and struggling to comprehend. *My mother's sister-in-law? This woman is my aunt!* Until this moment he didn't know he had one, or that his mother had a brother, a man called Yosef, Yosef Peled.

"But the name? Peled?"

"Stahlmann was their European name," Anna said. "When Ben Gurion ordered all military officers and civil servants to take Hebrew names, Yosef, who was an army officer, changed his to Peled, which means steel in Hebrew."

"I see...but you're still my aunt?"

Anna nodded and they stared at each other in silence, Alan trying to figure her out. She must have known this story all along, yet he'd had to drag it out of her. Why? What was she afraid of.

He broke the silence. "Yosef, your husband, is he still alive?"

"No."

"Too bad..." he said, then quickly recovered. "I'm sorry, but I would liked to have talked to him."

"Why?"

"I'm curious about the death of Thomas Penrose...my father. Maybe he could have helped me."

"I don't think so."

"But you said he and his father were angry with Penrose."

"It was so long ago. Are you going to write about this?"

"Why do you ask?"

"I just thought...I mean you're a journalist."

"No, I haven't considered it. I just want to find out what happened. Do you not want me to write about it?"

"Better to leave it alone."

"That's what Yitzhak said."

"He was right."

*

East of Cyprus, out beyond Larnaca Bay, a fat buttery moon eased up over the Mediterranean. A stream of yellow light snaked across the black swell of the sea like a rivulet of gold, flashing in the foam of the waves that broke on the sandy shore. Alan sat on the darkened terrace of his hotel with a drink, the sound of voices from the bar carrying through the open glass panels behind him, his face bathed in the paling light. He was not happy to be here on this island. He was still struggling with the fact of Anna Peled, his new-found aunt, and the information she had given him back in Israel about his mother and father. But he hadn't been back from Nahariya a single day before Noa was pressing him again about the LIS story. When he told her that the only way he could safely file such a story would be from Cyprus, she insisted that he do so.

The island and Larnaca, especially Larnaca airport, were familiar to Alan from his days in the early '80's covering the Beirut wars and the fate of hostages held there. The island had once been a place where Israel and the old PLO collided, years before the existence of Hamas and Hezbollah. In that dirty war they had car-bombed each other, attacked yachts, sabotaged ships and assassinated each other's agents. The island had been a center of intrigue, a crossroads for intelligence operations and illegal commerce. Some old hands in the espionage business compared Cyprus then to WWII Casablanca or Lisbon, or to Cold War Berlin in the fifties and sixties. Both the Soviets and the Americans had large embassies up in Nicosia and large KGB and CIA stations, listening posts eavesdropping on communications all across the Middle East. From the British airbase, sleek American U-2 reconnaissance planes slipped through the skies over the Levant, and at Larnaca airport an area was cordoned off for the use of American Nighthawk helicopters which sped low across the Mediterranean on clandestine business in Lebanon.

Cyprus still served as a place where foreign correspondents moving between Israel and many Arab countries changed to their second passports and laundered themselves. They'd stand on the tarmac beside a chartered aircraft ready to take them into Beirut and empty their pockets and bags in front of a Cypriot stringer - Israeli toothpaste, matchbooks, shekels, anything in their luggage or their clothes with Hebrew script that could mean serious trouble in an Islamic country. Or they came over from Israel to file a story that they could not get past the military censors in Tel Aviv, which was why Alan was sitting on the terrace of his Larnaca hotel. Not only was he concerned about the Israeli military censors, but he wanted to hide the origin and sources of the story he would file. To prevent the Israeli security services from eavesdropping on his internet or phone connections, he'd waited until he reached Larnaca before calling London. He explained to his senior editors there the delicate nature of the nuclear story he was dealing with and, after their initial surprise – the Alan Raskin they knew was a journeyman who didn't break big stories -- they agreed not only to hide his identity as well as that of the sources, they would also disguise the dateline of the story, slugging it as London.

Alan listened now to the voices from the bar, the languages being spoken, waiting to detect the distinctive sound of Hebrew. He had been in this hotel once before when the manager had asked a group of Israelis to stop speaking Hebrew as it drew the kind of attention that the management didn't want. The Israelis were both outraged and embarrassed, being made to feel ill at ease once again outside Israel. The only places where Alan had seen young Israelis completely at ease were India and Thailand, places where nobody cared about Jews or Palestinians. But for much of the world, especially in Europe, the name Israel was associated with the oppression of Palestinians, not with a beleaguered little state that wanted nothing more than to be a peace-loving homeland for Jews. That change had come in 1967, the seminal year when Israel showed itself to be a military powerhouse in war, when the occupation of millions of Palestinians had begun, and when Israel got the bomb. It was the tough guy now and sympathy always went to the underdog, even to a bumbling, incompetent, corrupt, and often murderous underdog.

Alan rose and went inside to the front desk. He asked for messages, was told that there were none. He slipped fifty dollars across the desk to the clerk.

"Anybody been looking for me or asking about me since I checked in?"

The clerk shook his head. "No Mr. Raskin."

He took the bill and Alan slid another fifty across the desk.

"I'd appreciate being tipped off if that happens. Understand?"

The clerk nodded, again taking the bill, and Alan, satisfied that so far he was secure and unobserved, went up to his room to work.

The room had sliding glass doors to a balcony and Alan opened them. He liked the sound of the sea. He went outside for a moment and looked at the moon, smaller now, sitting up over the dark water. He could hear voices and laughter from the bar and terrace below. Back inside, he moved a small table over by the sliding doors, then set up his computer and brought over his notes and a chair. Standing over the table he fussed with his notes for a while, went outside again and stared at the moon, came back in and, finally, forced himself to sit down.

Confronting his laptop screen, Alan knew that some Israeli journalists might have a problem with the ethics of writing what he was about to write. But he had rationalized his way through this problem and thought he had conquered his doubts. First off, he was not an *Israeli* journalist. He was a journalist who happened to be Jewish, yes, but that was different. He had been handed a story, an important piece of first-order evidence that Israel had nuclear weapons, *and* a novel way of producing weapons grade uranium by using lasers. His first loyalty was to the story, not to any country. He was not a soldier. Some of his colleagues had been hammered by the generals in Vietnam who claimed that by criticizing their conduct of the war the reporters had put loyalty to some silly journalistic principal ahead of loyalty to their country. He understood Dan Bergmann's statement that he was an Israeli first. That was fine for Bergmann. But he and other foreign correspondents in Israel thought it was a flaw in the Israeli press corps. Frank Harris had told him that during the first *Intifada* the American networks had to threaten to bring in foreign camera crews when the Israeli crews refused to tape their own soldiers breaking the arms and legs of the Palestinian *shebab*. The same Israeli press corps was absolutely mute when it came to the subject of Israeli nuclear weapons, obliging the government's obsessive secrecy and paying lip service to its bizarrely clever policy that "Israel would not be the first country to introduce nuclear weapons into the Middle East."

Alan placed his fingers on the keyboard and created a file. He opened it to a blank screen and began to type:

REUTERS – Dateline: LONDON

He stopped and stared at the screen for a while, then he got up and went outside again. He leaned on the balcony rail and stared south, across the sea. It was over there, in Cairo, that an Egyptian dilpomat had explained to him a few years earlier just how clever the Israeli policy was. Nuclear weapons are the ultimate deterrent and you have to let your enemy know that you have them, that you can annihilate him, otherwise their possession is pointless. That was the way most countries with nukes behaved – they declared their weapons by testing them, making detection possible by the intelligence services of their enemies. But the Israelis were different. It was by not "introducing" nuclear weapons into the Middle East that they hoped to prevent their spread to Arab and other Islamic countries. "An Israeli declaration of possession would be seen as throwing down a gauntlet," the Egyptian diplomat had said. "We would be humiliated and we would have to react. There would be great pressure on Arab countries to abandon the NPT and go nuclear. It would change the entire equation in the region."

Given the current attempt to stop Iran from building nuclear weapons, Alan knew that the disclosure he was about to make would be seen by the Israelis as very harmful. From their point of view it was a bad time to draw attention to their own nukes. On the other hand it was absurd to pretend that they didn't have them, and maybe it was their very *existence* that spurred Islamic nations such as Iran to get them too.

But, leaning on the balcony railing, he could hear in his mind the voices coming across the sea from the Israeli shore:

What about your conscience as a Jew?Don't you have any regard for your own people?

"It has nothing to do with being a Jew," he said aloud to the moon. *And, yes, I do have scruples as a journalist.* In Africa, he'd refused to witness executions that were being staged because of his presence. In Iran during the hostage crisis, his first foreign assignment, he'd spent a night under a blackout and curfew at the Canadian Embassy in Teheran, drinking scotch with the ambassador in front of the fireplace while half-a-dozen Americans were secreted away upstairs and he had never filed a word about them, ensuring their safety. He was not threatening Israel's safety by what he was about to do, and besides, Israel was the country that had the weapons. It could stand up for itself. That's what Noa had said and she knew better than he did...*and* she wanted him to do this story so very much. He loved Noa, although he hadn't told her this yet because he sensed she wasn't ready to hear it from him. But she would hear it, and he hoped she would love him in return. It was just a matter of time, and to get that time, to be able to spend it with Noa and to convince her, he had to write this damn story.

He went back inside, sat and stared at the screen. He was not an inspired writer, his prose was unstylish, flat and factual, the product of banging out wire service copy for many years. At last he placed his fingers on the keyboard and started typing the lead in short graphs, wire service style:

REUTERS-Dateline:LONDoN
Israelis scientists have developed a new technique
for uranium enrichment using lasers, according to a
documented source obtained by Reuters. The
technique is called "Laser Isotope Separation" or

LIS.

LIS avoids the need for thousands of centrifuges or gaseous diffusion plants which take up huge space. It also streamlines the processing procedure for nuclear weapons grade material by using tunable dye lasers.

Israel is a small country and the process enhances weapon miniaturization and supplies a bigger bang from a large number of small nuclear weapons, Hiroshima size, rather than trying to produce the big megaton city killers.

Thirdly, the technique produces a clean nuclear weapon, which is also important for a small country if it is fighting close to its borders.

(more)

***

Nine

When he heard the news on the Army Radio that morning, Gavri Gilboa knew the military censors had decided they couldn't bury the LIS story with its London dateline. Not in the age of the internet and cell-phones. Israelis were addicted to those, so instead they were trying to get ahead of the story, disparage the Reuters report as malicious anti-Israel propaganda spread by an unnamed source to create instability in the Middle East. Gavri scoffed when he heard that: *As if there ever was stability in the Middle East.* But he was sure he knew the source of the report and he lay on his bed for a while thinking of the implications of this. Noa Kagan, his divine *Shekkinah,* the tenth and lowest power in the realm and therefore the closest to the created world and to the sufferings of the people of Israel, had proved to be the most exposed to the machinations of the *Evil Powers.* In the Book of Bahir it was written that *The Emanations on the Left,* the sinister side, could influence the *Shekinnah*, capture her and bring her to the side of the Satanic enemy, *Samael,* where she became known as *Lilith.*

And so it had come to pass.

He arose, wearing only his boxer shorts, and padded across the floor of his bedroom to the adjoining room. Shades covered the windows, morning light seeping around the edges. It was a dim space, sparsely furnished. He lit the candles on a menorah that stood at the back of a cloth-covered table pushed against one wall. In front of the menorah sat a crudely made *aron kodesh* or ark. A small brass tetrahedron sat in front of the ark. From a sideboard drawer he withdrew the tiny black leather boxes and the leather straps of a *tefillin*, a *tallit* shawl, and a knitted *kippa*. He placed the *tefillin* and the *tallit* on the table beside the ark, put the *kippa* on his head. Then he drew back the curtain of the ark to reveal a cheap *sefer torah* scroll that he'd had written for him by a yeshiva student up in Jerusalem. He faced the scroll and started davening the *shema* prayer:

"*Hear, O Israel: The Lord our God the Lord is one. You shall love the Lord your God with all your heart, with all your soul, with all your strength...*"

He paused, picked up the *tefillin* and carefully placed a leather box on the biceps of his left arm and strapped it on with the long leather straps which he wound seven times around his forearm and hand.

"*Therefore you shall lay up these words of mine in your heart and in your soul, and bind them as a sign on your hand...*"

He strapped another box to his forehead, tying a knot at the back of his head.

"*...and they shall be as frontlets between your eyes.*"

He picked up the *tallit* and placed it around his shoulders.

"*And you shall have the tassel, that you may look upon it and remember all the commandments of the Lord and do them, and that you may not follow the harlotry to which your own heart and your own eyes are inclined, and that you may remember and do all my commandments, and be holy for your God.*"

He lifted a blue tassel on one corner of the *tallit* and kissed it.

Finished with the *shema* he went to a second table loaded with books and with the only chair in the room. Many of the books were old and worn, their spines taped up. Stick-it bookmarks with scrawled notes feathered the brittle pages. He chose the Book of Zohar and returned to face the ark. He opened the book at a numbered mark where much of the page was underlined in red ink. He commenced again to daven and intone:

"*When the Holy one, blessed be He, will bring about the destruction of the wicked Rome, and turn it into a ruin for all eternity, He will send Lilith there, and let her dwell in that ruin, for she is the ruination of the world...*"

He replaced the book on the table, picked up a small amulet designed to repel the power of *Lilith,* touched it to the point of the tetrahedron and placed it beside the ark. Then he picked up another volume titled *Emek haMelekh* opened it to the passage he wanted and resumed intoning:

"Lilith is a harlot who fornicates with men. She has no mating with her husband, for He castrated the male and cooled the female. And she becomes hot from the fornication of men, through spontaneous emission..."

His finger traced down the page, found what he wanted:

"Blind Dragon rides Lilith the Sinful – may she be extirpated quickly in our days, Amen! And Blind Dragon is castrated so that he cannot beget. And this Blind Dragon observes the union between Samael and Lilith. For the groomsman, the Blind Dragon, who was between her and Samael, will swallow a lethal potion at a future time, from the hands of the Prince of Power. And know that Lilith too will be killed..."

And he felt it now, as he continued through his Kabbalah texts, his scarred muscular torso bobbing in front of his Torah scroll. Felt that he had found himself, or rather that he *had been found* and transformed, newly ordained by the Prince of Power to his cause. The news report had made it necessary.

He would know himself henceforth as *Blind Dragon.*

*

Daniel Zentler drove his BMW with the seat pulled as far forward as possible, hunching his torso over the steering wheel, his soft belly pressing against the bottom of the rim. Gavri, sitting beside him, believed this was because of Zentler's crippled legs, a result of his time in the Nazi camps when he was a boy. The BMW came with Zentler's Shabak job and he had joked that its solid German comfort was one of the reasons he had been willing to come out of retirement when Kessar was sacked. They were driving against the aggressive flow of morning rush-hour traffic that snaked south towards Tel Aviv, their destination the Mossad complex at the Gelilot junction.

"You know this meeting will not go well for us," Zentler said.

Gavri, avoiding his glance, stared at the slow crawl of honking cars in the oncoming lanes. "You mean because of the Reuters connection again?"

"Of course."

"But this one has a foreign dateline...London..."

"Maybe, but not necessarily a foreign source."

Gavri shifted in his seat, glanced over at Zentler. "But there's no comparison between the two stories. This one has nothing to do with terrorists. It's all about scientific material. What do they have in common?"

"You said it yourself already. A wire service, Reuters. Why is that? The source in this second story has to have access to classified scientific information. How could Reuters have found such a source...here or abroad?"

"Are you suggesting it could be one of our scientists?"

"Remember Mordechai Vanunu?"

Gavri nodded. Vanunu was a Moroccan Jew who had worked as a technician at Dimona and had given the layout of the place and all that he knew about its nuclear operations to the British press back in 1986. He was later kidnapped by Mossad in Rome, extracted from Italy, and brought back to Israel for trial. He did 18 years in jail and was released with restrictions in 2004.

"It doesn't have to be a scientist," Zentler went on. "There are many technicians at Rehovot and down at Dimona. We have to start from the beginning. Get into the archives and personnel files. Name by name."

Now, within sight of the Mediterranean and just before a crowd of hitch-hiking soldiers gathered at the junction with the coast highway, Zentler turned to the right on a narrow road. He drove around the side of a grassy, artificial hill that hid the underground part of the Mossad complex and stopped at a gate. Every Friday morning, every week, the heads of Israel's security and intelligence services met routinely for breakfast - Shabak, Mossad, Aman (Military Inelligance), and Reshud (Police Special Branch) taking turns as host. This was not a Friday morning but a special meeting had been ordered by the Prime Minister's Office to deal with the Reuters story about Israel's nuclear weapons. The rotation had been ignored and the meeting was being held at Mossad headquarters because the "event" had, in the words of the Mossad Chief, Zvi Dolev, a foreign origin.

Azi Basri, the chief of Shabak, was waiting for Zentler and Gavri by the door of the meeting room inside the artifical hill. He wasted no time.

"Have you started yet?'

Zentler wagged his head. "I'm setting up inquiries at Rehovot and Dimona. I've ordered up all the personnel files and I'll be going down there personally."

"Fucking traitor, whoever he is. We'll crush his balls between two stones!"

Gavri had heard that expression and others like it before. Basri liked to give a lecture to the new officers in Shabak. "Note very well my friends," he would say, his dark Iraqi eyes darting across the faces in front of him. "Israel is very grateful to those we see as friends. But we are ruthless, vengeful, and relentless in our hatred against those who we see as enemies. And remember! There is no middle way! We'll crush their balls!" Men like Azi Basri and Yacov Kessar had risen in Shabak in the aftermath of the Six Day War in 1967. Along with the stunning victory had come the onerous task of running a police state in the occupied territories and Gaza. Shabak was given the job of ferreting out and crushing any incipient form of Palestinian nationalism. Sephardic Jews, most of whom came from Arab countries and spoke the language, were supposed to "understand" the Arab mentality and were considered good "human material" for this chore. Basri had risen to the top in that new era, as had his closest colleague at this meeting, Tamito Bouaziz, a Moroccan Jew who ran Reshud. They worked closely together, Shabak and Reshud. In Israel proper, the former investigated and fingered suspects while the latter made the arrests and processed the formal requirements of the judicial system. In the territories and Gaza, which had been under military administration and where Israeli law did not apply, Shabak's job had been much easier when it came to putting people away - the army did it for them with no legal fuss. Inside the windowless chamber where the session took place, Gavri observed that contemporary Israel was neatly depicted. Zvi Dolev and Moshe Eventov, both *ashkenazi* Jews, represented Mossad and Aman, respectively. Those two aloof and brainy outfits were in the hands of the Europeans. Basri and Bouaziz, the *sephardic* Orientals, ran Shabak and Reshud. They did all the dirty, hands-on, shit-kicking jobs.

Dolev opened the meeting by introducing a man named Chaim Sobel. Sobel was an executive assistant to the Prime Minister. His presence was meant to indicate just how seriously the Government was taking this issue.

"First things first," Dolev went on. "The censors were slow in getting a handle on this. Army radio should never have broadcast the Reuters dispatch this morning and they are looking into that now with the appropriate disciplinary measures. The only paper that published it was *Ha'aretz*...as we could expect. The other editors held off and called in for guidance. We have now put a total blackout on the story. So the lid is on and it's up to us to uncover who is behind this leak."

Basri smirked. "You mean up to you and Mossad. The story was datelined London."

"You give us no credit, Azi," Dolev smiled back. "We have our *sayanim* inside Reuters in London, hardly an impenetrable organization, and we are assured the story did not originate there but was filed from Cyprus."

"Still Mossad," Basri said testily.

"Not necessarily."

"How so?"

"It is conventional practice for foreign reporters to take material out of Israel that they know they can't file from here without getting into trouble with the censors. Cyprus has been used for this purpose before."

"Cyprus is your turf. You find out who it was."

Moshe Eventov, the only man wearing a military uniform, the rank of general, rapped his knuckles on the table. "Can we stop this petty turf war please? This is more serious than whose ego gets bruised. The information already put out by Reuters is enough to alarm the military command structures of our enemies, especially the information about miniaturization and the co-related delivery systems. We have to get to whoever is behind this leak, inside Israel, outside... it doesn't matter..."

Dolev waited a beat or two before continuing. "The bureau chief of Reuters here is relatively new, Alan Raskin. He filed a story a while ago about that bus hijacking down near Dimona, a story that contained classified information...."

Basri jumped in before the question could come. "We've been watching him. The boys up at Beit Agron had him in for questioning on that but got nowhere." He swung in his chair to Gavri and Zentler. "My people, Zentler and Gilboa here, have been on this..."

Daniel Zentler took his time speaking, a slow, hesitant cadence that always irritated Gavri and, he was sure, irritated others.

"We have had Mr. Raskin under surveillance since he filed the Dimona bus story. His phones are covered, both in his bureau and at home, his e-mails, his faxes." He glanced at Reshud's Tamito Bouaziz. "Also, as I'm sure you know, with the help of *Latam* officers from the Tel Aviv police we have had him under personal surveillance." He turned to Gavri. "Gavri Gilboa is the officer in charge of this operation."

Kick it down the line, Gavri thought. Just like bureaucracies everywhere. Of course, they also lacked insight, an understanding of the powerful underworld forces at work here. He didn't lack that insight, but he couldn't let them know that. They wouldn't understand. He hitched his chair closer to the table.

"We've been watching Raskin since the Dimona leak," he said, "and we've come up with nothing here. But a few days ago he did go to Cyprus and we watched him there..."

"Who gave you permission for that?" Dolev asked sharply.

"What does it matter?" General Eventov said. "What did he do there?"

"Nothing that could be regarded as suspicious," Gavri replied. "He was there for two days in Larnaca, but we couldn't monitor his communications."

"How about this American woman, Susan Miller," Dolev said. "I understand we gave you her name. Was she of any use."

"Not much," Gavri said. "I think she's either too nervous or too excited about working with us, and there's no evidence that Raskin sees her much anymore."

Eventov was edgy, tapping the table with a pen. As Director of Military Intelligence he was in charge of the Israeli Military Censor's office which had responsibility for news censorship. "Our people at the Military Censors office will ask him in for questioning, threaten him..."

"Bar him from Israel," Basri barked. "Bar Reuters from Israel."

Eventov nodded. "That's a possibility. We did that with a BBC reporter in the Vanunu affair. But we didn't bar the BBC. I think barring a major international wire service like Reuters will only draw more attention to this. After all we're supposed to have a free press here, aren't we?" He smiled at Basri. "The last thing we want is that Iranian lunatic Ahmadinejad raving about *our* nuclear weapons just when we want to stop him from getting them. As for Mr. Raskin, I think we should talk to him first. He may or may not be responsible, but later we may have to bar him from the country to punish Reuters."

Zentler raised his hand and Dolev said, "Daniel?"

"We have been talking here about Reuters and Alan Raskin because it is what the two leaks have in common. They both were published by Reuters. But that's all they have in common. One story is about terrorists the other is about nuclear science. Otherwise there's no connection..."

"Except for Dimona," Dolev said.

"Assume coincidence for the sake of argument," Zentler replied. "Then let us forget Reuters and Raskin for a moment and look at the scientific material of this story. Who could this have come from? Clearly from somebody who knows what goes on inside our nuclear weapons program. So what is required here now is some solid police work. Complete personnel file research and interrogations. We start at the bottom with the technicians at Dimona and the bureaucrats in Defense Ministry and work our way up. A clean sweep all the way to the top."

Eventov raised his eyebrows. "You're not suggesting that any of our top scientists are involved in this, are you? Remember, Vanunu was a technician."

"I don't know," Zentler said. "Not till I look."

Chaim Sobel, the man from the Prime Minister's Office, raised his hand for the first time. "The Prime Minister wants this handled with great care and sensitivity," he said, "so I must caution you to employ tact and discretion in all your investigations. The Prime Minister does not want any publicity whatsoever and certainly no scandal. We expect top security."

Dolev nodded. "Understood?" he said, scanning the table.

Heads nodded all around except for Gavri, who went unnoticed.

*

When they left the Gelilot Junction, Gavri asked Zentler about the presence of Sobel, the Prime Minister's man. "Is that usual?"

"Sometimes," Zentler replied. "It has to do with politics. They're worried about connections, important names. That could cause a problem for them."

"Do you know any of the top scientists who worked on the LIS project?"

"No. Do you?"

Gavri paused. "No," he said, shaking his head. "No I don't."

Zentler glanced over at him. "Don't worry," he said. "We'll get to them."

Gavri nodded, waited a moment. "What are you thinking?" he asked. "I mean where do you think this is going?"

"I'm thinking there's some connection between the bus and the nuclear leak," Zentler replied. "Some connection to Reuters and to Dimona. Somebody from Dimona, maybe, some technician coming from Dimona who was at the bus, who saw or heard what went on. We know Mr. Raskin was at the bus, so let's see if we can get the censors to ask him who he met there. It's a long shot that he'll tell us anything, but it's a start."

The Israeli Military Censor's office was in the middle of Tel Aviv near the Kirya, the Defense headquarters. Daniel Zentler had asked for permission to observe the meeting with Alan Raskin and he and Gavri Galboa sat behind a false mirror overlooking a room with a table and three chairs, two of them occupied by military officers, a captain and a lieutenant, the third by Raskin. They'd been sitting there for thirty minutes listening to Raskin deny any knowledge of the "nuclear story" that had been published by Reuters. Over and over again he said he knew nothing about the source for the story, that it had not been filed by his bureau, that it had originated in London. Finally, frustrated with their efforts to make any headway, the officers made a mistake.

"We know the story didn't originate in London," the captain said. "It was filed from Cyprus, *and* we know that you were in Cyprus at that time."

"*Schiess!*" Zentler cried. "He'll know now that we're following him."

"How do you know that?" Raskin asked the officer.

"What?"

"Either one. That it was filed from Cyprus or that I went to Cyprus."

"We have our sources."

Zentler was up out of his chair, pointing at the glass. "He's turned the game on them. They're supposed to ask the questions. Stupid! This is useless..."

Apparently Raskin had the same idea. He stood up too and said, "I think I'm finished here."

"By the way," the captain said. "That bus hi-jacking down near Dimona. You were there, we know that. We'd like to know the names of any Israelis you met down there."

"Stupid! Stupid!" Zentler hissed. "Not the way to ask that question. The captain doesn't care about the bus. He cares only about the nuclear story, he doesn't see that connection."

Raskin laughed. "You must be joking. Almost all the press were Israelis, and all the soldiers...forget it."

"You broke the rules and we can bar Reuters from Israel," the captain said.

Raskin smiled. "This *is* a democracy, isn't it? I don't think you'll do that."

"We can take your credentials away, bar *you* from Israel."

Raskin shrugged. "Obviously I don't want that. I just got here. But I had nothing to do with that nuclear story and I can't help you."

The captain tapped a pencil on the table, staring at him with obvious dislike.

"It's clear to me that you're not willing to cooperate, Mr. Raskin," he said. "You should start packing your bags."

Gavri looked up at Zentler who was still standing and staring at the glass. *Blind Dragon* did not want to let Alan Raskin out of his sight. He wanted him for himself and his justice. "If they ban him from Israel," he said, "we'll lose our surveillance and any hope that he can lead us somewhere. We must follow him, even if they expel him."

"I'll see what I can do," Zentler said.

*

Gavri spent an hour tidying his flat before Noa was to arrive. He cleaned up the living room, put away the prayer paraphenalia, but he left on view the little ark with the scrolls and the drawn curtain, the menorah, the tetrahedron, and especially the amulet designed to repel the power of Lilith. As much as he feared her, he wanted her to see that he knew. It was to be expected that she would try to avoid *Blind Dragon* and indeed she had been hesitant about seeing him when he called her. But that changed as soon as he said it had to do with Alan Raskin.

When he heard the downstairs buzzer he went to the intercom and verified her voice. He buzzed her in and then lit the candles and waited for the knock on his door. He was dressed all in black, black jeans, black polo shirt, black running shoes. There was a small vestibule so that a visitor could not see immediately into the living room. When the knock came he steeled himself, opened the door and watched her nose wrinkle with the smell of sulphur from the matches and the incense.

"What's burning?" she said, sniffing the air.

He said nothing and led her out of the vestibule and into the living room. She stopped just inside the threshhold and stared, legs apart, her bag dangling from both hands in front of her. It was her first time in his Tel Aviv flat and he watched for her reaction, pleased when he saw the shock on her face.

"It's true!" she exclaimed, whirling round to face him.

"What's true?"

"You've gone all religious. I heard rumors up at the kibbutz but I didn't believe them. Not the Gavri I knew."

He stared at her, looking for signs. He reached out and touched the amulet. "You're not the Noa I knew either," he said. "I am losing my *shekkinah.*"

She was busy now examining the stack of books and she swung again to look at him. "Losing you're *what*? What do you mean?"

"Alan Raskin is evil. He has seduced you and brought harm to Israel."

How could she understand that the divine flow of the shefa *had been diminished...that the* shekkinah *and her divine husband had been pushed apart and the people of Israel would suffer.*

She bristled. "Israel has brought harm to itself, to its sons. And what business is it of yours what I do with Alan Raskin."

"He is *Samael,* and I know that you are the source of the nuclear story he has written for Reuters."

Now she was furious. "*Samael?* Who or what is *Samael?*"

"He is the first of the divine evil powers and he is making you the seventh, the feminine one called *Lilith.*" He approached her, touching the amulet again and her eyes followed his hand. "I know it is not your will. Back in our days in Kefar Borochov and Safed you were the *shekkinah* and I was your servant, but the divine flow of the *shefa* has been diminished over time...." She was stepping back from him now, and he reached out and grasped her arm. "It is not your fault. *Samael* is responsible and it is the duty of *Blind Dragon* to bring about justice..."

She looked astonished for a moment, then her voice dropped in a cold level tone: "I'm not a girl anymore Gavri and you're mad. You've gone completely mad. These books, this Kabbalah shit..."

"Stop it!" he commanded, but she broke his grip on her arm, strode forward and swept the ark, the menorah, the tetrahedron and the amulet off the table, along with the candles. Hot wax spilled on the floor, some of the candles smashed out, others flickered on. She was moving for the books when he spun her around and slapped her hard across the face, knocking her to the floor.

"You do not desecrate the altar of the *Prince of Power,*" he shouted down at her, her bare legs flailing at him, trying to kick him.

"You poor bastard!" She wiped the spittle from her mouth. "First they fucked up your body and now they've fucked up your head."

Why couldn't she understand how serious this matter was? How the evil had entered into her through the person of Alan Raskin, how in the dynamic world of the *sefirot,* the situation always in flux, the realms on the left side, the evil side, had become stronger. He had to make her understand.

She was crawling across the floor towards the door. When she reached the vestibule she got to her feet.

He stepped towards her. "Noa?...Please!...Listen to me!"

She pulled the door open without looking back.

"I can have you arrested."

"Try it!" she shouted, slamming the door behind her.

He fell to his knees amidst the wreckage of what she had swept from his altar. Slowly, he began to pick up the pieces and place them back up on the table. It was not the *Shekinah's* fault, this desecration. She had been blinded by *Samael,* their real enemy, the one who he must not let out of his sight.

***

Ten

The desert air was dry but Noa's palms were sweaty. They left damp prints on the leather cover of the steering wheel in her Peugeot. She didn't like it that she was nervous entering Dimona. She had fantasized about her interrogation before being summoned, and in her fantasy she had triumphed, welcoming the questions and glorying in her devastating answers. She had imagined herself as absolutely fearless and defiant in confronting the power of the state – *To demand for ourselves, finally, the lives that we deserve to live.*

The interrogations had started days ago. The security officers had commenced with the technicians and worked their way up to the scientists. Noa knew that Chaim Nebenzahl, her co-author of the LIS report, had been called in on the second day. She had phoned him to find out what to expect but he said that he'd been told not to speak about his interview. Only after she was finally summoned herself did she begin to get nervous. She wasn't sure about Gavri, whether he had reported his suspicions about her or not. But if he had, why had they waited? On the other hand, who would believe him? Surely his superiors must know that he was demented. Also, if they had checked the archives at Dimona, her personal files, and noticed that some NATANZ documents had been replaced with an unclassified Weizmann document, then surely they would have arrested her already. They didn't suspect her, she concluded, and there was no reason to be nervous. It was just routine.

She parked her Peugeot in her slot outside the library building, wiped her palms on her skirt, got out of the car. It was near the time of the winter solstice and the desert air was cool. It helped her nerves and chilled the perspiration on her body. The "interview," as the summons worded it, was to be held in the library on the second floor. She climbed the stairs, steeled herself in front of the designated door, and knocked. The door swung open and she saw the chunky figure of Zev Rozow standing there.

"Ah, right on time," Rozow exclaimed. He stepped aside to let her enter and then introduced her to the other man in the room.

"Dr. Noa Kagan, this is Daniel Zentler from the *Sherut Bitakhon Klali* in Tel Aviv. Mr. Zentler is in charge of our investigation."

An elderly man with heavy glasses and a sad smile limped forward and shook her hand. "Please sit down Dr. Kagan," he said, indicating a solitary chair on one side of a table. She put her bag on the table and sat rigidly on the chair, her hands clasped in her lap. There was an ashtray on the table and she badly wanted to smoke, but she was afraid her hands would tremble if she tried to light up.

Daniel Zentler went around the table and sat in a chair facing her. Zev Rozow sat at one end of the table so she would have to swing back and forth between the two men if they both asked questions.

"Names," Zentler sighed, smiling at her pleasantly as he pressed back the plastic cover on a dossier. "In Israel it's always a matter of names, old names, new names, identities..." His hands fluttered about in front of him, touching some papers on the table, then moving to his black-framed glasses, then to the dossier. Finally, he clasped his hands on the table as if to quiet them and looked at her.

"Your grandfather was Sasha Kagan..."

She nodded before she realized this wasn't a question.

"...and your father is General Yosef Peled. I am honored."

"Thank you," she said.

"You use your grandfather's original family name, the Russian one, not your father's Hebrew choice or your husband's, can you tell me why?"

"I started using it when I set out to make my own career. I liked the sense of continuity with my grandfather."

Zentler studied her face, nodding slowly. "And a brilliant career too," he said, continuing to gaze at her as if he were looking back into her past. She felt uncomfortable for a moment until he suddenly twitched out of his trance. "Now then, to business and I'll try to be as brief as possible as I'm sure you're a busy woman. Would you like a cigarette before we start?"

As if on cue, Rozow slid a pack of Marlboros down the table.

Before she could catch herself, she lifted her hands from her lap and reached for the pack, paused, her hands suspended over the Marlboros, then she returned her hands to her lap and wiped them on her skirt. Quickly, she reached out again, took a cigarette and waited until Rozow leaned down the table and offered her a light. She inhaled deeply and blew the smoke off to the side.

"I don't know why I'm so nervous," she said.

"It's normal," Zentler said, watching her with his sad smile. "Do you know Alan Raskin, the former Reuters bureau chief?"

The question came like a slap out of nowhere.

"Why?...Should I?"

She knew the moment she spoke that it was the wrong thing to say. Too quick, too flippant. But she'd been taken by surprise with the snakelike speed of Zentler's strike, even though she'd expected the question to come up. He'd confounded her impression of him as a slow-moving, courteous old gentleman with manners.

"No, not at all," Zentler said reassuringly. "It's just that we believe that Mr. Raskin received classified information about our nuclear industry, specifically the LIS program that you worked on, and so we are trying to track down this breach in our security and close it."

"I only know the name because of what I've read in the papers and heard on TV," she said. "He's been banned from Israel, hasn't he?"

She knew, of course, the answer to her own question. Alan's press credentials had been confiscated five days before and he had left the country one day later for Spain. She knew he was at his house in Ibiza because he had left her a note with his phone number there. One thing Zentler's snap question had confirmed for her, though, was her hunch about Gavri Gilboa – Gavri knew that she knew Raskin and he hadn't reported this. Unless Zentler was leading her on.

She watched him carefully, his old white-haired head nodding in answer to her question while peering down at the dossier in front of him. "Yes, he has left the country," he said. "Shall we proceed."

For the next thirty minutes Zentler took her through her life. He read from the dossier, questioning, checking, confirming. The amount of detail they had surprised her. And gradually she began to feel exposed, not by any specific detail – each one, alone, seemed mundane – but by the portrait of herself that Zentler was assembling so thoroughly, piece by piece, and so compressed in time. It was invasive and she knew she was becoming angry.

Then Rozow asked his first question. "Your politics today...are you still active in Meretz?"

She glared at him. She knew that Rozow was a Sharon man and that he supported Likud - Kadima as did most of the security people at Dimona.

"Not in any meaningful way," she said.

"What does that mean? You don't want Peace Now?"

His crude attempt at sarcasm infuriated her. She snapped: "I don't expect it *ever* as long as nationalist fools like you are running things."

"Your grandfather was *Mapam*," Rozow said, as if old Sasha had a disease. "You're a kibbutznik and you grew up in that communist pioneer club *Ha'shomer Ha'tzair*. Kibbutz kids cause trouble in the army, they refuse to serve in Judea and Samaria. You want to make peace with terrorists..."

"My son died in Lebanon!" she cried in fury, her lips trembling. "He died because of a useless war started by that weak fool Olmert. You people are killing this country with your selfish pigheaded dreams and you'll kill all of us too unless you're stopped..."

Zentler, who had his head down as if he were ducking this exchange, suddenly waved his hands and raised his voice.

"Please!...Please!"

A silence followed in which he looked up at Rozow. "Zev," he said, "I think it would be best if you left the room."

Rozow opened his mouth, then closed it, nodding slowly. He rose from the table, shot a dagger glance at her, and snatched up the pack of Marlboros on his way out. She heard the door slam behind her.

"I am sorry about your son," Zentler said, "and I am also sorry that this happened."

He appeared to be embarrassed, his head down and his hands fussing again with the papers on the table. "I have only a few things left, your recent travel outside the country, for example." He clasped his hands and looked up at her. "Your last trip was to the United States, to Cambridge in Massachusetts?"

She nodded. "MIT, my old school."

"The Athens of America. Isn't that what they call Cambridge? Who did you meet there?"

"Dr. Jerold Raskin, a professor, an old friend..."

The name was out before she could catch herself.

"Any relation to Alan Raskin I wonder?"

She shrugged her shoulders, knew she had to say something. "All I know is that Jerold Raskin was my thesis advisor."

"Coincidence then," Zentler said. And he placed his hands flat down on the table and pushed himself to his feet. "Again, I'm sorry about Rozow. It seems increasingly difficult to have a civilized approach to politics in this country, although I'm not sure that we ever did." He looked down and poked at his papers. "Ah yes, one last thing I almost forgot to ask. I see that you grew up on a kibbutz called Kfar Borochov and you're almost the same age as one of my colleagues who is from there. Gavri Gilboa. Do you know him?"

"Gavri? Oh yes, we grew up together. We were very close."

"And now?"

"Well...not so close. We see each other now and then."

Zentler nodded. "That's it then. I'll give him your regards, and thank you for putting up with us."

After the security checkpoints, Noa blew out of Dimona at high speed. It had gone badly, she knew. She had made mistakes and she was sure that she had misjudged Daniel Zentler. He was smarter than the impression he gave. They could soon check with others such as Ofra or Dan Bergmann and discover that she did indeed know Alan Raskin. She had been stupid to deny that. And the bit about MIT and Jerold Raskin had been a serious blunder too. There was little time.

She raced through her options as the Peugeot sped through the brown stubbled fields outside Beer Sheva. Before he had been expelled Alan had talked about spending some time in Spain together for the New Year's holiday and she had checked online for flights. There was a daily Iberia flight from Ben Gurion to Madrid departing at 4:50 pm. She looked at her watch. She could make it with one quick stop in Neve Zedek to pick up her passport and a toothbrush. Gripping the wheel tightly, she could imagine Zentler peering at her, his owl-like gaze seeing right through her. She couldn't wait for his next move. Silently, her lips moving, she repeated the mantra she had adopted from the night at the Rabin rally – *To demand for ourselves, finally, the lives that we deserve to live.*

She still had work to do and she could take the Natanz document and the computer with her. But she knew she had to go... Now!

*

When Iberia flight 3753 left Ben Gurion and wheeled to the west across the Israeli shoreline, Noa looked down at the white line of surf with mixed feelings of relief and regret. Relief because she had slipped from the grasp of Daniel Zentler, a grasp that she'd been certain was about to reach out for her. She had arrived at the airport with plenty of time and she could have bought a ticket on an El Al flight to Madrid that left half an hour earlier than the Iberia flight. But even if Zentler was slow and she made it through airport security, there were Shabak security agents on all El Al flights and she wasn't taking that chance.

She used her cell phone to call her mother to tell her that she was taking a short vacation in Spain.

"Why Spain?" Anna asked.

"I have a friend who has a house there. An American journalist."

Her mother was silent for a moment. "What's his name?" she asked.

"Anna. You know we don't ask questions like that."

"I'm sorry," Anna said. "I just thought I should know in case...you know..."

"No, I don't know, and I've got to go," she said, and she disconnected.

Next, she called Alan in Spain and told him she was coming earlier than expected and gave him the arrival time in Ibiza for her connecting flight from Madrid. "What's wrong?" he asked, and she told him that was no way to greet a lover who was on her way to meet him. *He* sounded nervous when *she* was the one about to go through Israel's tough security screen.

When her turn came she placed her passport and her return ticket on the counter and watched the alert young face of the uniformed woman who scanned them. Her luggage, a single carry-on bag, was about to be hand-searched by a State-trained professional who would also be a keen observer of her answers to questions and of her behavior. She waited for what seemed an eternity, resisting an urge to tap her nails on the counter while the woman checked her passport on a computer screen.

If Zentler was going to stop her this was the moment, one phone call and she was trapped.

"Have you packed everything in your bag yourself?" the young woman asked, sliding her passport back to her and opening her bag.

She nodded. She was almost there. All she had to do from now on was continue to act normally. The woman took out the NATANZ documents and glanced at the Wiezmann stamp on the cover.

"It's my work," she said. "I can't get away from it even on vacation."

The woman, impassive as stone, didn't respond and she didn't open the document. She replaced it in the bag. "You have to put your computer through the screener," she said, and waved her through.

Not even a *shalom!*

Now, peering down at the darkening blue of the deeper water, the word exile leapt to her mind. It was true. Self-imposed exile! That was what she was facing and her realization of that fact was what turned her relief to regret. She knew this without any illusions, knew that in her flight she would be seen as a traitor, and reflecting on this her regret soon turned to anger. The State of Israel had been an ideal that her grandfather Sasha Kagan had created for her. It had been the defining entity of her youth and those of her pioneer compatriots in *Ha'shomer Ha'tzair*, a group that Zev Rozow had sneered at hours earlier that day. Their spiritual atmosphere had been the air of Israel, their mental horizons ended at the shores of the Mediterranean, and they expected that their lives would end under the soil of Israel. They had been born in Israel, shaped in Israel, so that they could serve Israel and die for Israel, and Israel would then remember them. Israel had been their cradle, their world, their grave, and their monument. But somewhere after the glorious Six Day War in 1967 it had started to go wrong. A cancer had started to grow in the body of the land. She had seen it personally in the corruption and cynicism that riddled Rafi's arms-dealing business and other slippery *laissez-faire* operators; she had watched the boastfulness and brutality of the military in the persons of her father and Arik Sharon; she had witnessed the Holocaust-obsessed Menachem Begin take over the government and turn much of the country into a paranoid version of himself. And government after government, left or right, had gone on building settlements after 1967, catering to religious nationalists, denying the Palestinians a viable state of their own. Israel, a great experiment in building a new, more humane society, had lost its moral bearings. She couldn't recognize her own country anymore. Her own son had expressed those very feelings in his will.

His will!...the will of a twenty year old boy who had been sent to Lebanon to be killed.

The stewardess interrupted her reverie, parking the service cart next to her in the aisle. She wasn't hungry and she ordered a *vino tinto*. She unscrewed the cap on the little bottle, poured some wine in her glass and sipped, staring out the window into the emptiness below.

Exile and traitor?...No! She was not betraying Israel. Israel had betrayed her. Israel had killed her son.

In the civilized world the State punished wrongdoers. But who punished the State when it had done a grievous wrong? How does the State punish itself? The answer was that it didn't. And that was why she'd had to act.

Noa the shaker would punish Israel!

At 30,000 feet over the Mediterranean, in her insulated and pressurized world, nothing loomed so large in Noa's view as her injured self. Nothing was too precious to be sacrificed to its hunger.

A few hours later when the pilot said they were flying over Ibiza, Noa looked down at the pin-points of light. Alan, her scribe, was down there waiting for her. The LIS story that he had put on the Reuters wire had already caused an uproar among the Arab nations and in Iran. The night before he'd left Israel he had expressed concern that it was having the opposite effect from what she intended. "From what *we* intended," she'd said. "I hope you're not going to go all soft on me." Alan was not used to living in Israel where war and threats of war were second nature to the people. Now, she ticked off the dates, looking for some possible mathematical progression that could predict the future – 1948, 1956, 1967, 1973, 1978, 1982, 1987, 2001, 2006. She would have to stiffen Alan up for the task of writing the NATANZ material. Only public knowledge of that nuclear plan would stop Israel from launching the next war, a "pre-emptive" war of course.

At Madrid's *Barajas* airport she faced her last nervous moment: passport control. She didn't know how it was done but she had no doubt that Zentler and *Shin Bet* could have her detained by Spain's *Guardia Civil*. She watched the hands of one of their officers as he flipped through her passport. He looked up at her face, then down to the document again; quickly he picked up a stamping devive, slammed it down on a page, and passed her passport back to her. Maybe she was overestimating Zentler, maybe she hadn't aroused his suspicion. In any case, it was too late for him now.

She was free and loose in Europe.

Es Colodar airport in Ibiza was deserted except for the arriving Madrid passengers. It was after midnight and she was bone-tired. She walked past the baggage carousels and the *Guardia* officers at the customs exit, the opaque glass doors sliding open to reveal a small group of people waiting for the arrivals. Alan was at the back and he raised his hand in greeting. She had never seen him dressed so casually – sandals, jeans, a battered Boston Red Sox sweatshirt over a tee-shirt. He had been in Ibiza only a week or so but he looked more tanned than he did in Israel.

She put her heavy shoulder bag down and opened her arms. When he stepped into her embrace she pulled his body to hers and kissed him ardently.

"I've missed you," she said, leaning back in his arms and looking up at him. .

He grinned, his awkward boyish grin, self-conscious, maybe also a little uncomfortable.

"I've missed you too," he said.

***

Eleven

He didn't know why, but Alan wasn't sure he was ready for this. Since he'd left Israel something had lifted from him, like a heavy load that he hadn't known he was carrying. After a few days he noticed he didn't feel the tension, the excited nerves and the claustrophobia that Israel inflicted on its inhabitants. He felt normal again, relaxed. Then, ten hours ago, as he was happily chain-sawing a dead almond tree into firewood on his property, his cell phone vibrated in his pocket. He turned off his saw, took off a work glove and fished out his phone. Noa Kagan was calling to say she was coming to Ibiza days earlier than expected. Now she was here, standing in front of him at the airport, and he didn't know what to say.

He pointed to the large shoulder bag at her feet. "Is that your only luggage?"

"I need to buy some clothes," she said. "I had to leave in a hurry."

Her call had come barely a week after he had settled in at his *finca* on a hillside near the town of Santa Eulalia. Since his arrival he'd had time to think of what he had done and he'd been having second thoughts about the wisdom of filing the LIS story and the cost to him personally. His London superiors – who had been wild about the story at the time -- had defended him dutifully and protested to the Israeli government when he was expelled from the country. But he thought he'd detected a certain coolness in his private conversations with them in the last few days, maybe some second guessing on their part due to the Israeli reaction. Plus, there was the question of his future. "You've pulled one the shortest tours as a bureau chief in Reuters history," his London boss had said, supposedly in jest. "What do we do with you now?" He'd always kept a low profile and never before in his career had he had this kind of trouble. It wasn't that he didn't desire Noa or want her here -- he could feel the excitement in his body just looking at her now. It was the tension crackling in the air surrounding her, standing right next to him now in the airport, enveloping her like a radioactive cloud. She had brought it with her, and it made him feel like he was back in Israel.

"You said that on the phone," he said. "Why? What happened?"

"Can it wait? I'm tired. How far do we have to go to your place?"

"Twenty, twenty-five kilometers. Too bad it's dark. You won't see anything."

"I don't care." She took his arm and smiled at him. "I came to see you."

And later, in his solid Spanish double bed with the moonlight and the smell of rosemary coming through the window, he believed her. He may never have had this kind of trouble before in his career, but neither had he ever had a lover like Noa Kagan. That night he could feel her orgasm coming, her sex pulsing and driving him into a thrusting frenzy, her hands, her legs, her voice, all urging him on to a deliriously convulsive climax. It was better than before, better than anytime before in his life.

When he awoke it was still dark and he went down to the spacious *sala* with the huge fireplace. The floor tiles were cold on his feet and he placed some newspaper, kindling, and *almendra* logs on the embers, stirred them into flames, then rubbed his arms in the glow. A feeling of well-being suffused him as he looked around the room, its three-foot-thick walls, its high timbered ceilings. He loved his old *finca* and he loved having this woman in it. How could he have had doubts about her coming here? It was right that she was here and that he should take care of her.

He walked out the door barefoot into a darkened stone courtyard open on one side and roofed over with bougainvillea. He crossed the courtyard and went out onto a dirt terrace. He stopped at the edge where the drop was about five feet down to the next terrace. To the east the sky was turning from grey to pink. A series of terraces with *oliva* and *algoroba* trees stepped down the hillside to the plain below, the Mediterranean just beyond. He stood there naked, facing the winter dawn, fondling his genitals and pissing over the edge with pride and pleasure in his masculinity. But the feeling lasted only for a moment before he recalled Noa telling him only hours before about Dimona and a *Shin Bet* man named Daniel Zentler and how she thought that Zentler was suspicious and that was why she had fled. He shivered in the cold morning air, felt goose bumps on his skin, his sex shriveling.

Only now did it occur to him: *If she had fled, would they not follow?*

The morning chill, it seemed, had permeated Noa's mood too when she awoke. He proposed a shopping expedition for clothes and told her the stores would be having sales. "They do that here after Christmas."

"I *have* lived outside Israel before," she replied sharply.

He was eager to show her some of the island's beauty that she had missed in the darkness the night before and he made a plan to combine shopping with a trip into the capital. The island was so green compared to Israel, the rugged hills thickly covered with pines. He drove his old Renault IV on a back road that dipped and curved through a series of breathtaking views of the cliffs and the sea. "The Romans called it the pine island," he said. But Noa did not seem impressed by the scenery. The city had the same name as the island – Ibiza, or Eivissa in Catalan – and the center of it was a fortified acropolis that came into dramatic view through a cleft in the hills. Philip II of Spain's massive 16th century walls surrounded a castle and a Christian cathedral where once a Moorish mosque had stood, and before that, in their turn back over the centuries, a Byzantine basilica, a Roman temple, a Carthaginian temple for the worship of Melkart and Tanit. Alan had found this history fascinating, but his attempt to share it with Noa fell on deaf ears. She seemed preoccupied. He drove on into the city and parked beneath the old walls. They had walked for only a few minutes in the crowded little streets when Noa first showed some interest.

"They're not speaking Spanish," she said. "What is it?"

"Ibicenco," Alan replied. "A dialect of Catalan. But they all speak Spanish if you want to try."

"No thanks," she said.

The islanders, he explained, were a genetic mixture of Catalans and Moors. They were used to invasions and now their home was the hedonistic clubbing capital of the western Mediterranean. Hordes of tourists descended every summer, adding to the permanent colony of northern Europeans, especially Germans.

It had been among these ex-pat Europeans that Alan had found friends on a visit fifteen years before. He discovered a lifestyle that was so casual and so sexually uninhibited that it scared him at first. But he came back again and again for holidays and eventually he bought his *finca*, a two-hundred year old farmhouse with an acre of terraces in front and surrounded on the sides and back by a forest of pines. He spent at least a month every year at the *finca* and rented it in the summer for a small fortune.

The jet set had brought Gucci and Armani and Prada and every other brand name to Ibiza and their stores were clustered in the part of the city jammed between Philip II's walls and the port. Noa was not indecisive. She selected quickly from several stores. A pair of slacks, a pair of designer jeans, T-shirts, a sweater, a silk blouse, underwear. She added a pair of sandals and a pair of walking shoes and said she was done except for a suitcase.

"Now for some sightseeing," he said. "OK with you?"

"If you wish," Noa said.

He drove around the outside of the city walls and began the climb to the *Dalt Villa*, the high part of town. "When we get up there," he said, "you can see how thick those walls are. We have to walk through them to get inside. The place was impregnable, especially from the sea, which is where the Turks would be coming from..." He glanced over at Noa. "It's a great view, you'll see."

Noa said nothing

On their left as they climbed they passed an open expanse of hillside dotted with small caves. "Guess what that is," he said.

Noa shook her head, not looking.

"It's a necropolis, one of the oldest in the Mediterranean. The Carthaginians buried their dead in there. Over 3000 tombs. They came over from Africa to spend their last days here because they believed the island was a magical ground, protected by the sacred power of the gods."

Noa turned and looked at the legendary necropolis. "Ugly," she said.

At the top Alan parked the car outside the wall and they walked in through a tunnel and up a ramp that took them to the plaza at the summit. He showed her the cathedral and the plaque with the names of the Franco martyrs who had been killed by the Republicans in the brief savage battle for Ibiza in the civil war. She had nothing to say. Then he took her to the archeological museum which held a collection of Punic artifacts. She moved through quickly, showing little interest until she came an ancient stone bust of a woman with coiled hair and a tiara. She stared at the woman's face, her blank eyes.

"Who's that?" she asked.

"Tanit," he replied. "She's the most popular goddess on the island, even today. All the new-age people love her. They celebrate her with parties on the beach up at Beniras. Bongo drums, lots of pot. She's a Carthaginian fertility goddess, a sex goddess I guess. She's really a version of Astarte, Phoenician in origin, from your part of the world. She was not averse to sacrifice, human sacrifice, children..."

Noa glared at him. "What are you trying to get at?"

"I'm joking," he said, taken aback by her ferocity. "It's the first thing you've been interested in all morning and I was teasing a bit by embellishing her. I'm sorry."

"You don't have to entertain me," she said. "Can we go?"

Outside, he walked her over to the cliff which plunged a hundred feet or more down to the sea. The sun sparkled on the blue water, flashed on the white spray flung up from the rocks. The view out to the island of Formentera was immense.

He pointed east. "Straight out there is where they came from. Ancient Phoenicia, the city of Tyre, right next door to you in Lebanon."

"Why remind me of where my son was killed?"

He looked at her, feeling helpless. There seemed to be nothing he could say that she wouldn't twist. "I'm sorry. I didn't mean to bring up your son. I mean it, I'm truly sorry if..."

"It doesn't matter," she said curtly, interrupting him. She patted her shoulder bag. "I've something to show you. Can we get in the car?"

Once inside the Renault, she didn't waste any time in explanation. She opened her bag and took out a document with a stiff vinyl cover. She passed it to him and he saw stamped on the outside the words WEIZMANN ISTITUTE. He stared at it until she spoke.

"Go ahead! Look at it!"

He turned the cover and looked inside at the title page. The first thing he saw stamped on at the top of the page was KMG – DIMONA, the same words that had been stamped on the LIS file. His heartbeat quickened. Below the KMG– DIMONA slug there was a title:

NATANZ
(Ordnance)

He knew that *Natanz* was the name that the media gave to the location in Iran where it was believed that weapons grade nuclear material was being processed.

"You know what Natanz is?" Noa asked.

He shook his head in disbelief at what he seeing in his lap, his pulse pounding in his ears. What was she doing?

"I don't believe you," she said, misunderstanding his reaction. "You're a journalist. Of course you know."

He nodded this time. "I do, but I don't know much about it."

"Few people do," she said. "What you're looking at is one of several ordnance reports on the Israeli plan to destroy Natanz with tactical nuclear weapons. I designed some of those weapons and the reports contain details on the types to be used, the warhead strengths. I have more, much more, including the targeting schematics on the laptop I brought." She was icy calm and clinical in her tone. "The weapons are all to be delivered by aircraft and the reason the strike will be nuclear is that we don't have enough aircraft and the logistical back-up to launch the multiple raids with conventional bombs that would be necessary. We can only go in once. I want you to write about it and file it on your wire service."

"Jesus!...Noa!"

"That's the only way to stop them."

"Stop who?"

"Don't be stupid! The IDF, the generals who Olmert won't be able to stop even if he wanted to. He's too weak with all the corruption charges against him. He's finished. And if Netanyahu takes over it'll be worse. He'll want to do it. "

"But how do you know they're going to do it? This could just be a contingency plan. Every military has those. Besides it's nuclear!"

She glared at him angrily. "You don't know these people and I do. They'll do it. Only the United States can stop them. And the Americans will need to see some clear evidence like this plan to jolt them. You have to write it."

She was rigid in her seat, her eyes burning with the intensity of conviction. He sensed that all morning she had been waiting to get to this. She frightened him. This passion of hers frightened him. The way she went at it with such manic vengeance.

Suddenly, her shoulders slumped and she reached her hand across to his thigh, her eyes softened with the hint of a sad smile. "I'm sorry, I didn't mean to call you stupid. Just look at it when we get home and ask me any questions you like. Please? Like you did before?"

But *before* was in Israel and look at what that had cost him. Couldn't she see that? He looked into her eyes, searching for help. They were intense with those steel flecks, uncompromising. Her righteous sense of purpose in betraying her own country was incomprehensible to him, an outsider. It had to have something to do with the deep, corrosive grief and anger she felt for the loss of her son. She was troubled and in trouble. In the past he had always walked away from trouble, but there had never been a woman like this in the past. He wanted to help her. But how? He felt the warmth of her hand moving on his thigh and it aroused in him thoughts of the night before. He didn't want to lose that. But he had to end this conversation, give himself time to figure out what to do with the NATANZ document. Also, he had to think about Reuters and what they might do with it, and with him.

He handed the document back to Noa. "OK. I'll have a look at it later, I promise" Then, quickly, he clapped his hands. "Now then! How about some lunch?"

Santa Eulalia del Rio got its name because the only river on the island ran beneath a bridge at the entrance to the town. After the bridge the roadway curved around a steep hill called the *Puig de Missa* which had a 14th century fortified church on top. The cemetery next to the church contained many foreign names, German, English, French, Dutch, a few Americans. For decades Santa Eulalia had been a haven for ex-pat artists, writers, British actors, vagabonds, con men, and world drifters. Alan had pitched up here when he first came to the island. The layout of the town was a grid of white-washed buildings and a modern marina clustered on the eastern shore of the Island. An old town hall or *Ayuntamiento* with a fountain in front stood in the central plaza with a pretty tiled *paseo* lined with plane trees running straight down to the shoreline. A couple of blocks off the *paseo* along the *Calle del Mar* was a restaurant named *Bes,* a favorite hang-out for the ex-pat community.

The place was half full when they entered. Christmas decorations still hung over the bar and a TV set was turned on to CNN in English. A cheap four foot plaster replica of the Egyptian dwarf God *Bes* – the original was in the Louvre in Paris – stood on a plinth in the middle of the main dining area. He looked squat and ferocious, arms on his hips, his genitals hanging between thick bandy legs.

Noa stared at him, grimacing. "I assume he's *Bes*," she said. "Who was he?"

"Egyptian God who drove off evil spirits," Alan replied, "protected households..."

"*And* he gives us the good things in life, music, dance, sexual pleasure," said Trudi Ballach, a broad and blowsy German woman who rolled out from behind the bar to greet them. "So Alan *dahling!* Who's the lovely *fraulein* you've brought us today?"

Alan kissed her cheeks. "This is the legendary Trudi," he said to Noa. "She owns the place. And this is Noa, who has just arrived from Israel."

"Ah!...From Israel!" Trudi exclaimed, wiping her hands on her apron. "Well, you know, *Bes* was also a very popular God for the Phoenicians, right next door to you. You should feel right at home here, yes?"

"Thank you," Noa said coldly. "I just love midgets."

"Trudi is a terrific cook, " Alan said quickly. He pointed to a large blackboard hanging on the wall with chalk listings of the day's specials. "All this stuff is great."

Trudi seated them where they could see CNN and then trotted off behind the bar to tell the regulars who the newcomer was. When Alan went up a few minutes later to order drinks he greeted some of the men, two of them Germans who had nice things to say about Israeli women.

"I'm sorry," Noa said when he returned. "I didn't mean to be rude. Maybe it's that she's German and I still have a problem with some of them. You're Jewish...don't you feel it too?"

He shook his head. "Not really. A lot of the Germans here are the self-hating types when it comes to Israel. It's the Brits and the French who are really down on you because of the Palestinian situation."

"Those great liberators," Noa scoffed.

Later, while they were eating, one of the Germans, a man named Axel who Alan had greeted at the bar, stopped by their table and invited them to his restaurant later on for drinks and dinner.

"He's got some of the best food in Sta. Eulalia," Alan said to Noa.

She shrugged. "Why not."

He turned to Aksel but before he could speak Trudi interrupted, remote in hand, calling their attention to the TV as she turned up the volume:

"You should look at this Noa," she said.

On the screen was a map of the eastern Mediterranean with arrows swooping out from Israel as far as Crete and southern Greece. The CNN reporter's voiceover said that Israeli aircraft had carried out an unusual training exercise over 1500 kilometers into the Mediterranean that morning, using dozens of F-15 and F-16 jets along with refueling tankers and rescue helicopters. The distance, the reporter said, was the same as that between Israel and the Iranian nuclear facilities at Natanz. The reporter quoted an Israeli military source as saying it was a rehearsal for an attack on Iran which would be a necessity unless that country abandoned its attempt to develop a nuclear weapon.

"Wow!" Trudi cried. "You really going to do it Noa?"

"Fucking madness!" a wizened little Englishman at the bar shouted. "The Israelis got their fuckin' nukes and don't want anybody else out there to have 'em too, the selfish bastards."

Axel leaned down to Noa and whispered. "Don't mind them. You've every right to defend yourself. Remember. Never again!" He looked up at Alan. "Come about eight o'clock? I'll speak to my chef."

Alan, his thoughts whirling, his eyes fixed on the TV, nodded. "Eight, that's fine."

He glanced at Noa. She was staring at Axel's back as if she'd just eaten something foul. Nothing seemed to please her here. It had to be the strain on her nerves after what she had done, and she was not in famliar surroundings. Or maybe there was another Noa, a person altogether different from the one he thought he knew.

*

The festive season in Spain lasted until Epiphany on January 6th. It was known as *El Dio de los Tres Reyes* – the day of the three kings, the Magi who came bearing gifts to the baby Jesus – and it was more popular among children than Christmas day itself. In the few days before *Los Tres Reyes,* Alan and Noa ate together, slept together, and made love together, but he had the feeling he was living with a relentless overseer and not a partner. They had never lived together before and he felt Noa's presence hovering over him each day, pressuring him to write. He worked on his computer in a small room off the courtyard, a former *cocina* or kitchen which he had turned into a study. He struggled with the NATANZ documents, tried to write a few leads, then tried to write separate sections, but he didn't like any of it and neither did she. She often sat beside him with her laptop open, supplying more details, trying to make him understand the complexity of the operation. They had little social life. Noa had refused to go to Axel's place after what had happened at *Bes.* "Never again?" she'd said sarcastically. "What right does he have to say never again?" In fact she refused to go any place where she might have to deal with Germans. And as he had predicted, when they did go out it was the Brits and the French who badgered her with questions about the plight of the Palestinians in Gaza and the West Bank. He began to feel sorry for her. It was hard to be an Israeli among Europeans, especially among the kind of know-it-all artistic types that populated Ibiza. The irony, he thought, was that Noa herself was far more critical of Israel *and* better informed about it than any of his friends. It was in her presence, putting himself in her place as he listened to the harangues and lectures she received from his ex-pat friends, that he began to hear and feel for the first time in his life something unfair, something too one-sided, something that gave off the stink of anti-Semitism. Had it been there all along and he had never noticed it until somebody he cared for was subjected to it? Another irony was that the Germans, especially the younger ones like Axel with their deep sense of shame, were the least guilty of this latent anti-semitism and that Noa, perhaps because of the deep conditioning of her Israeli culture, couldn't see that.

On the evening of the festival of the Three Kings he persuaded Noa that she shouldn't miss it and he succeeded in getting her out of the house. They drove down the hillside to Santa Eulalia and parked the Renault near the marina. Just outside the marina gate there was a wide cement landing ramp where the summer ferries tied up. Torchlight flickered over the large crowd that had gathered at the head of the ramp, spreading out along the *Paseo del Puerto* and into the streets behind. *Nina's* restaurant and *Donna Ana's* which over-looked the *paseo* were filled with drinkers and diners. A number of young men in Eastern dress and turbans stood at the water's edge on the landing ramp. Several of them held the reins of three horses, others held torches. The horses were saddled and decorated with plumes on their heads and flowers woven into their manes and tails. There was a noisy festive air and the night was filled with the excited voices of children who were anticipating the gifts they believed the Kings were bringing.

"What are the horses for?" Noa asked.

"Wait for it," Alan said.

Suddenly the sound of a horn, like a *shofa*, wafted across the water. Parents held their children up and pointed out into the harbor. *Mira! Mira!* Look! Look! And around the mole came a large fishing boat with an open deck. On the fore deck, under bright lights strung up the mast, three men wearing crowns and beards and magnificent long robes stood together. The children screamed and the crowd roared and applauded. The boat glided up to the landing ramp and

Los Tres Reyes were helped ashore by the attendants waiting for them.

"Pretty neat, isn't it ?" Alan said. "Up in San Carlos they bring them in from the fields in a horse drawn cart. But this one is the best."

"Who are they again?" Noa asked.

"They're gentiles, *goyim*. Melchior, Gaspar, and Balthazar. He's the black-faced one supposed to be from Africa, but they've got no blacks on Ibiza so they use shoe-polish. The three of them represent the non-Jewish people of the world being introduced to the baby Jesus, the Jewish savior of the world whom Herod, another Jew, wants to kill. They bring gifts to the baby, which is the part the kids love. It's New Testament stuff, Christian, where all the-Jews-killed-Jesus stuff begins."

"*Harah! Nimas li!*" Noa exclaimed in Hebrew.

"What's that mean?"

"I've had enough of this shit. Can we go?"

"Sure."

Alan took her arm and began to guide her through the crowd. The Magi would proceed on horseback up through the town to the plaza in front of the *Ayuntamiento* where they would hand out the gifts that the children's parents had been piling up there all day long. Alan heard the crowd laugh and when he looked back he saw that Balthazar was having trouble mounting his horse. Then, suddenly, the horse broke free from the attendants and bolted, riderless, clattering up the ramp, scattering the screaming crowd. The attendants, some of them still carrying their torches, ran after the horse. Alan turned away and pulled Noa back toward the barrier pole to the marina.

Then he heard a roar and when he looked again he saw that a man had grasped the reins of the runaway horse and was holding him in, handling him expertly. Torchlight flashed on the man's face for the briefest moment.

Alan was stunned. He was sure the man was Gavri Gilboa.

"Over there!" he cried, tugging on Noa's arm and pointing. "Isn't that your friend Gavri?"

"Where?"

"Over there! With the horse."

A mob of turbaned attendants now surrounded the horse, torches waving, the crowd surging around.

"I don't see him. You're crazy! What would he be doing here?"

"I don't know," Alan said. He searched through the crowd, but he couldn't find the face again. "I'm pretty sure it was him."

"Don't be foolish," Noa said. "Your nerves are getting to you."

A couple of days after *Tres Reyes,* Alan called Jerold in Cambridge. He went out on the terrace with his cell phone, walked down by the orange tree well away from the *finca,* well out of earshot from Noa. He'd never asked Jerold for advice or guidance on any story he'd ever worked on before, but he felt he needed to talk to someone about NATANZ and what Noa expected from him.

"Are you in Israel?" Jerold asked when he answered.

"No, I'm in Ibiza," Alan said. "I've been expelled from Israel by the military censors..."

"Good Lord! What did you do? Are you alright?"

"I should have told you earlier, but I'm fine..."

"Why were you expelled?"

"For writing about the Israeli nuclear weapons progam without submitting it to the censor. I had a really good source."

"Pah!" Jerold's dismissive P sound exploded in his ear and he pulled his cell phone back. "They can't expect to hide their weapons forever."

"I suppose not," Alan said, fingering the bark on the orange tree, "but listen, I've got another story about nuclear weapons that I'd like to run by you, get your opinion."

Jerold said to go ahead and Alan spent the next five minutes explaining where Natanz was, what it was, and the Israeli classified material he had his hands on – their tactical nuclear weapons and their targeting details for an attack on Iran. He finished by saying that his source was absolutely convinced that the exposure of such material – via a report that he would write on Reuters – was the only way to stop an imminent pre-emptive nuclear attack on Iran by the Israelis.

He waited for Jerold to speak...and waited.

"Dad?"

"Do *you* seriously believe this to be the truth, that the Israelis would launch such a nuclear attack?" Jerold finally asked.

Alan reached out and grasped an orange in his hand. "I don't know."

"But one thing you do know," Jerold said. "You're a Jew."

"So what?" Alan said. "You never placed any emphasis on that. You don't have any religious faith or a belief in Zionism and neither do I. What does it mean to be a Jew? Have a memory of the holocaust?"

"No, no, that's a terrible mistake," Jerrold said. "Too many American Jews indulge this Holocaust obsession. It confuses a means of remembering with a reason for doing so. Just because Hitler exterminated my grandparents is not sufficient reason for me to claim that I'm a Jew. It is the things that I do that reach beyond myself, things that contribute to the Judaic sensibility of questioning and truth-telling, no matter how uncomfortable those truths may be." He paused. "Are you doing this for the sake of some journalistic coup, a Pulitzer prize or something?"

Alan jerked on the orange violently, snapping it free from the tree. He didn't know how to answer this. He felt shallow, and embarrassed.

"I'm sorry," Jerold said. "I've put you on the spot and I didn't mean to do that. You have a good soul, my son. Look into it and decide for yourself what is best for you to do as a man...and as a Jew."

Alan stood on the terrace holding his orange for a long while after this phone conversation, watching the smoke from the evening cooking fires drift across the valley below, the dogs barking, and out beyond the shoreline the color of the sea tinting purple with the setting of the sun. He was looking straight to the east, down the Mediterranean towards Israel, peering as if he could see the country

beyond the horizon. Jerold had exposed something that he had long
buried or denied in himself:

He was a Jew... and he could not betray his own people.

It was as simple as that. And as he stared out at the faint pink
clouds over the sea, he shook his head as if in wonderment:

He was a Jew first, a journalist second.

Dan Bergmann would love it! He tossed the orange over the terrace and walked back toward the *finca*. Now all he had to do was find
the courage to tell Noa and hope he didn't lose her.

*

The village of Santa Inez in the northwest corner of the island was not
much more than a church, a few houses, and a restaurant with a very
good *tortilla espanol*. But at this time of year Santa Inez had a
spectacular show –almond blossoms turned the whole valley into a
faux winter wonderland. That show was how Alan sold the outing to
Noa, who was not happy with the progress of his writing. He needed a
break, he said. And he did, but it was from the game of deception that
was wearing him down, not the writing of the NATANZ story.

They drove up on Sunday morning and parked in the little plaza in
front of the restaurant terrace. He suggested they walk around the
valley before lunch – he'd made a reservation, knowing it would be
crowded with Germans, which he didn't tell Noa. The air was clear and
invigorating and on the first rise in the track that circled the valley
they stopped to admire the view. Thousands of almond trees stood in
ranks across the floor of the valley. The sun was passing behind a
cloud and they waited for it to emerge. When it came out a flood of
light bathed the valley and millions of white almond blossoms
shimmered like a blinding field of snow.

"They tell a story about this valley," Alan said. "A long time ago a
Moorish nobleman married a princess from northern Europe and
brought her here to live. She became homesick and was pining away

for her homeland. So the Moor planted a thousand almond trees and when they blossomed every winter she had a valley filled with snow."

"That's a sweet story," Noa said. "But did the princess stay?"

"I don't know. I hope so, otherwise..."

"A waste of almond trees?"

"You're such a hard-headed realist. I thought I'd soften you up with a nice romantic story."

"Why?"

Alan felt his heart beating faster. Why not now? Just say it!

"Because you're not going to like what I'm going to say next." He paused, looking at her, the whole of her. She was wearing the designer jeans she had bought and the sweater over a t-shirt. He wanted to take off her dark sunglasses so he could see her eyes.

"You're just staring at me," she said. "Go ahead! Say it whatever it is!"

"I'm not going to write NATANZ or file it on Reuters. I can't do it."

Her mouth tightened and she spun away from him, clutching her arms across her chest. He heard her deep sigh of irritation, saw her shoulders rise and fall. He raised his hands to her shoulders, then dropped them. The seconds that passed before she turned to face him seemed infinite. But when she did turn she smiled at him and took his arm.

"Let's go back to the restaurant," she said, "have a glass of wine and talk about this."

The restaurant terrace was filling up, but their reservation was honored and they were given a small table for two against the railing overlooking the plaza. They sat in the warm sun and listened to the singing coming from the white adobe church. Some people loitered under a huge eucalyptus tree near the church door. Alan ordered a *tortilla espanol* for two and a bottle of red wine. Noa waited for him to finish ordering, then leaned forward, her elbows on the table.

"You're being naïve," she said. "The Israeli military sees no alternative to this attack on Iran and it has to be stopped. Every intelligence agency in the world believes the Iranian program is geared toward making nuclear weapons and everyone knows that economic sanctions won't work without Russia and China going along, and they won't. Only a protracted conventional aerial assault can stop the Iranians and only the United States has the conventional military capacity to do the job."

Alan opened his mouth and Noa raised her hand.

"Let me finish," she said fiercely. "My point is that the United States does not have the will to do it because it is tied down in Iraq and Afghanistan and the American people have no appetite for another Middle East war in Islamic lands. Which leaves only Israel, and believe me, we will do it *and do it with tactical nuclear weapons*. The NATANZ document proves this and you have to expose it."

The waiter brought the wine, bread and *aioli*, and they waited silently for him to open the bottle and pour. The doors to the church opened and worshipers began to spill into the plaza.

"Let's talk about rationality," Alan said, leaning in over the table and keeping his voice down. "There's this Jewish lawyer my father knows in Cambridge. He's a very bright man, teaches at Harvard, a rational man you would say. But he's also a fanatical Zionist. Israel can do no wrong with him. He has this theory that Iran is what he calls *a suicide nation,* that for the first time in history we have a country and its leadership that are willing to commit suicide for a cause. He's saying that Iran *is not a rational nation*. That's like saying that Muslims don't love their children because they allow them to become suicide bombers. I believe he is wrong, that Iran is not a so-called suicide nation..."

"He *is* wrong," Noa interjected. "He's projecting. Israel is the suicide nation and doesn't even know it. It's a Masada complex and we'll do it again, and you *are* naive if you think we won't. Ever since Begin we have developed a victim psychology, we see only enemies. I think you're scared. You won't write this story because you're afraid for yourself. You think you saw Gavri and he's frightened you."

Alan shook his head. She was calling him a coward and that wasn't the reason at all.

"You're son wouldn't have wanted you to do this," he said sharply.

She winced, and quite suddenly she began to cry. She was facing out towards the plaza and nobody on the terrace seemed to notice. He reached out and took her hand and she squeezed it, shaking her head.

"It's not fair that he's gone," she sobbed. "He comes back to me without any warning...like a punch in the stomach...I hate them..."

"I'm sorry," he said. "I didn't mean to hurt you..."

She let go of his hand, took her napkin and blew her nose.

"It's OK. I'll find somebody else," she said, her words muffled by the napkin.

"You don't have to do that," he protested. "Just think about it. What could they say if you gave it back?..."

He stopped. She had dropped the napkin and the look on her face told him that she wasn't listening. She was staring at something behind him in the plaza, over toward the church. She hissed some words in Hebrew.

"What?" he said.

"It's Gavri!" she said. *"He's here!"*

He turned to the plaza and saw Gavri clearly, standing over by the eucalyptus. Old couples, short Spanish ladies and their men in dark Sunday suits, came out of the church and ambled past him. He was looking directly at them up on the terrace.

Then he waved.

"Harah!" Noa exclaimed. "He wants us to see him. He's mad!"

They watched in silent astonishment as Gavri turned and walked over to a motorcycle that was standing at the edge of the plaza. He mounted it, kick-started, and then drove off out of the village without looking at them again. They continued watching the bike and the man recede, diminishing in size down the straight road that ran from the village into the surrounding hills.

"Senor! Su tortilla."

"Sorry!" Alan swivelled on his seat to face a waiter who stood beside the table holding a hot dish with a towel.

"Let's get out of here," Noa said.

"*Lo siento,*" he said to the waiter, "*pero tenemos que partir.*" And he gave the puzzled man some money to pay for the food and the wine.

Alan's mind raced through the possibilities as he drove the Renault through the mountains south from St. Inez, choosing dirt roads and a circuitous route because he had some notion they could be followed. Gavri Gilboa was *Shabak* and his presence here must mean that they had followed Noa to the island. It also meant that they knew about NATANZ and had come to take it and Noa back. But what would they do with him? And how to explain Gavri's weird behavior. He glanced for the tenth time over at Noa, puzzled by her silence. He could stand it no longer.

"For God's sake say something! Are they...the *Shabak*...are they here? What will they do?"

"I don't think so," she said.

"You don't think *what* is so?"

She looked at him. "Don't worry. You're safe. It's me Gavri's interested in. He's completely deranged and I think he's here alone. But he wants me to know he's here."

"What do you mean deranged?"

"He's had a complete breakdown. He's gone into *Kabbalah* and adopted some occult religious nonsense. He thinks that he's a dragon or something who has to protect me from evil."

"And you knew this before you came here?"

"Yes. He asked me to go to his place and he let me see this bizarre set up he has, a kind of altar with weird symbols, and these medieval texts. He wanted me to know all about it. He became violent when I tried to leave. He knew that I was seeing you and that I had given you the LIS material, but he did nothing about it. He's quite mad."

"Am I the evil he is supposed to be protecting you from?"

"Maybe. But I wouldn't worry. He's more interested in me. We've known each other since we were kids growing up on our kibbutz and I think he may be trying to warn me about something."

"What do you mean? How so?'

"I'm not sure. But that wave. He meant something by that, and the sudden way he drove off on that motorcycle. Leaving like that."

Thirty minutes later when they arrived back at the *finca*, Noa's hunch proved correct. There was a note wedged between the large oak doors. It was in Hebrew and Noa read it and then translated for Alan.

"It's addressed to the *Shekkinah*, which is what Gavri calls me when he likes me. He warns me that the false protectors of Israel are closing in on me and that he can save me only if I flee from this island. He wants me to go to the airport, which he can help me do. He signs it the *Blind Dragon*."

"Jesus!" Alan swore. "What does he call you when he doesn't like you?"

"Lilith," Noa said. "The whore."

*

It was always damp inside the *finca* in winter and Alan stoked the fire with his fresh cut *almendra* until it was throwing out so much heat they couldn't sit on the banquettes on either side of the fireplace. Instead they sat at the thick slab of oak on a trestle that was the dining table. There was a new tension between them now, something that Alan had never felt before and he wasn't sure how to handle it. They had to eat and he cooked his version of a Spanish omelet while Noa stared at the television, a *liga* game between Barcelona and Athletic Bilbao. He split the omelet on two plates, opened a bottle of red wine, sat down.

"Those are two non-Spanish teams, the Catalans and the Basques," he said. "The Spanish call Athletic Bilbao *el equipo de las terroristas*...the team of the terrorists." She said nothing. "I didn't know you liked football."

"I'm not seeing it," Noa replied.

"What are you seeing?"

"That Gavri's right. I've got to leave here. Since you're not going to write about NATANZ I think you should give the documents and the computer back to me. I can fly to London or even to New York and try to find some journalist with the guts to publish it."

"Ouch! You don't pull any punches." He felt hurt, but he had to make his plea now and hope that she didn't really mean it. He took a swallow of wine. "I see it differently," he said. "I seeing us going back to Israel together and giving up the NATANZ stuff. I'm Jewish and I have the right to citizenship. They can't deny me that. We can be together."

Noa, eating some of her omelet, looked up at him. "What would you do there?"

"I could work as a journalist on an English paper like the Jerusalem Post until I learned Hebrew." He reached out and took her hand. Should he tell her he loved her? She was becoming so spiky he never knew how she would react. "I want to be with you," he said. "We could be together."

Noa looked down at their hands, a sort of wonderment on her face. "You would immigrate to Israel?"

He nodded.

Noa shook her head and and pulled her hand away. "You're too weak," she said. "You'd never make it there. And besides, do you think they're going to give me my job back? Get real!"

You're weak! Get real! That hurt badly, but he tried to respond as if he hadn't heard it. "What if you give NATANZ back to them, they would have to take that into account, wouldn't they? No harm would have been done if it isn't published."

"God! Your father said you had no ambition, but he never said you were so naïve and stupid." She was staring straight at him. "I'm sorry, I'm being cruel. Forgive me for that outburst, but I'm going to go to London tomorrow morning and take my chances there. Right now I'm going to bed."

She rose from the table. "I'm sorry for what I said."

Too far! Alan thought. *Weak! Stupid!* She had gone too far. He'd read somewhere long ago that there were some things you couldn't apologize for. That they changed who you were, and you couldn't change back.

"Jerold may have said I have no ambition," he said, "but he also said that I should give the NATANZ material back to the Israeli government."

Noa smiled. "Like father, like son."

Her smugness infuriated him.

"Wrong! Jerold isn't my real father. My real father died in Israel back in 1948, the year I was born."

"You were born in Israel?"

"No. My mother left when she was pregnant. Her name was Ruth Stahlmann. You're friend Ofra Gefen helped me track down the story with a woman named Anna Peled who married Ruth's brother. She turns out to be my aunt...lives on a kibbutz up north."

Noa sat down again as if she'd been knocked down, her face turning pale.

"What is it?"

"She's my mother," Noa said. "Anna Peled is my mother."

"What?"

Noa nodded slowly, her hands to her lips, her fingers trembling.

Alan stared at her, the intimacy of their family relation dawning on him. *Noa was his cousin! His first cousin!*

"I think I'm going to be sick," Noa said.

***

Twelve

G avri sat in the lotus position three terraces down from Alan Raskin's *finca*, the range maybe sixty to seventy meters. A Beretta 9 mm. pistol lay between his legs. His back rested against a gnarled olive tree and he was hidden from view by the surrounding brush. He had chosen this observation post over two weeks ago, the day after he had arrived on the island with Raskin, following him from Israel on Daniel Zentler's order.

He raised a small pair of Zeiss binoculars, found a space in the brush to peer through to the target. The architecture of the *finca* was peculiar, a cluster of white cubes connected to each other but at different elevations. Now, in the last light of day, blueish smoke curled up from the chimney, lights shone in the two small windows on either side of the massive door where he had left his message; also there was light in the window of the higher cube to the left of the door which he assumed was a bedroom. He trained his binoculars on that window and saw Noa Kagan move across the room. He had hoped that after reading the message he had left in the door she would have departed for the airport by now. All he could do was wait and improvise a plan to protect her. They would come for her tonight, he was sure.

*

Days before, when Raskin and Noa were out, Gavri had gone up to have a look at the layout of the *finca*, peering through the barred windows. He knew that the chimney was over a large room with a fireplace at the back where the *finca* had been dug into the hillside. That would be the kitchen/dining room where, he guessed, they would spend much of their time. There was no exit from this room directly to the outside. They would have to go through the front room and the large door into the courtyard. He'd also looked through a window into a smaller cube on the right side of the courtyard, saw a desk and a couple of laptops. Raskin's office, he guessed. But he made no attempt to break in and get the documents or the computer that the *yekke* Zentler had told him Noa had taken with her.

Zentler had called him on his cell phone early in the morning three hours after Noa arrived in Ibiza. The *yekke* had assigned him to follow Raskin only after he had pleaded that they couldn't let the American go loose outside Israel because the source of the leaks might contact him. He'd been right about that – he was at the Ibiza airport to witness Noa's arrival – but he was sure that it gave Zentler no satisfaction.

"Why did you deny knowing any of the LIS scientists?" the *yekke* asked him on the phone. "You grew up on the same kibbutz as Noa Kagan."

"What took you so long?" he replied. They were so slow and stupid. But methodical old Zentler let the sarcasm go by and told him that they had looked at the *LATAM* surveillance reports that he, Gavri, had kept in his desk and discovered that Raskin had been a frequent visitor to Noa Kagan's condo in Neve Tzedek.

"We understand now that you were protecting her," Zentler said, "and we know that she has gone to Ibiza, presumably to meet Raskin. But I'm telling you that she has taken some very important papers with her and a computer, something much more serious than LIS, something that could seriously damage the security of Israel. We must have them back, Gavri, and Noa Kagan too. You're an Israeli soldier and I have no reason to doubt your patriotism. I want you to stand down now and let us take over. "

When he didn't reply to this, Zentler said it was an order. Again he didn't reply and Zentler said they had been to his flat in Tel Aviv. "We think you need help Gavri, professional help, and we want to help you.

We don't want you to do anything else. Nothing rash. We can look after this from now on. Where are you staying?"

That was when he cut off the call.

They would send an extraction team, he was sure. *Sayeret Matkal*, possibly Unit 269 because it was a foreign job. He would be waiting for them. They would have no problem tracking down Raskin and the location of his *finca* on the island. But they had to make sure about Noa Kagan's presence here and only then could they set up the extraction. He didn't know how they would do it. Possibly by boat, working with the Navy's "Flotilla 13". That's how he would do it. Snatch her and smuggle her out to something bigger offshore at night. That would avoid any official papers or passports and possible trouble with the *Guardia Civil* at the airport. But it would take a couple of days to find a boat, set it up. Meanwhile they would keep the couple under surveillance. And that was how he would find them. Watch for the watchers and then let them see that he hadn't stood down. Knowing that they would have to deal with him could really fuck-up their operation. It would give them pause. Make them think.

A day after Zentler's phone call, last light of day, he had sat in his concealed spot below Raskin's *finca*. He hadn't let Raskin and Noa out of his sight since the Zentler call, had followed them on his motorbike into Ibiza town, watched them shopping and sight-seeing, and then followed them back to Santa Eulalia. That evening his patient stakeout had paid off. He heard the sound of a motorbike approaching up the track on the other side of the woods. Not an unusual sound. Some kids in a farmhouse further down the road had a couple of bikes. But then the engine sound stopped and the kids never stopped; they just roared up the track and then back down. He swung his binoculars to the woods and waited. Soon he saw two men emerge from the pines, crouching and moving rapidly towards him across a terrace. They wore black running shoes, blue jeans, black lightweight wind-breakers.

The two men stopped when they had a clear view of the *finca* and one of them raised a pair of binoculars and peered over the edge of a terrace to look. The other one raised his hand to his mouth and his lips moved. He was speaking into a microphone in his fist and to somebody else. That would be control, no more than a few kilometers away, probably down in Santa Eulalia. Not bad, he thought. Less than twenty-four hours after Zentler's call they had a *Sayeret* team on the ground, their target located, and a control set up. There would be at least four others besides these two. He studied the faces of the two men. They were young and he didn't know them. But they would be good, he was sure. Who was control, he wondered? Would it be Zentler himself? There would be hell to pay for allowing Noa Kagan to slip out of the country and the *yekke* would want to redeem himself...if they'd let him. He waited until one of the men left and then he slipped back down the terrace and followed him to town. The man drove his motorbike to a circular little plaza with a cluster of palms near the *Paseo del Maritimo*. He parked and went into a building with a sign that read *San Marino - Hotel/Residencia*. There were lots of winter rentals available and Gavri was satisfied that he had established the location of their control. Also, he was more certain that the extraction would be by boat and he had to find it.

He had rented a room at a small restaurant/hostel called *Axel's* on *Calle San Vincent* and that night he kneeled back on his haunches before a candle on the floor, his hands on his thighs. In front of the candle lay the amulet that protected him against *Lilith*. His meditation was supposed to help counter the power of her evil, but he found it difficult to concentrate. Memories of his years at Kefar Borochov with Noa Kagan kept filtering through, memories of their childhood and adolescence, their dreams. He understood Noa, what she was doing. A violent death, the loss of a son like Sasha, would bring despair and depression to most people. But Noa's response to loss was anger and aggression. Since childhood she had been that way and now she was seeking vengeance. How else could she rewrite history? Kefar Borochov had given them values, above all it had taught them to seek justice in all things for all people. But then the kibbutz had sent them out into a country where the people had commenced to worship the false Gods of the Americans. They were prostrating themselves before the idol of market capitalism. Selfishness and corruption ruled, not social justice; pride in military prowess blinded them to the nakedness of their territorial ambition. Noa's mistake was that she never could escape her scientific training. She had tried to fight them on their materialistic terms and in doing so she had been seduced by *Samael*. He, Gavri Gilboa, was a son of the same kibbutz, and he'd had the same values bred into him as Noa. But when he came to his breaking point he'd saved himself by transcending the temptations of modern Israel, the lust and greedy materialism that permeated the society. He had found a spiritual realm of peace and respite from the Sodom he saw all around him. It was not Gavri Gilboa but *Blind Dragon* who now picked up the Book of Zohar, held it in his hands. But he was too angry to read. His thoughts had shifted to the *yekke* Zentler and his words on the telephone: *You need professional help.* Who did the *yekke* think he was? They were the ones who needed his help. He had sacrificed himself to their bloody cause, suffered his wounds and soiled himself in gore and blood on their behalf. Now he had transcended their secular world view. He had been released by the *Prince of Power* into the spiritual realm. They were so twisted in spirit and beneath his contempt. They would see.

Blind Dragon would soon reveal himself and the contest would begin.

Catching the breakaway horse at the boat landing on the night of the Three Kings had been deliberate act on his part. Half-an-hour before the Kings had landed from their boat he had spotted the same two *Sayeret* men from the *finca*, one by the entrance to the marina, the second on the terrace of a *pasteleria*. They were following Noa and *Samael*, the American Raskin. They were talking, as if to themselves, holding their hands to their mouths. Was it Zentler they were talking to in the apartment nearby? When the horse bolted, he decided this was as good a chance as any to show himself to them, let Zentler see the agent of the *Prince of Power*.

He was not sure whether or not the extraction team had seen him that night, but he was soon tipped off that someone was looking for him. Axel, the German owner of his hostel who had taken a liking to him when he had registered with his Israeli passport, came to his table in the restaurant. "You should know that someone is asking about you," he said. "An older man who speaks very good German. In fact, I think he is German. But I think he is the wrong kind of German who is not a friend of your people so I didn't tell him you were my guest." An old German? It had to be Zentler. The *yekke* himself was here.

It was urgent now that he find the boat. The next day he staked out the *San Marino,* concealing himself among the palms in the little circular plaza, squatting beneath a curious metal sculpture of an elongated horse. It took less than a hour before he saw Zentler leave the building and walk with his limping gait down to the *Paseo* and along to the marina. The main concrete pier had half-a-dozen long finger-like pontoons with numbered slips. Most of the boats in the slips were moth-balled for winter. Zentler went to Pontoon B, walked out to a white sixty foot Sun Fisher tied up stern on and went aboard. Gavri walked out on a parallel pontoon until he was oppposite Zentler's boat and he could read the writing on the stern with his glasses. *Zeus* was the name, registered in *Palma de Majorca* -- and provided, he was sure, by some innocent *sayan* owner. They would use it to take Noa Kagan off the island, meet up with "Flotilla 13" at sea to transfer her to Israeli custody, then return the boat to Palma with a grateful *toda* to the *sayan*. They wouldn't kill Raskin, an American citizen, just immobilize him. All neat and clean. Now that he was pretty sure of their plan, he had to devise a way to counter them.

First, he wanted Noa to know that she was in danger and that he was there to help her, but he couldn't count on her having seen him capture the runaway horse. When she and *Samael* made their journey to the village of Santa Inez two days later he followed them. He quickly spotted the same two *Sayeret* watchers from the *finca* sitting at a table on the terrace behind Noa. One of them spoke into his hand, got up and came down the steps to the plaza and walked across to the church. He followed the young man inside, slipped into the shadows at the back and watched him hesitate, scanning the congregation. A service was being conducted but the young man paid no attention and walked up the center aisle, stopping halfway and then stepping into a pew beside an older man who was kneeling at prayer. Gavri studied the back of the older man's head. The man wasn't really praying. The man was Zentler. The young man sat and bent forward to talk to him.

If Zentler was here in person something was about to happen.

He quickly left the church, went outside and stood in the plaza and waved to Noa, making sure she saw him. He hoped to spook her and get her to leave. When he saw her and Raskin get up from their table on the terrace he went to his motorbike and left. He raced back to the *finca* and placed a message in the door. Then he had taken up his position under the olive tree.

*

Now, an hour or so before dawn, he saw the first movement. A sharp little crack of radio static had alerted him. The night had been cold and cloudy, darker after the three-quarter moon had disappeared behind the hill at the back of the *finca*. But he wore night-vision goggles and he scanned the forest behind the *finca*. First, he saw the greenish image of a man dressed all in black moving down the hillside through the trees. Quickly searching left and right, he saw another man on the other side of the house. A better look this time. This one was carrying an Uzi with a silencer, and he wore night-vision goggles too. With that technology they were definitely *Sayeret,* and that Uzi was not meant for Noa or Raskin. They were expecting him. He didn't move a muscle. Two at the back and how many at the front? The static had been closer to him. They had to be nearby, closing in on the courtyard. He closed his eyes and strained to listen until he heard a voice whispering harshly in Hebrew. He opened his eyes and peered through his goggles and found them, greenish figures crouched in the shrubs on the terrace above him. Two more, one with another silenced Uzi. They were facing the *finca*.

He was not hopeful. Too much firepower. He had only his 9mm. Beretta which he'd been able to bring on his *El Al* flight from Tel Aviv to Spain because he had security clearance at Ben-Gurion airport.

Why hadn't Noa left earlier?

The two men in front moved up to the edge of the last terrace before the courtyard. The two at the back were coming down around the sides of the *finca*. He calculated his chances again. Four was too many, especially with those damned Uzis. But if there were four of them here, wouldn't that leave Zentler relatively unprotected?

Blind Dragon could snatch too!

He pushed his Beretta back into his hip holster and slowly inched his way around the olive tree. He crawled across the terrace and dropped silently over the wall, moving away from the finca. The sky was barely brightening to the east. When he'd moved down several more terraces he rose and walked into the woods and removed the boughs that covered his motorbike. He wheeled it out on to the track, jumped on and rolled down the hillside without starting the engine. It was downhill almost all the way into Sta. Eulalia and when he did start the engine he headed straight for the marina.

Lights were on in the cabin of the *Zeus* but the deck of the boat and the dock were dark. He had scanned them from a distance with his night-vision goggles and saw no one. The only other light was in the harbor master's tower, at least fifty meters away from the *Zeus* on the tip of the quay at the entrance to the bay of Sta. Eulalia. The water in the marina lay flat and there was no wind. A good night to go out. He crept down the dock to where the cruiser sat in a slip without neighbors on either side. Zentler wouldn't want neighbors and in winter he would have had plenty of options in choosing a slip. Careless of him though not to have a man on watch.

A narrow gangplank spanned the gap between the pontoon and the rear deck of the cruiser. He could see a black clad young man through the window in the cabin door, sitting in a banquette with an Uzi beside him. No sign of Zentler yet. He heard the crackle of a radio in the cabin and he hunkered down to listen behind the service post which provided water and electicity to the boat.

"ZOHAR ONE, ZOHAR ONE *this is ZOHAR TWO...Over!"*

"ZOHAR TWO...this is ZOHAR ONE. Go ahead."

Zentler's voice, his strongly accented Hebrew.

"ZOHAR ONE...Target is secured...LILITH and her paperwork and laptop all retrieved. SCRIBE inoperative. No sign of DRAGON. Over!"

"Roger that. Proceed to marina ZOHAR TWO."

Gavri swore quietly in the dark. Zentler had indeed been to his Tel Aviv flat. He was using what he'd found there as code names for his operation. *No sign of Dragon?* They were mocking him.

That would soon change.

The door to the cabin was in a cockpit a couple of steps below the rear deck. The moment he stepped on that deck they would feel the motion below and know that somebody had boarded the boat. He would have to move swiftly to get that door open. He drew his Beretta from its holster, pushed the safety off.

He leapt off the dock. One foot hit the gangplank, the next was down in the cockpit, and he was at the door, pulling it open and thrusting his Beretta out in front of him. Zentler, sitting at a chart table, looked up at him, frowning. The other man started to rise, swinging the Uzi up from the banquette.

Zentler's hand shot out. *"Ari stop!"* he shouted in Hebrew, and young man froze, then slowly lowered his Uzi to the banquette.

Gavri stepped down into the cabin, pointing the Beretta at the *Sayaret*. "On the floor, on your stomach. Now!"

The young man did as he was told. Gavri reached in and pulled the Uzi down the banquette to his end. "Tie his hands behind his back or cuff him," he said to Zentler. "Use whatever you got. Then tape his mouth. Carefully."

Zentler rose to his feet slowly, reached into a locker and took out a bag of plastic wrist ties and a roll of gaffer tape. He knelt and pulled Ari's hands behind him, slipped a tie around his wrists, tightened it. He tore a strip of tape off the roll and slapped it over Ari's mouth. He grunted when pushing himself back to his feet.

"You're making a mistake Gavri," he said.

"Those are you're first words old man? Whose mistake is this?" He motioned with the Beretta for Zentler to sit back in his chair. "I'd say *you* need some professional help."

Zentler sat down. "What now?'

"We wait."

"That's your plan? To wait? For what?"

"You know what. I'm going to trade you."

Zentler smiled, shaking his massive head slowly. He took off his glasses and wiped them on the tail of his shirt. "Gavri, Gavri! I have no value." He gestured to the commando on the floor. "These young men won't trade the security of their country for me and neither should you. Sit down and talk to me."

Gavri sat on a corner of the banquette, keeping the Beretta on Zentler. He glanced at his watch. Only minutes now, he guessed.

"What's the hurry," Zentler said. "We're all Israelis here and I'm sure you're as patriotic as the next man. We've all had to make sacrifices for our country. We have no choice when our survival is threatened. What's your problem with that? Tell me what's troubling you."

"Israel troubles me," he said. The old fool! He couldn't see it. None of them could. "It has become Sodom. You are too blind to see it."

Zentler frowned. Water slapped against the hull in the long silence.

"Is that what your friend Noa feels too?"

"She seeks revenge."

"You planned this together?"

He shook his head. "She is innocent. She has been seduced by *Samael* and she must be protected and restored to *Shekkinah*. It is all written but you are too blind to read."

Zentler looked at his feet and sighed heavily.

"Do you know how fortunate you have been?" he said finally, his eyes squinting at Gavri through his thick lenses. "And how fortunate Israel has been to have had you, and her? Beautiful, talented, young people, unshackled at last from two millennia of oppression? Free spirits unburdened by the past and eager to build a new nation? What has so troubled your soul?"

"You have lost *your* soul to *Samael*. You have lost your conscience before God. You are animals in your worship of material well-being."

Zentler lifted his head and laughed. "We are all animals Gavri. We may love, hope, cry, rage, do all those things. But we're still animals. We face our neighbors across deeply rooted suspicions, we lift our noses and sniff the breeze for any waft of foreign smells. As for conscience? I remind you of the words of one of our poets:

It's foolish to pretend
There's something like a conscience
In a world which erased this face with Zyklon B."

He lifted his hand and pointed his finger like the barrel of a gun.

"Think about that."

The radio crackled through the cabin. *"ZOHAR ONE* this is *ZOHAR TWO*. We are entering the marina. Are we cleared for *Zeus* Over?"

Gavri nodded to Zentler. "Tell them to proceed."

Zentler picked up the radio:

"ZOHAR TWO...You are cleared. Proceed to *Zeus*."

Gavri waved his Beretta at the door. "You and me out on the dock. Now!"

They stood off the stern of the boat in the half light and watched the column of people approaching down the narrow pontoon. A single man with an Uzi in front; a man on either side of Noa, holding her up; the last man at the rear with an Uzi. When they were close enough to see him, he stepped partly behind Zentler and raised his Beretta to the side of the older man's head.

"Do as he says," Zentler called out, and he stumbled forward a bit on the dock, away from the service post. "My leg," he said, as Gavri moved with him, pressing the gun behind his ear.

"Have you doped her already?" Gavri called out to the men.

Noa lifted her head at the sound of his voice. "Gavri? Is that you?" Her speech was slurred, her head sagged.

"Answer me!" Gavri barked.

Impossible to handle her if she was unable to walk. Hopeless trying to get her down the dock, let alone to the airport and on a plane.

"How much?" he shouted

He shoved the muzzle of the Beretta harder into Zentler's neck. The *yekke* moved his head to escape the pressure of the muzzle, shifted his weight off his bad leg and shuffled a bit forward again.

"Tell him!" Zentler shouted.

"Luminal...320 mg per..." came the reply when Zentler shifted again.

And suddenly he was gone. Off the pontoon and straight down into the water. Just stepped off. The old *yekke* had fooled him.

He stared down at the splash and bubbles for a second before spinning to Noa and the *Sayeret* men. He saw their Uzis rising, saw Noa's empty eyes, her vacant smile.

It was all over.

Blind Dragon had failed the *Prince of Power* and he deserved to die. But he would not let these men be his executioners. In one swift motion he jammed the muzzle of the Beretta up beneath his chin. The last word he heard before he pulled the trigger was Noa's scream:

"LO!"

***

Thirteen

Her memory of her last morning on Ibiza was fractured into parts which refused to cohere, refused to gel and form a whole again and make sense. Lying in a room that felt like a hospital room, she struggled with this. She knew she had been on a boat but not for how long. She remembered the figure of a man, dripping wet, standing over her in the cabin of that boat. And that fractal of memory put her back up on a dock where she saw the same man go into the water. And then?... And then the top of Gavri's head flew off. Bits of bone and flesh and a shower of blood. And the needle shoved into her again, savagely.

Noa Kagan didn't know where she was, but if she had been able to go to the window and open the shade she would have seen a dark blue slash of sea in the distance, lush green fields in the foreground, and in between the black ribbon of the Haifa-Tel Aviv highway. Beside the highway was a small abstract sculpture. It was a monument placed there at the Gelilot Junction to commemorate the brutal massacre of civilians by terrorists who, years before, had come ashore, highjacked a bus, and headed for Tel Aviv. Although the terrorists didn't make it, there was a certain irony that the end – a fiery, bullet-riddled finale – had come at this spot on the highway opposite Mossad Headquarters. The men who worked inside had nothing to do with the shoot-out. That wasn't their job. But it was their business to know in advance about enemies who had plans to hurt Israel. Their obsession at the time of Noa Kagan's arrival at the Junction was with Iran and its nuclear program. One of Israel's possible responses to that threat had been compromised by this woman and those men were enraged. Even a little bit frightened by the incomprehensible fact that someone with Noa Kagan's background could be a traitor. Being so angry themselves, none of them noticed those feelings in the others, so there was no restraining voice to the severity of the interrogation that was to ensue. She had been heavily overdosed with drugs in getting her here, and now she was to be drugged ruthlessly again and again with a graduated sequence of methamphetamines, including desoxyn combined with sodium amytal variants to keep her awake and probe her mind, regardless of the danger of destroying it. These were rational men at the Gelilot Junction and they could not believe it was rational that she had acted alone. They wanted to crack Noa Kagan as quickly as possible while she was still disoriented. And it was only after days of drugs and relentless questioning, when still they had failed to find their conspiracy, that they let Daniel Zentler try to get them an answer.

Noa's face was pale and damp. The harsh lights accented the dark puffy shadows under her eyes. She sat slumped in a straight-backed chair and her hands were in constant jittery motion, touching the table in front of her, rising to her hair, then back to the table. Her thick hair was disheveled by the constant combing and twisting with her fingers. Her eyes were closed and she did not see the man come in. When he pulled out the chair on the opposite side of the table and the legs scraped the floor, she opened her eyes.

"Know you," she mumbled, her words sticking together.

"Yes," he replied. "I'm Daniel Zentler and I'm here to ask you some questions."

"Water?...Mouth is dry...."

Zentler brought her some water and took out a pack of Marlboro cigarettes. He gave her one and lit it. She inhaled and coughed. Smoke billowed up into the light.

"Your eyes," she said. "They're sad like Gavri's. Are you grieving for him?"

"That was unfortunate," Zentler said. "We brought him home for burial. But help me if you can. We're trying to understand his role in all this. What was he doing with you in Ibiza? Was he helping you and Raskin?"

She laughed and closed her eyes. She wanted to go back to the music she had been hearing before, a faint distant theme with violins and singing voices. All she had to do was close her eyes and she was in the hills of Safed near home, riding her horse with Gavri and the other boys.

"Gavri used to be my friend," she said, her eyes still closed. "My closest friend once. But they drove him crazy, a warrior crazed by war...divine madness the Greeks called it. Gavri couldn't help me. He couldn't help himself. Listen to the music. It's beautiful."

"What am I supposed to be listening to?" Zentler asked.

She was puzzled. Couldn't he hear it? "The music...it's so peaceful. This is the way it was meant to be...we couldn't help what happened."

"We? Who's we Noa?"

She opened her eyes. "Us.....Those of us who have been made to suffer."

"You and...?"

"All of us. Sasha, me, and Gavri too. You're not blind. You must see what we're doing to ourselves."

"What are we doing to ourselves Noa?"

She closed her eyes again and rolled her head back and forth. The music was fading and she was losing the hills of Safed. The bloody eruption from the top of Gavri's head jolted into her mind. Her bottom lip pushed out as if she were pouting and her face contorted with horror and disgust. Her eyes popped open.

"Symmetries!" she screamed. "Can't you see the symmetries?" She leaned forward, her eyes flashing with fury. "Fools!....Fools! We're tearing ourselves apart again. We've turned back. Greedy, bickering, murdering fools. They're killing our children and they have to be stopped."

Her face softened, pleading. "I tried to stop them."

"Israel may be all those things, Noa, but it's ours."

And the fury was back. "No, no, no...it's not! Don't you see? They're destroying us."

"Who's destroying us? Yosef? The army?"

Her eyes widened and she nodded eagerly. "You can see now that I had to stop them."

Zentler picked up her hand and squeezed it. "Yes, I can see now. But you couldn't do that alone, could you? What about your relationship with Alan Raskin?"

She grimaced, a face of disgust. "I don't want to talk about that. It makes me sick."

"Why?"

"He's my cousin...my first cousin." Her laugh was harsh, contemptuous. "But I didn't know that when I chose him. I seduced him but he was weak. He failed me in the end."

Suddenly her head slumped to her chest, then rose slowly. Her nostrils flared and she was hyperventilating. Her head started rolling from side to side, faster and faster, she kept on hyperventilating. Then she started convulsing and urinating on the floor.

Zentler hurried around the table and grasped her shoulders. "Get a doctor in here!" he shouted. And in seconds the door burst open and two men, a doctor and a medical assistant, ran into the room. The doctor produced a needle and thrust it into Noa's upper arm while the assistant held her still.

"It should counteract the disorienting effects of the desoxyn," the doctor said to Zentler. "I've been listening and you should know it's not just the drugs doing this. She's hallucinating, that stuff about the music. The drugs may have had some catalytic effect, but clinically she's showing the topology of a personality disorder that's psychotic, like it's some kind of breakdown. I'd have to know more about her pre-morbid qualities to understand the form of the psychosis." He bent over Noa, rolled her eyelids up with his thumb, one after the other, and shone a pencil light into her eyes. "You can go ahead in a few minutes," he said. "She should be alright for a bit."

But she wasn't. When she opened her eyes she looked at Zentler fondly, smiled at him. "Oh Gavri!...Gavri!" she moaned in a dreamy voice. "Why don't we go to Safed again, search for mysteries? Remember?" She closed her eyes. "Soft dark nights...and the sounds from the synagogues and the light spilling out the doors into the narrow streets ...and the old black-hatted men moving in the shadows. They had secrets, mysteries, and we were going to expose them." She opened her eyes, looking directly at Zentler. "You have exposed my mystery Gavri, haven't you?"

And she laughed then, a deep guttural laugh.

"I am *Lilith,* the whore."

***

Fourteen

The notes of Erik Satie's *Gymnopedies* tip-toed lightly across the terrace to where Alan Raskin sat, Anna Peled's touch on the piano keyboard soft yet confident. The terrace overlooked the village of En Karem, nestled in the Judean hills outside Jerusalem. The view was like an early cubist landscape: a jumble of sharply defined sandstone planes – houses, churches, a monastery, a convent, a mosque – with vertical slashes of dark green cypress and cedar. A Mediterranean vista, not unlike that from Alan's old *finca* on Ibiza which he had sold in order to buy this house in En Karem. The colors changed with the light and the light with the season. Winter was coming again and the late afternoon sun was low in the southwest, its light skimming across the tops of the ancient terraced hills, suffusing the sandstone of the village with a magical glow. The flattening rays of the sun caught the top of the bell tower of the Franciscan church with its green-coppered spire, the *Visitatio Mariae*. John the Baptist was said to have been born here and Mary was supposed to have visited his pregnant mother Elizabeth. When he brought his aunt Anna here to live with him Alan had remarked that the Franciscans had been here forever. Anna then reminded him that the Jews had been here *longer* than forever and that *he* was a Jew.

It seemed absurd to sit here now, absorbed in the light and the music, and think of his roots back in the bronze age. But yes, he did indeed feel rooted.

Alan Raskin...latter day Zionist!

*

With Dan Bergmann's help, Alan had found a job as a copy-editor at a small English-language publishing house in Jerusalem, something to keep him in pocket money until he learned Hebrew and could get work as a reporter again. But he wasn't sure he wanted to do that anymore. He could afford to wait and see what would happen as he tried to assimilate in his new homeland.

It had not been easy at the start. Although they could not turn him away in his bid for Israeli citizenship, many in the government bureaucracy had made it clear that Alan Raskin was not to be welcomed with open arms. He was detained at Tel Aviv airport on his arrival in April and subjected to an intensive closed investigation by *Shabak* for his part in the Noa Kagan affair. And it was only after an elderly officer named Daniel Zentler was able to show the panel that in the end Mr. Raskin had refused to continue to assist Dr. Kagan – "an unfortunate demented woman" – in her deluded effort to publish classified secrets that he was cleared and allowed to begin his new life.

Alan learned little from Zentler about what had happened on Ibiza. All he remembered of that early morning raid was the speed of the men who broke down his door, dark figures moving through the main *sala* to the back room where he'd been lying on a banquette beside the fireplace. He hadn't slept much. *I think I'm going to be sick,* Noa's words, had stung him like an ice-cold shower. *His lover was his cousin.* Those words had kept him awake, looping through his mind, over and over. The noise of the splintering door brought him to his feet quickly, only to be knocked down just as quickly by a black-clad man. Noa screamed up in the bedroom. He felt the prick of a needle on his shoulder muscle and then a swooning rush into darkness and oblivion.

"You are a journalist, Mr. Raskin," Daniel Zentler had said at the investigation, his blue eyes squinting through his thick lenses. "Why did you not file a story about the break-in at your house in Ibiza and the kidnapping of Noa Kagan?"

His answer was his only lie. How could he tell this slow, thoughtful man who had spent days combing through the story of his first months in Israel that when he woke up on the floor of his *finca* in Ibiza he had wanted to run away from his *intimacy* with Noa Kagan as fast and as far as he could. He wanted *nothing* to do with her.

"If I had filed that story," he told Zentler, "I would have had to explain why she was kidnapped and that would have led to the exposure of the NATANZ material, something I'd already told her I wouldn't file because I thought it would jeopardize the security of Israel."

Zentler studied him for a moment. "But you were lovers."

Not a question...a statement of fact. "If you say so."

"She has said that she seduced you."

"I'd rather not talk about it."

Zentler nodded. "Your answer about not filing the story will help you with your citizenship application. Once you are a citizen you will, of course, respect our laws and our silence with regard to all nuclear matters. I wish you luck."

"One other thing?"

"Yes?"

"Where is she?"

"At a mental health center in Beer Sheva. Unfortunately she was heavily overdosed with drugs in Ibiza. She suffered brain damage and a severe mental breakdown."

"Will she be put on trial?"

Zentler shook his head. "That won't be possible...and nobody wants it."

"And Gavri Gilboa?"

"Unfortunately he died. Took his own life, and Noa Kagan's too in a way."

"How so?"

"The men who witnessed Gilboa's death reacted badly. They overdosed Dr. Kagan, an act of vengeance, we assume, of which we disapproved."

Disapproved? Alan stared at him. Too much! Too much for him to comprehend. He didn't want to know any more.

"Thank you," he said.

*

Anna Peled called him a couple of months after his return to Israel. She said that Ofra Gefen had given her his telephone number and that she needed to meet with him. He had only one question for himself – *Did Anna know?* He would be embarrassed to meet with her if she did know and at first he put her off. But Anna insisted that it was important for her to see him and he reluctantly agreed. They met at a café in Neve Tzedek where Anna said she was living for a while. Alan hardly knew her. The coiled braids had gone and the sack-like brown dress she'd worn at both their previous meetings. Her hair was cut short and layered and she had bangs; she used makeup, and wore a silk blouse and a tailored skirt. But that was just the exterior. She hadn't lost weight, but she seemed lighter, buoyant in spirit, happier.

"You've transformed," he said, and she blushed like a girl.

"It's the city," she said. "Getting away from Kfar Borochov...and from Yosef."

He frowned. "Yosef? Your husband Yosef?"

Anna nodded. "And your uncle. I have to apologize to you. I told you he was dead when that wasn't true."

"Why did you say that he was dead?"

Anna sighed. "Yosef can be violent. After you told me the first time I met you about you're meeting with a man called Yitzhak, I knew who you meant. His name is Yitzhak Gavish and he and Yosef would do anything to stop you from digging up the story of the death of Thomas Penrose. They are proud and powerful men. This is a small nation and their reputation means everything to them. I hoped that if I told you that Yosef was dead you wouldn't dig any further."

"What would I have found?"

"There were three of them. Your grandfather, Benjamin Stahl-mann, his son Yosef, and his friend Yitzhak Gavish who was Irgun. Yitzhak lived in Jerusalem and was able to get the truck. He hunted down Thomas Penrose, learned his routine, and then Benjamin and Yosef went down to the city and they killed him."

"Yitzhak said the Haganah had a court-martial..."

Anna shook her head. "That's not true. They were never caught or punished. At the time, to the few people who knew what they did, they were heroes. Thomas Penrose wasn't a well-liked man and those people who approved of his death knew nothing about his affair with Ruth. That's why they're afraid of you. If you bring up that part of the story it becomes a sordid family revenge killing and that diminishes them."

"I had no intention of writing anything," he said. "I just wanted to know for myself, that's all." But he was curious now. "You talked about getting away. Have you left Yosef?'

Anna stared at him. "Our daughter Noa, who I believe you know, had a severe mental breakdown a few months ago. Yosef has connections in the government and over time he learned that it had something to do with her work, something that he felt dishonored him. He wouldn't tell me what it was, but he was shattered. He couldn't face his old friends. His anger and his rage turned on me. I couldn't live with him anymore. Noa has been confined to a psychiatric center down in Beer Sheva and her condo here in Tel Aviv was empty so I moved in. Yosef's not happy with this arrangement and I'm afraid he will try to force me to go back to Kefar Borochov."

She paused. "Alan?..."

He had been only half listening and Anna had noticed it. He was still dwelling on her first sentence – *Our daughter Noa, who I believe you know*. So Anna knew! But how much did she know? And why hadn't she told him earlier that she had a daughter? His cousin! But why should she have told him? He couldn't blame her for what had happened.

"Yes, I'm listening."

"Can you help me? I'm afraid of Yosef, what he might do."

"Help you? Why yes, of course...if I can..."

"It's not just for me. It's for Noa's sake too. I have to sell her con-do, for the money, and I need a place to live. Ofra tells me you've just bought a house up in En Karem. If I could share it with you for a while I would be so grateful. I mean you *are* family now and you'd be helping Noa as well..."

She left it lingering there for him to choose, floating out over the café table – *You'd be helping Noa as well.*

Did he really have a choice?

If he had told people that he was sharing his house with the wife of the man who had killed his father they would have thought it a bizarre thing to do. But it was not at all difficult. He had never known Thomas Penrose and he very quickly grew fond of his aunt. Anna was very helpful to him. He was after all a true settler, a man attempting to plant himself in a new country, to start a new life, and she helped to ease his entry and his frustration with the bureaucracy in which Israelis entangled their lives. At first he wondered if he would become like Susan Miller, who had packed it in and returned to the United States, claiming she would always be an outsider who was never accepted by the *sabras,* would never really belong here. But doing *aliyah* for Susan had never been more than an adventure. He was done with adventure. He had roamed enough of the world and he wanted to settle in some place where he hoped he could belong and do something to help his adopted country. After a little while he consid-ered himself lucky to have formed the nucleus of a small family with Anna. Ofra Gefen was a constant visitor to their home, and Jerold Raskin finally completed his aborted trip to Israel and announced that he was coming back in a few months for Passover.

"Nothing to do with your conversations with Anna?" Alan teased.

"Absolutely!" Jerold replied.

Trouble from Yosef Peled was to be expected, Anna had warned, and it had not been long in coming. When the retired General learned that his wife had sold Noa's condo and moved into a house in Jerusalem with a "friend," he threatened to bring her to court. Not long after Alan had started working in Jerusalem at the publishing house where Dan Bergmann had found him a job, he and Bergmann went down to Tel Aviv for a visit. They sat in a café near the *Kirya,* the Defense Ministry, and waited for Yitzhak Gavish, with whom Dan had requested an interview. When Yitzhak arrived at their table, Dan stood up.

"I believe you two know each other," he said and he left.

"What is the purpose of this?" Yitzhak asked imperiously, still standing.

"Sit down," Alan said. "This won't take a minute." And when Yitzhak sat he spelled it out. If General Yosef Peled did not leave his wife Anna alone, he, Alan Raskin, would write and publish the story of the General's family scandal and of Yosef's part in the murder of Thomas Penrose – assisted by his father, Benjamin Stahlman, and the Irgun terrorist Yitzhak Gavish – for fucking around with his sister Ruth.

"Tell Yosef that I'm Ruth's son and his nephew," Alan said, "and I believe that it's best to let sleeping family dogs lie."

Anna and Ofra drove down to Beer Sheva every second week to visit Noa. Alan never volunteered to go with them. On their return he inquired politely for a moment or so about Noa's condition – her diagnosis was toxic psychotic dementia – and listened to Anna's chilling description of her daughter's latest fantasies, her mind meandering in myth and distorted memory. Only once, early on in their time together at En Karem, did Anna criticize her daughter and, indirectly, herself as a mother. It sounded to Alan like something she wanted to get off her chest:

"You know, Noa's life before you met her, her marriage, her affairs, it was all a mess. It was that way for years. Sometimes I think she was a very lonely person. She grew up like a boy, competitive, aggressive. Her grandfather, Sasha Kagan, who she idolized, encouraged that streak in her. Her father didn't seem to care what she did. He was off in the army all the time, always fighting somewhere, and when he was home he was fighting with me. He used to beat me and that wasn't hidden from Noa. It must have had some effect on her. I think deep down she despised me. She thought I was weak because I never stood up to Yosef."

"You have now," Alan said in sympathy.

Anna smiled, waving her hand as if brushing something aside.

"Noa was a willful and difficult person, Alan. She used people. A man you don't know, Gavri Gilboa, grew up on the kibbutz with her. The poor man took his own life some months ago and they brought his remains home to Kefar Borochov in a box for burial. He loved Noa, worshiped her, but she just teased him, led him on. I think she drove him crazy. Especially when she went off and married Rafi Bourla on a whim. Then there's the way she treated him. She was oh-so-intelligent and had all these values. She always acted as if she disapproved of what Rafi did, but I never noticed her refusing the money he made and the life it gave her. And friends like Ofra, who idolized her, she used them too and criticized them. The only person she never criticized was her son Sasha. He could do no wrong. She worshiped him and tried to shape him. When he was killed up in Lebanon last summer it destroyed her. I think that was when she started losing her mind. She told me that she visits the spirit world now and talks to Sasha. That he's apologized to her for going in the army. She's insane, of course. They all have to go in the army and that was when she started to lose him, and for that she blamed her father. But she put the young boy up on the kibbutz with us in the first place so she could pursue her own life, and then she complained about Yosef's influence on him. I told you before that she always had difficulties with Yosef, but after Sasha went in the army she hated her father." Anna paused, pushed her fingers through her short hair. "She talks about visiting with Gavri too, but when she does that she becomes another person. She calls herself Lilith."

One night Alan sat with Anna and Ofra and watched a quiz show on state television. A Holocaust quiz show on location in Auschwitz. Israeli school kids answering questions about what had happened in the camps, competing with each other and getting points for the right answers. There was an audience but applause was not allowed. That would be in bad taste the announcer had informed the viewers.

Alan still had his journalist's perception that the gap between the actual physical security of the State of Israel and the people's perception of their security was enormous. As a new citizen he'd tried to understand that gap. What was it that made them feel so vulnerable?

"Another Holocaust," Ofra said.

"That's irrational," he'd replied. "The country is a military powerhouse. It has one of the most efficient, best-equipped armies in the world. Immensely superior air power. And above all it has tactical and strategic nuclear weapons and delivery systems."

Ofra shrugged. "You must understand emotions. They are not rational. We have a man in Iran who says he wants to wipe us off the face of the earth. We're supposed to ignore him? With our history? What has happened to us in the past? Why should we?"

The future is only the past again, entered through another gate. Maybe that explained it, Alan figured. The powers that be at Israeli TV were cunning with their Holocaust quiz show. Despite all its military might, Israel's real secret weapon *was* the Holocaust. And when it came down to popular perception in that part of the outside world that mattered to Israel, namely the United States, the Palestinians didn't stand a chance against it.

*

Anna switched to Chopin's Preludes and Alan shifted in his chair. The twilight air was getting chill, lights had come on in the houses across the valley. The hospital with the Chagall stained glass windows blazed like an ocean liner. One day, not long ago, he had walked over there with Ofra to see the windows. In one of them, white doves of peace flew over green headlands and a tranquil blue sea, a benevolent yellow sun above. A peaceful vista.

"Noa would like this," Ofra said, and then she told him a story about the passage of time, a bit of scientific information really, that she had learned from Noa. Apparently, if you bolted together two metal plates, one of them iron and the other titanium, and left them for nine thousand years, then you would no longer need the bolts to hold them together. They would have blended chemically into each other, rendering the fasteners unnecessary.

"She loved knowing things like that," Ofra said.

"But where would I get the nine thousand years?"

"Exactly Noa's point. 'Time is indeed magisterial' she would say, 'but we haven't got that much of it, so we need a blow-torch to speed up the fusion."

Ofra had introduced him to her friends in Peace Now and Alan had become a member. He worked for them in compiling reports on the illegal settlements and their data was far more complete than information the government was willing to put out. From his terrace he could see northeast beyond the Jerusalem Forest and Yad Vashem to the new suburban settlements of Jerusalem beyond the old Green Line. He worked with aerial photos, government data, and personal visits to Palestinian villages on the other side of the wall with an Israeli group called Anarchists Against The Wall. He'd been tear-gassed and arrested for a short period in the village of Bil'in during protests. Settlement construction in the territories was intensive, doubling over the previous year. If it continued, the two state solution was in jeopardy. And with it any hope for a permanent peace with the Palestinians. He considered his work a small contribution towards helping to restore Israel's moral standing in the world.

The Chopin piano music stopped and Alan rose from his chair on the terrace. Ofra would be coming soon and he had some Peace Now work to finish up for her. He walked across the terrace to his study, turned on a light. On the wall opposite the door to the terrace there was a medieval map which he had bought in a shop in Jerusalem. It had a title:

MONIALIUM EBSTORFENSIUM MAPPAM MUNDI

A window on the map of the world. It looked like a game of snakes and ladders. Sinuous blue rivers twisted around on themselves; crenellated brown walls marched back and forth, up and down snowy mountains, dividing the land and its tribes. At the center of it all sat ancient Palestine and Jerusalem. The map presented a myopic and xenophobic view of the world. But it was a circular map, and from the distance of the door Alan liked to think it could be mistaken for a view of our planet Earth from outer space, like one of those glorious blue and white photographs taken by astronauts. He had not chosen the map for that reason, but having that perception of it from the door had made him keep it there. For better or worse, it said to him that our whole planet was our country now. Jews could not turn back in on themselves again. They had too much to teach this one world country, a place in which, because of the tragic nature of their history, their wanderings had made them the first true citizens of Earth.

***

About the Author

Sam Jon Wallace is a psuedonym for the author who has lived and worked throughout the Middle East from Israel to Iran.

Made in the USA
Lexington, KY
29 October 2012